Dream Lover

Mortal Immortal Series

Book 1

Eunice D. Colvin

iUniverse, Inc.
Bloomington

Dream Lover
Mortal Immortal Series

Copyright © 2012 by Eunice D. Colvin.

All rights reserved. No part of this book may be used or reproduced by any means, graphic, electronic, or mechanical, including photocopying, recording, taping or by any information storage retrieval system without the written permission of the publisher except in the case of brief quotations embodied in critical articles and reviews.

iUniverse books may be ordered through booksellers or by contacting:

iUniverse
1663 Liberty Drive
Bloomington, IN 47403
www.iuniverse.com
1-800-Authors (1-800-288-4677)

Because of the dynamic nature of the Internet, any web addresses or links contained in this book may have changed since publication and may no longer be valid. The views expressed in this work are solely those of the author and do not necessarily reflect the views of the publisher, and the publisher hereby disclaims any responsibility for them.

Any people depicted in stock imagery provided by Thinkstock are models, and such images are being used for illustrative purposes only.
Certain stock imagery © Thinkstock.

ISBN: 978-1-4759-1782-6 (sc)
ISBN: 978-1-4759-1855-7 (ebk)

Printed in the United States of America

iUniverse rev. date: 05/25/2012

This book is dedicated to my daughter Heather-Jayne who has shared my passion for reading and my books.

Contents

Glossary of nouns and meanings ix
Prologue xi

Chapter 1:   The Beginning 1
Chapter 2:   The Dream 4
Chapter 3:   Six Months Later 9
Chapter 4:   Confession 32
Chapter 5:   The Letter 47
Chapter 6:   Revelations 58
Chapter 7:   Kaspir's Tale 74
Chapter 8:   Plans 87
Chapter 9:   The Journey 96
Chapter 10: Together at Last 109
Chapter 11: Onwards to Scotland 119
Chapter 12: Home at Last 135
Chapter 13: Preparations 149
Chapter 14: Prophecy and Legend 170
Chapter 15: Getting Married 184
Chapter 16: The Ritual 202
Chapter 17: The New Queen 217

Glossary of nouns and meanings

Vardesh—A vampire race with limited immortality, they usually live between 500 and 1000 years.

Clan—A group within the Vardesh, comprising of Dragon, Wolf, Cat, Eagle or Phoenix.

Avardi—Enemy of the Vardesh. Alchemists and Scientists who will use any means to extend their own lives.

Solelae(m)—Human soul mate of a female Vardesh.

Solelil(f)—Human soul mate of a male Vardesh.

The Keeper—Record and history keeper of the Vardesh.

Rhysae—One who will rise again and be reborn.

Guardian—Protector of the Sacred Temple.

The Black—Death and the Afterlife.

The Veil of Light—Mystical place where time does not exist, as such. Where all the Phoenix clan reside (females only, rarely are males born). High Priestesses and attendants live there.

The Shaman—Leader of the Avardi.

Assists—Lower Shamans.

Maiden Healers—Nurses and Herbalists.

Eunice D. Colvin

Initiates—Avardi recruits and are subservient.

Story Tellers—Verbal record keepers of the Avardi history.

Channeller—Talisman to help channel telepathic energy for communication.

Transform—An elite warrior vampire who can change into the creature of their clan. They tend to live much longer than other vampires, maybe twice as long.

Sisters of the Phoenix—The Priestesses of the Veil of Light, who perform clan rituals.

Year of Yearning—The time when the Vardesh have to seek out their mates.

Sacred Temple—A place where all Vardesh rituals and ceremonies are held.

The Deliverer—A nurse or midwife who helps with birthing.

Ritual of Ascension—The ceremony in which Vardesh offspring reach maturity and become as their parents, a full vampire.

Ritual of Transcendence—The ceremony in which human mates become Vardesh.

Doric Translations

Braw—Good/Great/Nice

Braw nicht—Great/Nice night

Wo tae?—Where to?/Where do you want to go?

Whit's adae?—What's wrong/What's the matter?

Prologue

The Transcendence Ritual was ready to perform, representatives from the four main clans were gathered in the sacred temple deep beneath the ground. Despite the lack of a breeze flames danced in the torches lining the walls, casting shadows that appeared to creep across the lofty ceiling. The High Priestess and her sisters waited behind a shimmering curtain, known as the 'veil of light', which kept 'Sollest' the High Priestess and the other priestesses from ageing. They were all members of a fifth clan called 'Phoenix'. Only females from this clan could enter the 'veil'. Living beyond the veil they only come out to perform the rituals of their people. It was rare for a phoenix child to be born and when they were, most were females. They entered the 'veil of light' immediately. Males however, rarely survived past their 'Year of Yearning'.

Kaspir of the 'Dragon Clan was there with his Solelil Anya, he had found her at the eleventh hour. Well . . . actually that's not true, he had found her in a bar he chanced upon as he was travelling round the world looking for her. Kaspir had been getting desperate, he had only ten days left before his journey into the black. Unlike most of his race he had been convinced by someone that he would be able to find his Solelil quicker if he physically travelled in search of her. When he walked into the bar that night, he was on the verge of despair. Then a thread connected, it was like a lightning bolt shaking him to the core. Kaspir swung his head round and looked for her. There she was, his Solelil standing behind a long counter. From his vantage point at the top of the stairs he could see she was small but perfectly formed. Long red hair pencil straight led down to her narrow waist. A delicate face held within it a pair of large emerald green eyes. The sight took his breath away.

Anya had been staring at the handsome stranger ever since he had walked through the door. In the five years since she had been working at the bar she had never seen anyone like him. She had been eighteen when she started working at the bar after not being able to find any other work. For some strange reason she felt a pull towards him. This tall, fair haired man with long curly hair, that looked like a perm from the eighties. His bold chiselled features gave him a very masculine almost grecian look, which seemed at odds with his clothes. Clad in black leather pants with matching waist coat over a black shirt. The look was finished off with black silver tipped cowboy boots and a black duster style overcoat. His dark clothes seemed to reflect his mood. His face was sombre and his eyes held a sadness that seemed incomprehensible.

As he entered the place he began looking around the room, he hadn't noticed the bar that was over in the far corner. It wasn't until he expanded his mind that the connection was made. As their eyes met, his breath stilled. Before he realised what had happened he was standing at the bar. It was as if he had floated across the room on a cushion of air. As he stood there, Kaspir smiled at the vision before him. Anya's breath got stuck in her throat, his smile dazzling her. Perfect white teeth surrounded by full luscious lips, slightly pink against his pale skin. A mouth to die for and when he spoke, well . . . she all but melted on the spot.

"Hello," he said his voice rich and deep, with a slight lilt to it.

"Hi," she said, the word coming out like a sigh. The way she had said the word almost dreamily reminded her of a soppy romantic movie, which made her blush from head to toe.

"My name is Kaspir, may I ask yours?" The words dripped off his tongue like melted chocolate all rich and smooth. His ice blue eyes sparkled like frozen lakes in winter. The sadness she had seen when he had first walked in seemed to have gone. It was replaced by a look of hope and excitement.

"Anya," her voiced squeaked as it caught in her throat. His ice blue eyes seemed to study every inch of her face, taking in every detail of her. He looked like a man half starved, ready to devour her. The thought caused heat to pool in her stomach. For some reason she felt an instant attraction to him, which she found very disconcerting. Just then a man with a gruff voice, balding head and a large beer belly shouted to her from the games area, breaking the spell. Anya hadn't realised that when he had spoken to her, she had heard nothing around her. No chatter of peoples voices. No music from the Jukebox and no cracking of the pool balls as they connected with each other on the tables. Everything else had been silent, that was until Jack her boss had pulled her back to reality by bellowing at her. She blinked and looked towards Jack.

"Anya! You're supposed to be working, not socialising. Serve the man and then go and collect some glasses!" Anya nodded sheepishly.

"Sorry," she said, clearing her throat and coming to her senses. "What would you like?" she asked him.

"You." He said simply. Anya was shocked by his bold reply and blushed again, this time a deeper shade of red. Averting her eyes as an embarrassing shyness came over her. "Please do not look away from me Anya". His quiet but gentle plea made her stomach flip. "Your face is too beautiful to hide." Kaspir leaned across the bar and lifted her chin with the tips of his fingers. As soon as their skin made contact an arc of electricity shot between them. Anya's eyes widen in shock and she stepped back, making the bottles on the shelves behind her bounce off each other with a clinking sound.

Rephrasing the question Anya asked. "What would you like to drink?" Kaspir's mouth lifted at the side slightly in a half smile.

"Red wine, please." Anya nodded and turned around to pour his drink. It gave Kaspir an opportunity to admire more of her. She could feel his eyes on her, watching every movement, no matter how small. It felt like he was boring into her soul, heat began to spread through her whole body. She had never in her life experienced such sensations before. No man had stirred her the way this man did. All he had done was look at her and spoken a few words. And she had almost dissolved into a puddle. Anya returned with his drink, her hand shaking slightly.

"There you go, sir." She tried to give an air of professionalism, but it wasn't working. Her mouth was dry, which made speaking difficult. And no matter how many times she swallowed, it didn't make any difference. As Kaspir paid for his drink, he held onto Anya's hand.

"May I ask you two questions?" His eyes held her just as his hand did. She hadn't noticed before but there were flecks of gold in his piercing blue eyes that seemed to glow. Anya wanted to looked around just in case her boss decided to have another hissy fit, but she couldn't so she nodded slightly. Kaspir then released her hand to Anya's relief. Her temperature had been rising steadily and she thought that she might just burst into flames if he held it any longer. "Will you please call me Kaspir?" his voice was low and seductive, almost hypnotic. Anya turned away and went to the till to charge up his drink, as she did she ran his name over in her mind. Then quietly she tested it on her lips. Kaspir with his excellent hearing heard her and smiled to himself. When she came back with his change, she hoped that she could just drop the coins into his open palm, but he was too quick for her. Once again retaining possession of her hand.

"Here is your change . . ." Although he did not let go of her hand, he did not hurt her either. His grip was firm but gentle. She realised that until she had complied with his request, there was no way he was going to let go. Eventually, she relented. As his name rolled off her tongue it felt like a butterfly had just stroked his skin with its velvety wings.

"Thank you, Anya." She tried to pull away, but he held her fast, she realised that until he had asked his second question she was going nowhere.

"And the second question?" she prompted slightly taken aback by this handsome stranger. Her arm was getting a little cramp in it and she was starting to feel more than just a little uncomfortable with his touch. Not that he was hurting her. The fact was that the longer the contact, the more sexual heat she felt. Anya could feel her core burning and her arousal had dampened her panties. In desperation she looked at him. "Kaspir, the second question?" she pleaded. Kaspir released her hand to her relief. He could feel the sexual heat building between them. He was glad he was standing at the bar and wearing a long coat, although it was not fastened. He very much doubted that he could sit at this moment in time. The constriction of his leather trousers was making things difficult for him. Kaspir held her gaze for a moment longer.

"Anya, may I please see you home?" Anya was speechless, but before she could respond her boss bellowed again.

Dream Lover

"Anya! If you've finished making googly eyes at that man, then maybe you could do some work. We're closing in twenty minutes." The red faced man then rang a bell. "Last orders folks, if you haven't finished in twenty minutes, then tough your outta here regardless." Anya was then swamped by customers wanting a final drink before leaving the bar. Once she had finished serving them she had to start collecting the empty glasses. Kaspir turned round and leaned back against the bar watching her. His coat fell back revealing his obvious attraction to her. She was wearing blue jeans cut off at the knee, black pumps and a cropped green tee shirt that matched her eyes. Kaspir drank in the sight of her as her hips swayed, whilst she moved from table to table. Leaning across them tightened the denim around her curvaceous behind. Sometimes she would have to stretch up to retrieve glasses off the shelves in the pool area, revealing even more of her creamy white skin, which her hair stroked tantalisingly. He wondered what it would feel like against his bare flesh. Kaspir groaned inwardly, as if he wasn't hard enough already. He had to stop thinking those thoughts, his erection seemed to grow and thicken even more.

Anya was well aware that Kaspir was watching her every move. She found it exhilarating in a strange kind of way and his impressive bulge hadn't gone unnoticed. She started to make a little show of things by bending over tables and stretching more than necessary. Occasionally she glanced out of the corner of her eye and could see him squirm, trying to adjust his stance to something a little more comfortable. For some strange reason she was being a tease, something she had never done before and she was enjoying it. Smiling to herself, it felt quite exhilarating to return the favour. After all, he had made her all hot and bothered. Suddenly the bell rang again.

"Time please, people," the baldy headed man said. "Time to go home, if you haven't finished your drink by now, tough. Anya collect everything in now." The man opened the door to the outside and people started making their way out of the bar. Everyone went without argument, bidding him goodnight, saluting or nodding to him. Kaspir hung back until he was the only person left. "You to pal," he said to Kaspir. Kaspir looked at Anya, holding her in his gaze.

"You never answered my second question?" he prompted, as she placed empty glasses on the bar. She could see that her boss was starting to get annoyed with him.

"Come on you, out. No lock-ins here." Kaspir had no idea what he was talking about. He just stared at Anya. She sighed.

"Yes," she whispered to him as she walked away, exasperated by his behaviour. What she really wanted to do was kick him for making her boss growl at her again. Jack never normally got grumpy. Then again she wasn't usually this distracted. "Now go and wait outside". She shook her head as he smiled and closed his coat before walking out into the night.

Anya came out from the bar thirty minutes later and saw him standing on the corner, leaning against a street light. The orange glow seemed to make him look almost ethereal. 'Persistent', she thought to herself and smiled as she walked over to him. They walked in silence as Kaspir escorted her back to her apartment, his huge form dwarfing hers. Not a word passed between them, he hadn't even tried to hold her hand. By the time they reached her apartment Anya was exasperated, not to mention frustrated. She turned to face him.

"You haven't said one word to me all the way here. Why?"

"Because . . ." he hesitated for a moment. "I wish to kiss you, but not in public." Anya was taken by surprise and thought it kind of strange. Lots of people kissed in public, what makes him so different. 'Perhaps he's shy', she thought. Kaspir looked at her.

"No, Anya. I am not shy. I am just a very private person."

"How . . . how did you know what I was thinking?" she looked at him curiously. Kaspir smiled.

"It is written all over your beautiful face." This time Anya didn't just blush, she turned crimson. No one had ever called her beautiful and he had said it twice in one night. "May I enter your home with you?" he asked. Anya couldn't help but laugh at the way he had asked to come in. He spoke in such a formal and old fashioned manner, she almost wanted to laugh. Instead she just smiled and shook her head. Kaspir thought that she was declining his request, disappointment flashed across his face briefly.

"How do I know you won't rape me or something?" It was a stupid statement really but she could not hold in her sarcasm. After all he hadn't even tried to hold her hand on the journey to her place. She instantly regretted her words when she saw the look on his face was one of horror. Anya felt guilty, she never expected such a reaction. "I'm sorry Kaspir, I never meant to . . ." Kaspir cut her off by holding up his hands.

"Anya I would never do such a despicable thing. I would never take your virtue without your consent." Anya laughed at the use of the word virtue. Kaspir got serious then. "Anya in truth, I do desire to make love to you. But I would have your permission and I would ensure every pleasure would be given to you before such an act". Anya felt as though she had been punched in the stomach, heat exploded through her whole body. His words were like a torch setting her on fire. As she turned she felt slightly giddy from his words, she retrieved her key from her pocket. With unsteady hands she managed to unlock her door. Briefly she looked over her shoulder at him. Anya put her hand behind her and grabbed Kaspir by the coat dragging him into the hallway of her apartment. If Kaspir had not picked up on her thoughts, she would not have been able to move him. The mind thread was there, although not very strong. But at least it was there. He hoped that the rest of the mesh would begin forming soon. Kaspir closed the door with his foot and Anya turned to face him.

"Who are you?" she whispered. "And why do I find myself so attracted to you?"

"You are?" Kaspir tried to sound surprised. He knew that soul mates always had a deep and powerful attraction to each other. The pull between them was impossible to ignore.

"Yes." Her reply came out breathy, as she stared in awe at this handsome stranger in her hallway. Kaspir cupped her face in his hands. Gently he stroked her cheeks with his thumbs. He began to lean into her; Anya licked her lips in anticipation. Ever so softly his lips brushed hers; he then licked her lower lip making her lips part slightly. He applied more pressure as he deepened the kiss. Anya's mouth responded automatically and began moving of its own accord. She lifted her arms and put them around his neck bringing her body closer to his. Kaspir moved his arms to encircle her body as he deepened the kiss even further. Kaspir's tongue delved deeply into Anya's mouth, tasting the sweet honey that was her. When Kaspir had the strength, he pulled away resting his head on hers, as they tried to gather enough oxygen. Anya felt so hot and wet; her sheath was swollen beyond comprehension. Her bones seemed to be dissolving and if he hadn't been holding her, she was sure that she would be a heap on the floor. "Wow," she laughed breathlessly. "No wonder you wanted to kiss in private." Kaspir smiled at her, his eyes sparkled with excitement and passion. The gold flecks in them seemed to glow even more.

"May we venture further into your abode or do I have to leave?" 'Leave? Leave?' she thought. That was the last thing she wanted him to do. It was also the last thing he wanted to do, but he would not force her, no matter what the time frame. Anya slid her hands to the front of his coat and undid the buttons. Her hands trembled as they slid along his coat. Breathing in deeply to steady her nerves, she could smell his intoxicating fragrance of leather and spice.

"You can hang your coat behind you, on that peg," she said pointing behind him. "And take off that waist coat too." She didn't know why she said that but she didn't want him to have so many layers on. Kaspir nodded and did as she requested. Anya took her coat off too and hung it on one of the pegs. Anya headed for the kitchen, she needed to get some space between them, so she could think straight. "Coffee?" she shouted back, as she looked over her shoulder at him. Kaspir shook his head. "Well, I need one after working that shift." Kaspir came up and stood just a few inches behind her. He was so close that she could feel the heat from his body. Anya's breath stilled in her throat. For a moment nothing happened, then he slowly slid his arms around her waist. His hands travelled around the front of her body. Spreading his fingers wide he pressed his hot palms onto the flat of her belly. Heat scorched her body, fire burned in her veins as flames licked over her skin. Leaning down he smelled her hair and bent forward to kiss her neck just under her jaw. Anya responded automatically tilting her head to the side for him. Anya moaned as his lips caressed her skin. "Are you sure you don't want anything?" she said drowsily as his lips did their work. Suddenly she stiffened. 'Shit, I've done it again,' she thought. Kaspir smiled against her skin and kissed the sweet spot between her neck and shoulder.

"Yes," he whispered against her neck. "I would like something very much." The words sent tiny shudders coursing through her body. "I would like you naked on a bed, so I could explore every inch of you, with both my hands and my mouth. Then if you wished you could do the same to me. Afterwards, I would make love to you for the rest of the night." Anya felt her legs buckle, melting at his words. If she had not been holding onto the counter to stop herself from falling, she would be in a heap on the floor.

"Oh, God!" Moaning as she leaned back against him, no longer being able to hold herself upright. She could feel his swollen length pressed into the small of her back. How could she resist him, when mere words made her react this way? Erotic pictures flooded her mind of the two of them, naked and entwined. Kaspir's hands began to slide up under her top, over her smooth milky skin. Kaspir sucked in a breath as his hands moved over her skin. Heat began to consume both of them. His hands continued their exploration of her skin. Suddenly he was at the edge of her bra, Anya gasped in anticipation. She could feel her nipples harden, straining through the cotton material. Slowly his hands crept over her clad breasts, cupping and squeezing them firmly. Gently he brushed his thumbs over her taught buds. Heat erupted in her already wet channel. Kaspir moaned at the softness of them and Anya moaned at his touch, an ache spread to the junction of her thighs. As Kaspir teased the hard buds through the fabric, his erection throbbed almost painfully. Anya pressed her hips into him, causing him to suck a breath in through his teeth. His own body was desperate for relief. Anya raised her arms to put them round his neck. But before her hands got to their destination he took advantage by removing her tee shirt. Anya froze. Kaspir just stood there with one hand on her and the other clasping her top. Eventually she gained enough courage to twist round and face him, she could see the stark hunger in his eyes. Lowering her face Anya felt a strange urge coursing through her, she started to unbutton his shirt. After each button released a piece of flesh she took the opportunity to explore it with both her hands and her mouth. Kaspir stood there gritting his teeth as he let her explore him. He did not want to force her in any way. The sensation of her small hands and slender fingers caressing his skin was unbelievable. Her mouth was soft and warm, her tongue left streaks of fire in its wake. Eventually she was at the waistband of his trousers. Anya risked glancing at him, he was looking down at her through hooded eyes, a fierce desire in them. Tucking her fingers in his waistband she pulled him round with her as she stepped out of the kitchen. Kaspir held his breath as her fingers almost brushed the head of his erection. She led him backwards as she headed for the bedroom. Pressing her back against the door, she fumbled for the handle with her free hand. She felt a little afraid; she had never experienced such intensity. She had had a few relationships, but they paled in comparison to what she was feeling now. As she reversed into her room, Kaspir had no choice but to follow her. Before she realised it Anya had bumped against the end of the bed, causing her to sit down abruptly. Kaspir stood before her, not moving, her tee shirt still clasped in his hand. He was giving her every opportunity to stop what was happening. Kaspir was on the edge of his control, but he would not rush things or force her to do anything she wasn't willing to do.

Anya was now eye level with the very large bulge in his trousers. She swallowed hard and licked her lips. The sight of her sitting on the edge of the bed with her fingers still ensconced in the waistband of his trousers, was nearly his undoing. Her fingers were so close to his erection he could feel the heat of them. Anya's breath quickened causing her breasts to push against the light cotton material that covered them, he groaned. He wanted to lavish attention on those breasts with his mouth. His shaft twitched and strained against the restrictive material of his trousers. Slowly with shaky hands Anya reach for his button and undid it. Kaspir held his breath, resisting the urge to grab her and fling her back on the bed and be damned with anything else. With excruciating slowness Anya pulled down the zip. She did not know that beneath the trousers he wore nothing, so inch by slow inch he was revealed to her. When she finally released him, she gasped in astonishment. Kaspir was enormous in every sense of the word. He could take no more, stepping back he kicked off his boots and removed what was left of his clothes. Free at last he was able to gather what little control he had left. He held out his hands to Anya and lifted her up onto the bed, she was slightly taller than him now. Placing a hand at the back of her head he brought her mouth down to meet his. The heat of

Dream Lover

his naked body burned through what little clothing she had left on. After several long drugging kisses he let her go. While they had been kissing he had managed to rid her body of her clothes. Anya hadn't felt anything, losing herself in the passion of his kisses. She felt a little exposed as Kaspir released her and stepped back. He explored every inch of her with his eyes, until her image was burned onto his retinas. He worked his way down her milky white skin from her little upturned nose, down to her narrow jaw line, her long slender neck flowed into smooth white shoulders, and he noticed that they were dusted with light brown freckles. From them hung slender arms with small hands and long fingers. Her breasts were not on the large size but were pert and perfectly shaped, tipped with dark pink nipples. A narrow ribcage led to a narrow waist, ample hips, followed by short, sculptured legs. To Kaspir's surprise he seemed to harden even more.

Whilst he studied her form, she studied his. Kaspir had a strong jaw and a dimpled chin. Ice blue eyes that seemed to flicker with gold and shimmer in the light. Broad shoulders held up strong muscular arms, his torso was sculptured and ribbed. He was narrow at the hips, legs like Grecian columns. And well . . . his mighty sword was thick and heavy. Anya looked at him with trepidation.

"You're so big." Her words a mere whisper as her breath hitched. "How can you possibly think . . . ?" Kaspir stepped forward and pressed a finger to her lips.

"Ssh, Anya," he said to quieten her. "I would never hurt you . . . only pleasure you." Anya nodded, strangely trusting his words. She had no reason to, but she could hear the truth in his voice. Kaspir scooped her up and laid her on the bed, placing himself beside her. He laid one leg across her thigh, holding her gently to the bed, while his mouth and a hand began their exploration. He cupped the furthest breast in one hand, teasing and stroking the nipple between his finger and thumb. The other he laved with his tongue and sucking the nipple into the cave of his mouth. Anya arched into him as his hot, wet mouth was unrestrained on her breast. His hand then ventured slowly south, spreading an intense heat across her body as he ventured to her secret cavern. Sliding his fingers through her forest to her entrance. He could feel the heat and the moisture there as he cupped her. Kaspir slipped a finger through her folds and brushed slightly over her nub, making her squirm under him. Then he slipped his finger inside her channel, rotating gently, stirring her up even more. Then he slipped in a second, plunging deeper inside to stretch her. Anya clutched the covers as he worked them in an out, moaning incoherently that it was too much but not wanting him to stop. Then a third finger delved into her channel, she was so tight and he had to make sure she could accommodate him. Not only was he long in length, but he was large in girth. Even Kaspir was worried that he might hurt her. Kaspir kissed his way down whilst his fingers continued thrusting in and out of her preparing her for his invasion. Anya bucked and writhed under him. As he reached her entrance he could see the sweet nectar dripping from her core. Kaspir inhaled sharply catching the heady scent that was Anya.

"Anya, I need to taste you." He pleaded, she was burning with desire. Vibrations of pleasure washed over her in waves, she couldn't focus on anything.

"Kaspir please," she begged, her breath coming out in short gasps. Anya didn't know if she was begging him to stop or to relieve the ache that consumed her. Kaspir bent down and took one long slow lick over her entrance. At once Anya crashed over the edge, her orgasm making her scream and buck so hard; Kaspir had to hold her down. Little lights sparked behind her eyelids as she tried to climb up the bed. Kaspir held her firmly and placed himself at her entrance.

"Anya, I need you to breathe deep and slow for me." Anya panted as she struggled for breath. "Look at me, Anya, focus on me and breathe." Anya looked at Kaspir, his hooded eyes full of lust and desire. She nodded briefly and started to take long slow deep breaths. Every time she exhaled and relaxed he nudge his way in a little bit more. He was so big and she was so tight, the pressure on him made him wonder if he would fit. But breath after breath he managed to inch his way in until he filled her completely. She was hot and wet but he dared not to push himself all the way home for fear of hurting her. Anya started to rock; she was so tight he did not know if he would be able to move.

Dream Lover

"Kaspir please, do something. The pressure is too much like this." He knew what she meant, it felt like he was being squeezed in a velvet coated vice. He began with short slow strokes lengthening them a little at a time. His thrusts became longer and harder bringing both of them to the brink. Kaspir was spiralling out of control, with one final thrust he buried himself up to the hilt. Anya's scream caught in her throat as he poured his seed into her, her own orgasm sending molten lava coursing over him. The look of shock on her face, having him so deep inside of her, was terrifying. Kaspir was mortified as he released himself from her as carefully as he could. Anya moaned as the pressure subsided, causing several aftershocks to hit her. Kaspir sat up and turned away from her, unable to see the look of condemnation he was sure was on her face.

"I am so sorry, Anya. I never meant to hurt you." Pain and anguish coursed through him, he held his head in his hands. Ashamed that he could not keep his promise to her. Pink tears dropped silently into his palms. Anya smiled, she was sore but not in pain. She reached out her hand and stroked her fingertips down his side, but he ignored her. She rolled onto her side and put her hand flat on his back.

"Kaspir look at me," her voice was soft and gentle. He raised his head wiping his eyes and looked over his shoulder, his face still lowered unable to look at her face. "Kaspir, turn around and look at me, please." He twisted his body round so she could see him better, although he still hung his head. He could not look her in the eyes, he had disgraced himself. Anya sat up; placing a hand under his chin and lifted his head. "Kaspir," she smiled at him, her eyes sparkled in wonderment. "Kaspir, you kept every single word. You said you would pleasure me and you did. Despite your size, you did not hurt me." She gazed into his sad blue eyes and repeated her statement with more vigour. "Kaspir . . . You . . . Did . . . Not . . . Hurt . . . Me!"

"But what about . . . ?" she sat up and kissed him into silence. When she released him Anya looked him straight in the eye.

"I was just a little shocked to find out that you could fit all the way in. That's all." She laughed and her face lit up. Relief spread through Kaspir's body and he could feel another thread take hold.

"May I tell you something? It is really important and I want you to understand what I am saying to you is the truth. I do not lie and I will never lie to you."

"Okay?" Anya was perplexed by the urgency of his tone.

"I believe we are meant to be together." Anya was just about to speak when he shook his head. "Please Anya, I beg of you. Just listen, then we can talk about it afterwards." Anya nodded and pressed her thumb and forefinger together, moving it along her lips, as if to zip them shut. "You are my Solelil, my soul mate. I have searched for almost a year to find you. Please, I ask that you give us the time to talk and get to know each other. Will you give me some precious time with you?" His words tugged at Anya's heart and nodded.

"I would like to get to know you to. I will call in sick for a few days, okay." Kaspir nodded and smiled as another fine thread connected. Kaspir hoped they would have enough time to finish the mesh.

They spent a blissful five days virtually in each other's arms, talking, sharing, confessing and making love. By the end of it he had convinced her to go through with the ritual, although she still had a few concerns. But Kaspir promised he would be with her throughout and at the end of it she would know the wonders of what it was to be Vardesh. Perhaps because everything had been like a whirlwind and she had just been swept up by the intensity of it all, not giving herself enough time to think things through properly. Anya hadn't seriously considered what Kaspir had been saying.

It all seemed like a dream, a fantasy as they made their way to the secret temple. With one day left they were now standing in front of a pedestal. On it sat a bejewelled golden chalice with an inscription in some strange language. Standing beside her was Kaspir. She was besotted with him after their brief but intense affair. However, now it came down to actually going through with the ritual she was unsure. No, that wasn't true, she was terrified. He had not given her enough time to understand and digest the implications of what he had said. He had sounded so desperate, verging on despair. His eyes pleaded, they way he had spoken it was almost as if his life depended on it. But she knew that was silly, wasn't it?

At last the veil lifted and three stunningly beautiful women walked out, they were dressed similar to her. Pale green floor length togas held together with a white plaited thong, tied at the waist. On each upper arm held a silver armlet one with a phoenix design and the other a different creature. As they approached the pedestal they separated to reveal a woman dressed in head to foot in gold. Her body covered in a golden toga that shimmered in the torchlight. Her arms and her hair were adorned in gold jewellery.

Everyone who was there bowed their heads in respect. The woman in gold raised both hands towards Kaspir and Anya. She then began to chant in a language Anya had never heard before. As the woman in gold continued to chant she took one of Kaspir's hands and one of Anya's. She held them above the chalice and got them to entwine their fingers. Leaving one of her hands on theirs she reached into her hair and retrieved a small golden comb which had the image of both a dragon and a phoenix on it. Kaspir tightened his grip on Anya's hand. Within the blink of an eye she struck their wrists with the comb and blood began to pour into the chalice. Kaspir's and Anya's blood mixed together. Anya gasped and felt a rise of nausea, which she tried to hide from him. After a few moments the hand maidens wrapped their hands in a tight bandage containing some sort of salve. Once their arms were back by their sides the woman in gold lifted her own hand above the chalice. She cut herself with the golden comb and bled herself into it. After mixing the contents she handed the chalice to Kaspir.

In English so his Solelil could understand he recited the ritual. He did this so she could repeat the words.

> My mind is your mind.
>
> My heart is your heart.
>
> My soul is your soul.
>
> My body is your body.
>
> My breath is your breath.

Eunice D. Colvin

And leaned down to kiss her briefly.

My blood is your blood.

With that he raised the chalice to his mouth and drank, he then turned to the woman in gold and held it out, she took the chalice and held it out to Anya. Kaspir held his breath; if she refused it would be a death sentence for him. She looked at the chalice in the woman's hands in horror. She shook her head retching and backed away, and then everything went black.

The Beginning

When Dayton rose that evening, he knew something was different, he felt a change inside of him. From tonight an important journey was about to begin. He knew this day would come eventually and he greeted it with mixed feelings. Feelings of dread along with feelings of anticipation coursed through his veins. His blood seemed to be on fire. He remembered with great sorrow his friend Kaspir, who had died over twenty years ago. He was not allowed to go to his Transcendence Ritual, because he had not gone through one himself and from all accounts it had been a disaster. His friend had only lived a few days after bringing his Solelil to the temple. Just enough time to return her back to her previous life and seek his final resting place, before entering the black.

The realization set in that tonight was his time to seek her out, his other half, his 'Solelil' (his soul mate). For the last ten years he had dreamt of her. What she might look like, the colour of her hair, her eyes, the feel of her skin. His mind began to wander again. Dayton berated himself., he had no more time for fantasies, now the time was at hand. Tonight he would begin to seek her out. He would be certain that he would not make the mistakes as his friend had done all those years ago. It was realised that the mesh had been too weak, the connections were not strong enough. It had shattered at a crucial point in the ritual and both of them had suffered, but in different ways. His friend lost his life and his friend's Solelil would have a half life, never really being fulfilled. She would always know that there was something missing, but never really knowing what exactly.

Dayton dressed himself in his favourite clothes, tight black jeans that hugged his long muscular legs. A white v-neck sweater that fit him like a second skin caressing over his ribbed torso and black converse trainers. His clothes complimented his long wavy black hair that rippled down his back, like the ocean at night. Tonight he wore it tied back with a black satin ribbon at his nape. Within his strong angular features were a set of deep blue eyes. Eyes the colour of the deepest ocean. He smiled to himself, 'now it begins'.

In his study Dayton sat in his favourite chair, a high winged back covered in soft dark brown leather. Positioned on the right hand side of the marble fire place he could look out over the ocean. No fire was lit in the hearth that evening, as it was unusually warm for April. He took a deep breath to steady himself, as he made himself comfortable. He was now ready for the task ahead of him. He was hungry, but not for food his appetite was sated. Dayton knew he would need a great deal of strength this night, so he journeyed to Aberdeen. Whilst there he visited many public houses and had consumed almost three times the amount of blood that he would normally have. He felt bloated and a little sick, he could not tell if the sickness was because of the blood or the anticipation. All he wanted to do now was to stretch out his mind and find his Solelil, he may not even succeed this time. Dayton had no idea in which direction she would be. This night would prove to be one of the most difficult nights of his life, he might have to try many times before succeeding. Taking another deep calming breath Dayton centred himself. Sending his mind out into the aether he sort his target.

He had no idea of the passage of time as his consciousness travelled in every direction searching for the smallest of connections. After what had seemed an eternity Dayton felt a tingling sensation course through his body. This was what he was looking for, he turned all his energy to that direction using the feeling to guide him. Although, he did not know the whys or the wherefores, he knew deep in his heart that he was on the verge of reaching his destination. Then he saw it, a small spark of light. Dayton suddenly felt a wrench as his soul raced towards the light, instinct took over he was no longer in control. He knew when the connection had been made because his eyes flew open from the sheer impact. Breathlessly Dayton looked over to the grandfather clock which stood in the far corner of the room. He was amazed to see it was almost dawn, through the window he could see the horizon beginning to lighten. There was no more time, his body felt leaden, he was not really surprised how drained he felt. Despite his preparation he had used virtually every ounce of energy in his body. He desperately needed to rest and replenish himself before he could attempt another contact with her. At least he had found her and the connection had been made, however tenuous. Next time she would be much easier to find because he could follow the thread. Dayton heaved himself out of the chair, his legs were weak, threatening to buckle under him. Thankfully the entrance to his sleeping chamber was just to the left of the massive oak desk. Travelling down through the secret entrance he entered his room, just in time to collapse on the bed.

The Dream

Erysah woke with a fright, her heart beating like a drum. Thankfully it was not because of her usual nightmare. She usually woke most nights, after revisiting the death of her family. It was almost the same every time. She found herself running along a road that was on the side of a hill. On either side of her were steep slopes. Travelling on one of these roads was dangerous, giving the driver three options and only one of them was good. Erysah always found herself on the same place each time. She got there just in time to see her grandfathers car go through the barrier and tumble down the slope carrying her mother and grandmother with him. As she watched it tumble in horror she knew once again she was too late. She always woke when the car exploded at the bottom. Although Erysah had not witnessed it, she had made the mistake of visiting the crash site. Ever since then she had relived the accident like a repressed memory. Somehow she had picked up on the echo of the event and began to relive it in her dreams. The past week had been the worst, she had had the dream every night without fail. The stress was getting to her, the last time she had had it this bad was just after the incident when she had gone to lay flowers where they had gone off.

Erysah had no family left now and she had never known her father. Her mother had always insisted that she was a result of a one night stand and that she never saw him again. Despite that fact she said that she never regretted it, because she had been given a most valuable gift. Erysah was nineteen when her mother and grandparents died. Her mother had never married, she never even went out with men. Even though, they were queuing down the street to date her. She just never seemed interested, Erysah never understood why. Her mother was a very beautiful woman and everyone said that Erysah looked like her in every way. But she wasn't interested in another relationship. The only way she could describe it was almost like part of her life was missing and she had no intention of finding it. She had dedicated her life to bringing up her daughter and then looking after her parents.

Erysah still grieved for them, even now. She had lost all three of them in the same car crash, two years ago. She supposed that in the great scheme of things two years was not very long. At the inquest they said it was an accident. That her grandfather had had a heart attack whilst at the wheel, causing the car to veer over the edge of a cliff and crash into a ravine. Erysah's nightmares came only some nights now. At first they had been constant, so much so she wished she had never visited the site. Erysah had gone to counselling to help with the dreams. Her dreams had persisted and the sleep deprivation was taking its toll on her. Six months down the line, Erysah and her counsellor had parted company. She felt as though they were just going round in circles and getting nowhere. The nightmares had subsided slightly, but they had not gone away. There intensity was the same as it had always been. The only useful thing to come out of the sessions was the 'dream diary'. The diary had helped her refocus after the terror of the nightmares.

However tonight she did not have the nightmare, tonight she had a very strange dream. In her dream she felt like she was floating in the middle of a lake or sea at night. No matter where she looked she could not see the shore line. The moon was full, then she noticed a glowing thread in the black water, as she pulled at it she saw it was attached to something. When it got closer she saw it was a man but all she could see was his face. Erysah's breath caught in her throat. He was amazingly handsome, although his eyes were closed he looked in pain. Erysah reached out and touched his face, when she did his eyes flew open. Erysah gasped at the colour of his eyes as he fixed his gaze on her, moments later she woke up. Erysah reached into her nightstand drawer and got out her diary, then she started to write what she could remember of her dream.

Diary entry—April 12th 2015—03:03am

> *Tonight I had another dream. This one was not like the others. It was completely different to the ones I usually have. It was the strangest of all dreams. I remember seeing the face of a man. A very handsome man with angular features, his dark hair pooled*

around his face in the water. His skin was smooth as cream and it had a soft glowing appearance. I did not recognise him, so I know it wasn't someone I had seen at the bar. His eyes were closed and had heavy brows that matched the colour of his hair. His brow was creased as if in pain or concentrating very hard, suddenly his eyes flew open. It was like he had seen me. His eyes were the deepest blue I have ever seen. That's when I woke up.

After Erysah had written the dream in her diary, she lay back down on the pillow. Without realising it she was rubbing her left hand. Not that it was sore, there was just a slight tingling sensation there. She was still feeling rather breathless after the bizarre dream. Leaving the light on Erysah closed her eyes and then had to sit back up and open them again, the face of the man was still there in her mind. Her mind was filled with it, especially his eyes. She couldn't believe those eyes, they were the deepest blue she had ever seen. They seem to sparkle with a slightly paler shade of blue. Like pale stars in the nights sky. There seemed to be a hunger in those eyes, as if searching for something or someone. Who was he, she wondered?

Feeling restless she got out of bed. Looking at the clock it was still only 03:30am. Twenty seven minutes ago since she had been woken by the dream. After using the bathroom Erysah went into her kitchen and put on the coffee machine. While she waited for the coffee to brew she went into the living area and looked around her apartment. Erysah was the envy of all her friends, she had been left a sizeable inheritance and could afford to be self sufficient. She owned a reasonably sized open plan loft apartment. In a newly renovated part of town. Erysah walked across to the windows and opened the curtains slightly and stared out at the lights sparkling in the streets below. It was in a fairly new building, part of a regeneration scheme within the city. Her grandparents had left it to her in their will. What Erysah hadn't realised it was supposed to have been a 21st birthday present. They had put a deposit on it before it was even complete.

However, after the accident everything went to Erysah anyway. There had been three properties left to her. Her grandparents house, which was in the country. A big property set in 50 acres of land. With ten bedrooms, several reception rooms and bathrooms. A splendid manor house indeed. But it was far too big for Erysah. Her grandparents had bought it when they retired after selling their haulage business. On which they made a very good profit. Then there was her mother's house, a four bedroom detached property in a mock Tudor style. Neither of the properties appealed to her for a number of reasons, the main one being too many memories. She had asked her solicitor to sell them and most of the contents. Erysah just kept a few of her favourite pieces, which she gave pride of place in her home. She loved her two bed roomed loft apartment and it was more special because it had been bought for her by her grandparents. It was spacious and open plan with a living room, dining room and kitchen that occupied the main space. Then there were two bed rooms both with built in storage and en-suite bathrooms.

When everything had been finalised the solicitor sent her a cheque, Erysah found herself quite rich, even after heavy death duties, which had taken at least half of the inheritance and of course there were the solicitors fees on top of that. Erysah had also donated to several charities at the request of her mother. Unbeknown to her, both her mother and grandparents had considerable savings. So she still had a sizeable amount left, the actual figure was only a few thousand pounds shy of three million. As she stood there staring out at the night she began rubbing her hand again. Looking down Erysah saw that she was rubbing the tattoo that was there, resting just above her thumb on the front of it. A single tear slid down her cheek as she remembered the day she had gotten it. It had been the only thing that Erysah and her mother had shared. Her mother had said she wanted to give Erysah a present to remind her that she was part of her mother and that despite everything she loved her daughter. They had spent the whole day together doing mother and daughter stuff. For the first time in her life Erysah had the mother she always wanted. They went to a salon and had their hair and nails done, then they had lunch, finally going to a tattoo parlour and getting identical tattoos. It was a small black dragon of tribal design about three centimetres long. The tattoo lay from her wrist to the junction between her thumb and fore finger. Erysah had been so happy that day. She could remember them putting their hands together and looking at the tattoos in the mirror. Another tear fell as she moved away from the window, her eyes blurred as more tears threatened. She wasn't going to go down that road again, she had promised herself that she would not cry any more. Staring out at the night seeing the lights on the darkened landscape reminded her of the strangers eyes in her dream, she would rather focus on that than be reminded of her family.

Erysah headed back to the kitchen area and grabbed a cup of coffee then made her way back to the sofa. Tucking one leg under her she thought back to the night out with her friends. It had been her 21st birthday and Erysah had gone out with a couple of old friends from college for a meal. A quiet birthday party in her favourite restaurant. Erysah had never been one for clubbing and partying despite the fact she had spent the last three years working in a bar. Apart from a few college friends who she saw occasionally when she wasn't working, she had no other friends. There was her boss Greg and his mother Violet, but they were more like family to her. They had had a sumptuous meal, a few drinks, good conversation. Her friends had mainly moaned about the men in their lives. But when they took her to task about not having a man in her life, she just threw their own words back at them. She was not ready to settle down and to be truthfully honest she didn't know if she would ever be.

As Erysah reflected on the conversation with her friends she realised she had a rather sad and lonely existence. She began to rub the tattoo again absentmindedly. Even as a young girl her life had been very insular, mainly revolving around her family. Her grandparents and her mother. The only time it didn't was when she was at college. Somehow she felt like she was continuing where her mother left off. As an adult she was living the same way, apart from the fact that her family was now gone. Had she substituted Greg and Violet for them. Her heart ached, sighing she closed her eyes. Once again the vision of the handsome man appeared in her mind. Instead of opening her eyes, she studied his face. For some unknown reason she felt drawn to it. Was this hope she was glimpsing at or just a fantasy of what she wanted, no needed. Erysah knew there had to be more to her life than what she had now. Existing was no longer an option anymore, she wanted to live. Erysah had made her mind up, she was going to grab every opportunity that came her way. No more being content with what she had. With that decision made, Erysah headed back to bed hoping to try and get a few more hours sleep before her shift started at the bar.

Six Months Later

Dayton had not realised how much energy he had used in the first attempt at finding his Solelil. He had been laid up for almost four months. Then it had taken another two months to rebuild his energy levels, before he could even think about making another attempt. After he had fed Dayton had come back into the library and settled down once again into his favourite chair. The soft brown leather cocooning him in its gentle embrace. He had sat there every night for the last six months while he recuperated, reliving his first contact with her. The weather had turned colder so there was now a fire blazing in the hearth. Along the far wall flames danced creating shadows that darted around in anticipation. The flames took him back briefly to a time when his parents had helped him use his talents. They would sit around a fire and his father had suggested he use the flames to help him focus. At times he still used this method to help him, especially if the task was a difficult one. Clearing his mind of all thought he focussed on the fire, taking a deep breath to centre himself, Dayton closed his eyes and began to expand his mind, this time knowing in which direction he had to go. He reached for the fine thread that had already been made by the initial contact. Sliding his mind along it, he felt its energy the thread would become thicker and stronger with every contact made. It behaved a bit like electricity, it could travel with ease but unless there was a destination to ground itself it was inert. Dayton knew the more times he used the thread the stronger the connection would become, as long as she connected with him at the other end. Within minutes Dayton was there in the back of her mind. This time he was careful to take it slower, he did not want to frighten her. The first time he connected was like being struck by a thunder bolt. All he could really remember of it was the flash of her green eyes as they connected.

Dayton was surprised to find that she was awake. He sat there in her subconscious watching through her eyes and waited. She was sitting in front of a mirror brushing her hair. This was his opportunity to have his first look at her. He stared out through her eyes amazed at the reflection he saw. She was so beautiful; her skin looked like the colour of alabaster. Smooth and creamy, magnificent large emerald green eyes and full luscious deep pink lips filled her face. Her hair was long and thick and the colour of fire. Curls sprang up as the brush released its hold on the strands. Dayton was transfixed by her, a desperation came over him that he nearly forgot himself. Calming his emotions he became resolute, he had to strengthen the thread. It would be the only way he would be able to find her in the physical world. As reluctant as he was, he had to pull back. As gently as he could he slipped away from her, feeling slightly bereft he returned to his body. Dayton had every intention of returning again later that night, in her dreams.

Erysah sat there staring at her reflection in the mirror. Her hand seemed to have frozen in place on the last stroke. She couldn't seem to move or blink. For some strange reason she seemed to be transfixed by her own image. After what seemed like hours she came out of her trance. '*I must be more tired than I realised*,' she thought shaking her head. Getting up from her dressing table she walked over to her bed, she stopped briefly pulling back the covers and glanced back at the mirror. A shiver ran through her body as if someone had walked over her grave. She felt her hand began tingle as she climbed in. Curling up she rubbed her fingers over the tattoo, then she cuddled her pillow and drifted off into a deep dreamless sleep.

Dayton had hoped to return to his flame haired beauty again that night, but because the thread was still new and extremely fine, he had not got the energy to return to her. He needed to feed again before dawn came. Since making contact he was getting more anxious to find her or perhaps it was more in anticipation. He was feeling confused by his emotions, it seemed they had increased since he had started his 'year of yearning'. Although the Vardesh had emotions they became muted after ascension. Now they had definitely increased since that first contact. He took a deep breath to calm himself, he needed to plan and think of a suitable dream for their first meeting. Thankfully he still had the time to make sure everything was done properly. He would not leave anything to chance unlike . . . he did not want to dwell on those thoughts. Now that he had seen her face, it was all that he could focus on. Tired, drained and frustrated, he ventured out into the forest to seek out sustenance. A few miles from

Dayton's home was a small village where he could gather enough blood to replenish him. He would have to be very careful this close to home and he would have to do something he wasn't keen on and more often than not frowned upon. Grazing was deemed unseemly and dangerous because it would affect too many people, but Dayton was convinced that he did not have any choice. On careful consideration he decided to visit every fifth house and take a little from each male there. With his ability to slide in and out without being seen or heard by anyone or anything, he could ghost through the doors without a problem. By the end of the night he had visited a substantial number of the healthy male populace there, most of them had been drinking and would feel as though they were slightly hung over from their previous night's libations. It was an hour before sunrise, barely enough time to get home and secure himself safely in his chamber.

Erysah woke the next morning feeling more refreshed than she had been in the last few years. She realised that she hadn't dreamt at all last night, well not that she could remember, it left her feeling rather disjointed. The thumb of her right hand caressed the dragon on her left. She had got so used to dreaming every night, whether just a dream showing a memory of her family or whether the nightmare of their deaths. She had always dreamt something, or so she thought. As Erysah sat in front of her mirror she had the strange feeling of 'deja vu', perhaps she had dreamt of sorts. A waking dream . . . a dream about her face, she laughed at how preposterous that sounded. Getting up she went to her bedside drawer and got out her dream diary. Then turning to the last entry, she read it. It was the dream about the face of a man in a lake or something attached to a silvery thread. A very handsome man but what would he have to do with her? What was really strange was she was almost certain that she had had other dreams but for some reason she hadn't written any down. Not since the dream about the man's face all those months ago. Had it really been that long and why on earth would she dream about her own face. Once again her mind drifted to the features of the handsome stranger and his amazing eyes. She could drown in those eyes, two pools of deepest blue she had ever seen. She could imagine falling into them and not wanting to leave. Erysah shook her head and chastised herself. *Pull yourself together Erysah*, she thought, as she closed her diary with a resounding thud. Over the last few months she had often thought about the man in her dream.

Fantasising about him in every way, *'boy did she need to get a life.'* She laughed to herself as she returned the book to its home.

Tonight she was on the late shift at the bar. Normally she wouldn't, but Greg had asked her as a favour. His mother, Violet had been taken ill unexpectedly. Erysah wasn't comfortable with the idea but she had met Violet on numerous occasions and got on with her really well. She was as shocked as him when Greg told her that she had had a heart attack. Violet had always treated Erysah like a daughter. Greg said she sometimes seemed to prefer Erysah to him, which made her laugh. Although, he didn't mind really. Greg always thought that if he had had a younger sister, he would want her to be exactly like Erysah. She didn't need to work but she wanted to. She had to have some purpose in life. She could have travelled the world but never had the inclination. So she got a job as a part time bar maid, just so she could keep busy. Erysah found that she was very good with the customers and Greg said she was good for business. Ever since Greg had given her a job, business had more than doubled. She was young and attractive, but not trashy. Erysah didn't go in for all this peacocking business. She dressed simply but well, especially as money was no object. Usually she did the lunchtime shift but tonight Greg was feeling vulnerable and needed someone he could trust to close up for him. He had been devastated when it had happened. Luckily he was at home at the time. Greg had said that she was making a cup of tea when it happened. He had been in the living room watching the television when he heard a crash in the kitchen. When he got there his mum was on the floor clutching her chest, broken crockery all over the floor. Greg was grateful it was only the cups and not the teapot which had been brewing, otherwise she could have been scalded too. Despite the fact that Greg had a couple of other guys working for him, he never seemed to trust them the way he did her. How could she say no to him or Violet? Erysah was upset by what had happened, the memories of her own loss still fresh in her mind. She prayed that Violet would recover quickly. She was a tough old bird and Erysah had a feeling she would be back on her feet in no time.

As Erysah walked into the bar she was met by the look of relief on Greg's face, he smiled at her briefly. She could see the strain and the worry on his face. Dark patches shaded his eyes and his skin was pale from lack of sleep. As she reached him she gave him a reassuring hug.

"How is she Greg?" It pained her to see him like this. She always knew him as rock steady with a shy confident air about him. Now he was a mess, worry and doubt were his bed fellows at the moment, tinged with a little fear. She could understand that Greg was devoted to his mum and if god forbid he lost her well . . . She was his rock, all he had except for the bar.

"She's stable, the worst is over thankfully." Erysah didn't really know what to say, so she said the only thing she could think of despite the urge to bite her lip.

"Come on Greg, Violet's tough, she'll be home before you know it." Erysah smiled briefly but it didn't reach her eyes. Deep down she was just as worried as he was. She doted on Violet almost as much as Greg did. They had both been there for her when she had lost all her family, especially Violet. She had been very patient with her in fact she was grateful to both Greg and his mother. Without them she didn't know what she would have done. To her they were her 'family' now, the only family she had since her mother and grandparents had died. That's when she realised that yes, she had replaced one with the other. Oh, how sad. It almost made her want to cry but for who? She gave Greg another hug and held out her hand. "Keys", she said wiggling her fingers. Greg dug down in his pocket and gave Erysah the keys to the bar.

"Thank you for doing this Erysah, are you sure?" Greg knew he didn't have to ask the question but he felt obliged to. At the moment his life seemed full of doubt and he needed that extra bit of reassurance. Since Erysah had come into their lives things had been much brighter. Although there was that time a couple of years ago when she had lost all her family. That almost tore her apart, thankfully that was past now and she had regained her bubbly self. Now it was his turn to lean on her as she had on him and his mother. Not that it was demanded, it was like she was just part of the family. He felt a closeness, a connection of some kind and he loved her, not like a man loved a woman but as a brother who loved his sister. Erysah shook him out of his thoughts.

"Go before I change my mind and give Violet a kiss from me." With that she took the keys turned him around and pushed him towards the door. It was a quiet night for a Thursday, so quiet in fact, she let Kenny go early.

Eunice D. Colvin

Sometimes Erysah thought the quiet nights were the worst. Whilst Kenny was still there serving customers she took advantage and cleaned the whole of the bar area, from one end to the other. She took off every bottle and every glass off each shelf and cleaned the shelves, bottles and glasses before putting everything back. Kenny had laughed at her and called her the 'dust buster'. Erysah swiped at him with her cloth and told him to wash the bar down for his cheek. By the time she got home that night, she was exhausted. It was 3am and all she could think of was sleep. Dragging herself into her room she flopped onto the bed, she was asleep before her head hit the pillow.

Dayton had been trying to reach his 'Solelil' for hours but her mind was too active that he couldn't connect to her. He was worried and frustrated, he desperately needed to strengthen the thread between them. Going out as soon as it was dark he travelled to a village south of him and fed. He had got back about midnight and headed straight back to his library. Dayton had tried every hour since then to connect with her, to no avail. It was now 3:30am and Dayton was getting tired but he refused to give in, he needed to know she was okay. Once again he let his mind follow the thread, this time it connected, relief washed over him. Her mind was heavy with sleep as he slipped into her sub-conscious as gently as he could. He stroked her mind softly with great care trying to ease her exhaustion. He sent her waves of warmth and affection, even though he had not met her yet he knew he was falling in love with her. The feeling was all encompassing. All it had taken was that one look at her beautiful face. Her green eyes that were the shade of deepest emerald reminded him of the forests of home. He had not thought of the place since he had left nearly three hundred years ago. He wanted to fall into her eyes and lose himself. Before he left he brushed a kiss in her mind and smiled. '*Soon my love, soon I will find you*', he whispered to her and then retreated. Before he came back to himself he checked the thread, it was much thicker now. He had made contact three times, although he had been down the thread at least twice that many. Unfortunately, it only grew stronger when a connection had been made. So despite all his attempts earlier it had not made any difference. Dayton was resolved even though he was getting tired. Tomorrow he would make plans to start the important task of connecting properly with his Solelil. He already selected the dream and could not wait until then. Dayton rose wearily and headed down to his sleeping chamber, he was eager to start this journey. But could do nothing until tomorrow night, when they would have their first true encounter. Then they would start a journey that would change their lives forever.

Erysah was not surprised to find that she had slept late. She had even slept through the phone ringing. Her answer phone was flashing with at least one message. Whatever it was it would have to wait until she had had something to eat and drink. Erysah desperately needed a shower, a coffee and some food. She had slept in the clothes that she had worn last night whilst working at the bar. They smelt of stale beer and sweat and so did she. Walking into her bathroom Erysah turned on the shower then went back into the bedroom and stripped. Leaving her clothes in a pile on the floor, Erysah padded back into the bathroom. When the warm water hit her skin she groaned in ecstasy. Letting it fall over her it washed the tiredness away. Washing her hair she gently rubbed her scalp, then suddenly stopped. She had the faintest memory of someone stroking her hair in a caress and then a kiss. Erysah raised her fingers to her lips, it was as if she could feel a kiss lingering there. Her fingers began to tremble as the tingle started on her tattoo again. Erysah shook her head trying to erase the feeling and finished showering. Sitting on the end of her bed still wrapped in a towel she questioned herself. *'Did I have a dream last night?'* She began to rub the tattoo again. She had been so tired she had just flaked out. Ever since she had dreamt of the man with those deep, deep blue eyes, she had felt more relaxed and rested. It was a strange realisation but in some way also comforting. Her thoughts were disturbed by the phone ringing. Jumping she headed into the living area, picking up the phone Erysah spoke.

"Hello."

"Erysah, Erysah, thank heavens you're okay!" Greg's frantic voice bellowed down the handset, it was so loud she had to hold it away from her ear.

"Greg? Calm down.! What's wrong?" Her ear was ringing from the decibels he had been speaking at.

"I've tried ringing you three times today, didn't you get my messages?" His breathing was still erratic from his outburst.

"I haven't long got up and then went straight in the shower, I never heard the phone ring, sorry."

"But I rang at eleven, then twelve and then twenty minutes ago." Greg sounded a little exasperated. Erysah looked at the clock, it was well after one in the afternoon, she was shocked. "Erysah are you there? Are you listening to me?"

"Sorry Greg, I must have zoned out for a moment." She decided to change the subject. "How's Violet?"

"That's what I was ringing to tell you about. She's coming home tomorrow." The excitement in his voice made her feel relieved. She had every faith that she would be okay.

"Oh, Greg, that's fantastic news. Will she need some help at home? Are they sending a nurse to look after her?" Erysah knew she was babbling but she didn't care, she was just happy that Violet had survived.

"Slow down, Erysah, for crying out loud. Are you okay?" Greg was concerned he had never heard her run off at the mouth before, he would have found it comical if the situation hadn't of been serious.

"Yes, sorry Greg. It was just a really long night I didn't get home until after three this morning. I guess I'm still a little out of it, I haven't even had chance to get anything to eat or drink yet."

"Erysah I'm sorry. Listen I have decided to close the bar for a while, so I can spend some time with mum and by the sounds of it you could do with some time off yourself."

"But . . . what about Kenny and Charlie? Couldn't they look after the bar for you?"

"No, I wouldn't feel comfortable with them running it by themselves." Greg felt a little guilty at his words because they had been with him for some time.

"You'll have to trust them at some point." Erysah felt sorry for them. They had been there before she had even started. Charlie had worked for Greg for almost ten years and Kenny for nearly five. But for some unknown reason everything changed when she had started three years ago. She had to give them their due, they were really good about it. Mind you the pair of them were so laid back, they were almost horizontal.

"I know, but not today Erysah, my decision is final. It won't do them any harm either." Greg couldn't actually remember when any of them had had an actual holiday. Between the four of them the bar was manned every day, both shifts. But he had made an executive decision and that was the end of it. "And thanks so much for last night. Now get off the phone and eat!"

"Yes Dad," Erysah laughed.

"I'll ring you in a couple of days, okay." Greg was not letting her get away with hiding, he knew full well that's exactly what she'd do.

"Okay, bye." Greg could be such an old man at times, but he was good to her and she was really grateful for that.

"Bye and thanks again. Oh, by the way can you drop off the bar keys at the house later?"

"Yeah, sure."

"Just pop them through the letter box because I don't know when we'll be back from the hospital."

"Okay, bye." Erysah's stomach began to rumble, giving her a subtle hint that she needed to eat.

After Erysah put down the phone she went and got dressed quickly, choosing a set of grey sweats for comfort because she had no intention of going anywhere. Going into the kitchen area she made herself some brunch and a coffee. As she ate Erysah listened to the messages Greg had left. Not once did he mention closing the bar. *'Perhaps . . .'* she thought, '*it must have been a last minute decision*'. She hoped it wasn't because of the conversation she had had with him this afternoon.

A couple of hours later Erysah was weaving her way across town towards Greg's house to drop off the bar keys. She wanted to talk to Greg about his decision but when she rang the door bell no one answered. '*He must still be at the hospital*', she thought. So she posted the keys and headed back to her car. It was already dark and the air was bitingly chilly, frost was already forming on the metal of the lamp post as she walked past it to her car. Erysah always made a habit of parking near or under a light at night, for her own safety. Even in the safest of places you had your unruly populace. Once in her car Erysah felt much safer, her ragged breath steaming the cold windows. Turning the key the engine roared to life, the sound deafening in the dark. A few minutes later her screen was clear enough for her to drive off.

By the time she got back home it was early evening. Erysah was still feeling the effects of the previous night as a wave of tiredness hit her. So she grabbed a frozen meal and put it in the microwave. Once it was ready she grabbed a can of juice and sat in front of the TV and began flicking. She had travelled through all the channels at least twice but found nothing of interest to watch. Bored with what was on the television she finished her meal and decided to have an early night. As she lay on her bed her mind went back to earlier today in the shower. The strange memory of being caressed and kissed were still on her mind as she fell asleep.

Erysah found herself walking on a beach the soft warm sand cushioning her bare feet. In the distance she saw a dark figure standing motionless staring out to sea. She should have felt afraid, she was alone in a strange place with a mysterious figure in front of her. Erysah didn't know if they were male or female. From where she stood the figure was just a shadow, the moon silhouetting them. She felt the strange urge to approach. Erysah was trying to decide if it was just curiosity or something more compelling that was pulling her as she continued to walk towards them. The closer she got the more she noticed. Erysah now saw that they had long dark flowing hair that billowed behind them in the breeze. But that didn't mean anything nowadays both men and women had long hair. The shadowy figure seemed very tall and as she drew closer, a feeling of trepidation grew inside her. Butterflies seemed to take flight in her stomach making her skin rise with goose bumps. Erysah expected the person to notice her approach, not that she was deliberately being quiet but they just stood statue still gazing out over the sea. Within minutes she was standing only a few metres from them. It was then she noticed that the dark figure was a man. Erysah froze, her gasp stilled in her throat. As if he had heard her breath, his head turned slowly towards her. The moon was full and high in the sky giving off enough light so she was able to see his face. 'His face', she thought as her eyes widened. 'I know that face'. She had seen it before but where . . . Her hand flew up to her throat as the realisation set in. 'From the dream.' The shock on her face was apparent as her chin dropped.

"Hello," he said with a smile that was as bright as the moon itself. It made his eyes glow as the smile reached them. Erysah immediately closed her gawping mouth. 'Oh, god! Those eyes, his eyes'. Erysah's mind was in turmoil and she thought she might faint. "Hello," he repeated. "My name is Dayton, may I ask what your name is?" His voice was just a whisper on the breeze but she felt it brush against her skin from head to toe. Erysah shuddered at the sensation and realised she had been standing staring at him, well his face anyway. Erysah shook her head slightly trying to come to her senses.

"Who are you?" Despite the fact that he had already introduced himself, it hadn't registered with her, bewilderment came across in her voice.

"Dayton, and you are?" There was no impatience in his tone, Erysah must have seemed like a love struck school girl the way she was acting. She cringed inwardly at the picture.

"Erysah," she croaked. Then cleared her throat so she could speak more clearly. "My name is Erysah." Then Dayton turned all the way around. She was still far enough away to be able to see all of him and there was a lot of him. He was tall at least a foot taller than her five foot seven inches. Long, strong muscular legs that were hugged by his tight black jeans. His feet were bare like hers but his were large with long slender toes. Broad shoulders topped a ribbed torso and muscular arms that was sheathed in a light v-neck sweater. He was beautiful, built like an Adonis and his skin had an luminous shine to it in the moonlight. He held out his hand which was also large with long pianist fingers attached to those strong arms of his. Dayton started to move slowly towards her with his hand extended, obviously he did not want to frighten her.

Eunice D. Colvin

"Hello, Erysah. I am pleased to make your acquaintance." His voice was as smooth as the silk caressing her skin and made the butterflies dance even more in her stomach. Without thought she extended her own hand towards his. Suddenly her hand was wrapped in his and he raised it to his mouth and kissed the back of it. His lips were deliciously soft and warm as they pressed onto the back of it. As he looked over their hands at her she felt herself melt. "I have been waiting for you," he said simply, a small smile touching his mouth. Erysah couldn't help but give him a puzzled look.

"Waiting for me?"

"Yes. Would you walk with me Erysah?" Erysah didn't have the strength to resist him but she also forgot how her legs worked and was rooted to the spot.

"Walk where? There is nowhere to go." Dayton smiled again, this time it reached his eyes making them sparkle in the moonlight. Erysah had forgotten he still had hold of her hand as he gently tugged her into moving with him. They walked hand in hand for a few minutes without saying a word. The whispering sound of bare feet on wet sand and the gentle rolling of the waves on the shore serenaded them as they walked. Before Erysah realised it they were near some flat rocks.

"Shall we sit Erysah?" She couldn't speak so she just nodded and followed him onto them. Helping her up he placed his hands on either side of her slender waist and lifted so she could sit. The rock felt warm under her but not as warm as the feeling of his hands burning through the fine material of her nightgown, as if it wasn't there. Leaving what felt like hot brands on her skin, letting go he sat next to her. He turned his body towards her so he could drink her in and the feel of her body for those few brief seconds left his hands scorched. Her long curly flame red hair reached almost to her waist which meant that when it was wet it would be much longer. Her emerald green eyes sparkled in the moonlight against her alabaster skin. Now that he could see the rest of her he was more in awe of her. She was dressed in just a pale pink nightdress, made of a silky material which finished just above her knees. Thin spaghetti straps held it up revealed slender shoulders and the delicate bones below her throat. Her décolletage led to ample breasts which stretched the material so taught that it held them tightly. The cool breeze teased her nipples into hard peaks, his eyes were automatically drawn to them. Immediately he felt a stirring in his groin, he shifted slightly adjusting his position. Moving his eyes he looked at her shapely legs, although he could not see all of them he knew they would be long and slender. Erysah had ample hips and a slim waist. She was perfect in every way possible.

Erysah wondered why he did not speak but just sat there and stared at her. She was beginning to think there was something wrong with her. She felt like he was devouring her with those eyes, it made her feel very strange. A warmth spread through her body and coloured her cheeks. She had the strange feeling of being caressed all over even though all he did was look at her. It left her feeling hot and needy which was very disconcerting. The only way that she knew he had not gone into shock was from the movement of his eyes and when he shifted slightly.

"Is there something wrong?" His eyes darted back to hers. "You were staring at me."

"Yes, no, I am sorry." Dayton felt slightly confused and embarrassed. He never expected to have such a reaction to their meeting. "I just have not seen anyone as beautiful as you." With his statement she blushed even more and her core heated. Boldly he said, "I have this urge to kiss you, may I?" Erysah had the urge to laugh but she stopped herself, she was strangely curious and wanted to know more. Was this just another dream, a fantasy. Because if it was, it was a really good one. Was her life that bad that she had to conjure up an imaginary man.

"Why do you always seem to be asking me questions?" Erysah seemed to have found her voice again.

"I would not want to do anything to hurt or upset you. I would feel remiss if I did not ask for your permission."

"You never asked permission to pick me up and sit me on this rock." Her statement took him by surprise. She was right he had not done so. Was he so struck that he had lost his manners.

"My apologies Erysah, I regret I forgot myself. I beg that you do not take offense by my forwardness." His voice held a sincerity Erysah had never heard before.

Although the way he spoke was a little unusual. This made her smile despite herself. Her smile lifted Dayton's heart, such a gift she had bestowed on him. He repeated his question. "Please Erysah, may I kiss you?" Erysah found herself wanting the very same thing. Even if it was a dream, she might as well enjoy it. She remembered the touch of his lips on the back of her hand and was intrigued to know how his lips would feel on hers. Erysah nodded and smiled again. He looked at her intently and she realised that he wanted a verbal response, not just a nod. Erysah sighed.

"Yes Dayton, I would like you to kiss me." There she had said his name, it just rolled off her tongue so naturally, suddenly she felt very shy. Dayton was aghast when she had said his name, another gift. He could not believe his luck; he took both her hands in his and leaned in towards her. Erysah responded and leaned into him, as she did one of her straps slipped off her shoulder revealing the curve of one of her breasts. Dayton could not fail to miss it. He closed the distance of their bodies so he could feel the heat of her. His hand slid up her arm to her strap and replaced it carefully. The softness of her skin as he touched it made him moan inwardly causing a constriction in his nether regions. In turn Erysah's pulled her other hand from his and it travelled up his muscular forearm continuing over his bicep to his shoulder stopping at the nape of his neck. At the same time Dayton's hand had reached hers. Both seemed to close their eyes as if wanting to savour the moment, the feel and the taste of each other. Who moaned first they did not know, they were lost in the sensation of lips against lips. Electricity seemed to pass through him as Dayton deepened the kiss. Erysah gasped and he explored her mouth with such ferocity, he could not continue the dream.

Erysah woke up gasping from the dream, unable to comprehend what had just happened. It had felt so real she could still feel her lips tingling, where he had pressed his lips to hers. She could still taste him in her mouth, he tasted of the sea and exotic spices. The touch of his hand on her skin, the feel of his muscles under her hand. What would her counsellor make of this dream? Even though, she was so confused, she was still determined to log it. After all, what good was a dream diary if you didn't use it. She almost laughed at the prospect of re-reading this particular dream and analysing it later. As she went to get her diary the dragon tattoo was tingling again. Erysah rubbed it with the heel of her hand, irritated by it. Grabbing her diary she opened it. When she looked at the last entry made it was on the 12th April, that was over six months ago. *'How can that be?'* she thought. She must have dreamt, she always dreamt. Erysah cast her mind back a few days earlier when she was sitting in front of her mirror, yes that had been a waking dream, her first. She quickly noted it down. Then there was the night before when she remembered the feeling of being caressed and kissed. By the time she had finished filling in her diary it was close to ten o'clock. Erysah thought that perhaps she was slowly losing her mind. She could have sworn that she had picked up her diary the other day and written in it, obviously not. Deciding to eat, before taking a shower she headed for the kitchen. Erysah realised that she was officially on vacation and she had no idea what she was going to do. She had never had a holiday or even travelled anywhere. She wouldn't know where to begin. After showering she tried to come up with a plan of action. She scanned the internet for holidays but there was nothing that attracted her attention. Erysah tried reading a book but seemed to keep reading the same few lines over and over again. Her next attempt was with the TV, still no joy. Her restlessness was beginning to annoy her. She stood by the window and looked down on the world. As she watched it go by her mind wandered back to the previous night and the dream. How vivid it had been and to still have sensations after waking, well she had never heard of such a thing happening. Turning away she went into her bedroom and fetched her dream diary. If truth be told it had been calling her all day but she had been trying to ignore it. Propping herself up with the pillows she opened it and started with the entry date April 12th. After reading them she was hoping to make some sense of them all.

Dayton sat back in his chair with a look of satisfaction on his face, his heart was full of joy. The fact that he could conjure the dream meant that the thread was good and strong now and he could return to Erysah. Erysah . . . Oh yes, now he knew her name and she had spoken his. This night she had given him three special gifts. The first had been her smile, it had lit her whole face up and made her eyes shine like jewels. The second was that she had spoken his name, he remembered the whisper of it over his skin. The third had been the kiss. Oh, the kiss it made his blood heat and his body harden. The softness and sweetness of her lips, the taste of oranges and blossom still lingered in his mouth. He could feed on her kiss for eternity and he fully intended to. Okay perhaps not eternity, but at least for the next five hundred years. He was determined their next encounter would be even more fruitful, he would find out in which country she lived and then make his way to her. Dayton stopped himself, perhaps not he conceded. As eager as he was to find her, he could not risk taking things too quickly. The memory of his lost friend reminded him that last thing he would want to do was to scare her. He knew he had only five more months before his time ran out. But that would be time enough, it had to be. If he and Erysah did not complete the ritual it would be the end of him. Erysah would survive but she would never be whole again. He did not want to put her through that.

He had reached his five hundredth year and was in his 'year of yearning'. If his race did not find their 'Solelil' or 'Solelae', they would cease to be. He had known a many of his race that had gone that way. Some had tried to just take someone, anyone, but it never worked. Although some had loved their women and some women had loved them back, there was no connection, no mesh. Without the mesh they would lose themselves and die anyway. Finding their true soul mates was the only way to survive, it doubled the lifespan of a Vardesh. The Vardesh were a race of vampires that had existed since the beginning of time. One of their weaknesses was their mortality. Not allowed to live for more than five hundred years alone. However, if they found their other halves during the 'year of yearning', they would live for further five hundred, they would be able to procreate. Unfortunately, for the Vardesh their 'Solelil' or 'Solelae' only existed in the human race. It was not until a specific ceremony was performed that their true natures would be revealed. Those that were never found would live a normal lives without knowing who they were or what they could be. Dayton hoped that because the mind thread was so strong already, that fate would be generous to them. Now he had made contact with Erysah, she would now feel the loss if he did not succeed. Dawn was almost upon him, time to retire and take with him the memories of the night.

"Until tomorrow, Erysah, my love," he said to no one in particular. With a smile on his face he made his way to his chambers.

Erysah had spent most of the day lounging around, apart from a brief call to Greg to find out how Violet was doing and if she was back home. Greg had said it would be okay to visit her on Monday. She was looking forward to that, being at home with nothing to do was driving her nuts.

She felt like a caged animal pacing around her apartment not being able to concentrate on anything. Well . . . actually that was not strictly true she had spent most of the day reading the same bit of her diary, over and over and over again, until she knew every word off by heart. She tried to be logical by trying to decipher those dreams. But she couldn't get away from the feeling that there was more to them. The counsellor had said that if she had a particular clutch of dreams that she found disturbing or were related, her best course of action was to read through them carefully. When she had time to digest what she had written then hopefully she would be able to rationalise them. It had worked in the past, but with these dreams it was different. She found herself wanting, needing perhaps even craving. That was a really strange thought but craving what? She had no idea and the more she thought about them the more exasperated she got. Surely the dreams were just a coincidence, perhaps after having the conversation with her college friends had instigated them. The whole evenings topic had been about men and relationships and the fact that there was no one in her life. Dreams could not progress and change, could they? Despite all her musings Erysah found herself hoping she would dream of Dayton again.

He had awakened something in her, in both mind and body that seemed almost primal. She began to wonder if she could will herself to dream about him. She laughed at herself. *'How pathetic do I sound'*. What was she thinking he was not real? He was just a figment of her imagination. *'I need to get a life, find a real man and not a fantasy one'*, she chastised herself and began to list the reasons why. He was too perfect, his hair, his face, his body and those lips, just at the thought of his lips had her breathing a little harder. She touched her own lips in remembrance, his warm mouth pressed against hers guiding and caressing, and the taste. Erysah moaned at the memory, how could they have been so vivid that she could recall every part of them. She was suddenly frustrated with herself and decided to have a shower before retiring. Stepping into the shower she let the water warm her skin, revelling in the sensation. Her body seemed to hum with life, putting some gel into her hands she began to wash herself. As her hands touched her skin she closed her eyes and a vision of Dayton appeared before her. As her hands travelled over her body she remembered his touch. She ached and began to moan as she caressed herself in abandonment and began to wonder how his touch would feel. Erysah started to sob and found herself in a heap on the floor of the shower cubicle. What was she thinking! Erysah began to get angry with herself. *'Pull yourself together, woman.'* With that scolding thought she got out the shower and dried herself so hard she almost took a layer of skin off before getting ready for bed. Her skin glowed pink with the burn of the towel. She needed to calm down and cool off, so she went into the kitchen and made herself one of her specials. A hot chocolate drink loaded with marshmallows, whipped cream and grated chocolate. She didn't care if it was decadent, she needed it. Erysah sat on the sofa cradling her indulgence trying to clear her mind. But it was no use, every time her thoughts turned back to Dayton. After finishing her 'hot chocolate delight', as she called it Erysah felt more relaxed. Climbing into bed she curled up and drifted off into another dream.

This time Erysah found herself standing in front of a magnificent grey stone manor house, surrounded with lush green grass. The moon was bright enough for her to make out that much. There was a light shining through a glass panels which stood either side of the wooden door. Slowly the front door opened and framed in the dim lit hallway was Dayton. Erysah's breath hitched she knew it was him, but how? His face would have been in shadow if it hadn't have been for the moon shining down on the scene. A feeling of relief washed over her, a strange reaction but she didn't really care at that particular moment. Her heart leapt, 'could this really be happening, could it be real. No, it was just some fantasy she had conjured up for herself'. Despite her conflicting thoughts it didn't stop her from looking at all the possibilities. Questions flew into her head, too many to contemplate. Dayton stood there smiling at her, his eyes shining in the moonlight, slowly he raised his hand out towards her in invitation. Erysah walked cautiously towards the steps the cool grass springy beneath her bare feet. Erysah stopped and sighed looking down at them, 'couldn't I have had some footwear on in these dreams'.

"Erysah." Her head snapped up and locked onto him. At that moment she had the urge to run to him, fling her arms around his neck and kiss him. 'Was that her thoughts?' She blushed and almost laughed at herself. As she approached him she asked him.

"Are you real Dayton or is this just a dream?" He answered with one word, his voice was so low she could feel it vibrate through her whole being.

"Yes." His answer annoyed her and she was determined not to be swayed by his charms.

"Yes?" Erysah was annoyed. 'Yes, to what?' she thought. Erysah look harassed, "what do you mean, yes? Yes, to you being real or yes, this is a dream?"

"Yes and yes Erysah." The corners of his mouth lifted slightly in amusement.

"Wait a minute, let me try again. Are you real?" Erysah was completely confused. How could she be having a lucid conversation with him in her dream. Was her mind that taxed? Was she that lonely? Regardless of these thoughts she continued with her questions, it was as if she couldn't help herself.

"Yes." He could not contain his amusement any longer. She looked so tempting in the way she tilted her head and scrunched her face trying to figure things out.

"Is this a dream?"

"Yes." Dayton smiled wryly.

"How can it be both?" Erysah thought she was losing the plot somehow. Or missing some important clue that would help her to decipher the mystery. She noticed that his hand had never moved and was still held out to her.

"Come inside Erysah and let me explain." Erysah stomped up the steps and was going to barge past him, but he reached for her catching her arm to stop her. His grip was firm and gentle sending a warm tingling sensation through her body. "Welcome to my home, Erysah." He whispered in her ear, making her shudder. She glared at him briefly and then looked past him into the hallway and stopped.

"You live here?" She couldn't hide the surprise in her voice. "How can I be here?" Dayton didn't answer her he just slid his hand into hers and led her into a library. As he closed the door he closed the distance between them. This time he didn't ask and she was glad, the question was in his eyes and the answer was in hers. Erysah slid her arms around his waist as Dayton slid his hands up her arms and cupped her face between them. As their lips met Erysah prayed that the dream would not end here. His kiss was gentle at first but Erysah wanted more and demanded more, so he responded with an eagerness of his own. To her relief it didn't end and when they came up for air, Erysah rested her head against his chest as her lips throbbed from the passion of his kiss. "Talk to me, Dayton. Please tell me what's happening." The sound of her voice vibrated through his body sending licks of heat in every direction. Erysah raised her head to look at him.

"Ask your questions and I will endeavour to answer them." He said with a smile that lit up his whole face.

"Won't you just tell me." She pleaded. Dayton shook his head.

"How can I tell you anything when I do not know what you want to know."

"You talk so strangely and cryptically." Erysah said with a frustrated huff. Dayton held her at arm's length and looked straight at her. "Stop, I can't think properly when you look at me like that."

"Like what?" he said innocently.

"Like . . . like . . ." she was having trouble stringing a sentence together. Dayton saved her from finishing it by changing the subject.

"Can I ask a favour?" Erysah saw a mischievous grin appear on his face. She considered it briefly, perhaps a little too briefly.

"Yes." It was hard to believe it, but she felt as though she couldn't deny him anything.

"Will you sit on my lap and ask your questions, that way I can hold you close and you will not have me staring at you." There was humour in his voice and Erysah could not help but laugh as she nodded to his terms. Dayton led Erysah over to his favourite chair and placed Erysah on his lap so she could rest her head on his shoulder. He slid his right arm around her back resting his hand on her hip, whilst his other held one of her hands. "Are you comfortable?" He asked as he looked down at her, his eyes were attracted to the cleavage that was cresting the top of her nightdress. He almost groaned aloud at the sight of it and had to hold himself in check lest his ardour began to grow. Erysah nodded, her silken curls caressed his neck and chin, the rest flowed over his arm in a river of fire. For the first time in his life he knew what it was like to burn. 'How am I going to survive this night,' he thought to himself. Erysah relaxed into Dayton slipping her arm around his back, he adjusted himself to accommodate it. The warmth of the fire on her back and Dayton's body surrounding hers, made her feel warm and safe.

"Okay," said Erysah taking a deep breath which did nothing more than push her breasts further up her nightdress. Dayton needed to focus on some other than Erysah, raising his head slightly he stared out to the sea. "Let's go back to my first question, are you real? I mean really real, do you exist in the real world and not just in my dreams."

"Yes, I really do exist," Dayton chuckled and closed his eyes briefly lest his gaze drift back down.

"Stop laughing at me!" Erysah was irritated by him, if he hadn't have been holding her hand she would have thumped him. He was stroking his thumb over the spot where the tattoo was, only it wasn't there. It puzzled her briefly but she couldn't dwell on that right now. She had much more important things on her mind. "Okay if you really exist, how can I be sitting here in this room with you holding me, it feels very real. And after the last dream from the beach when we kissed, I could still feel the sensation and the taste of your lips on mine."

"That is a very good question, it is difficult to know where to begin." Dayton mused.

"Try the beginning," she said sarcastically. Dayton opened his eyes and slipped his hand down and squeezed her bottom, which made her squeal. Erysah looked up and glared at him. Dayton took the opportunity to brush a quick kiss on her pouting mouth. Dayton kept his hand where it was he like the feel of her soft flesh through the satiny material. He had to stop thinking like this or things could get very uncomfortable for both of them.

"Sorry, I could not resist those luscious lips of yours," he said with a big grin. He neglected to mention the fact that his hand was still on her bottom. He had taken the wind out of her sails and that was all that mattered. Not that she minded in the slightest, as she snuggled back into him. "Right to answer your question. The reason the dreams are so real is because we are connected on a very deep level." Erysah looked up at him and was about to say something when Dayton shook his head. "Let me finish, please." Erysah put her head back on his shoulder. She was getting far too comfortable in his lap, but she didn't care. "What I am about to reveal my seem unimaginable. But I want you to listen very carefully and not say anything until I have finished." Erysah nodded against him and the movement sent her hair bouncing over his arm in a silken caress. Dayton swallowed hard and steeled himself before continuing. "At the moment I am creating these dreams so we can communicate and get to know each other. I have been searching for you, you are my 'Solelil'. The sun to my moon, the other half of my soul, my soul mate if you must call it something. When I connected with you over six months ago I left a fine thread between our minds. With each passing connection the thread gets stronger and thicker. There will come a time when we will need to meet outside of these dreams. In the real world, when that time comes a choice will have to be made. This choice will determine both our futures. My choice has been already made." She looked up at him puzzled.

"What choice?"

"To continue this association because I know in my heart I am already in love with you." Erysah's heart pounded at his revelation, how can he say such a thing like that with so much surety. The whole situation was so surreal. They hadn't even met and they certainly didn't know each other. Erysah gasped, but said nothing. Her mind was in turmoil, she already knew that he was constantly in her thoughts. She was besotted by the idea of him. But to know this was real and not her imagination, was difficult for her to comprehend. How could he be in love with her, was it that easy? Dayton just sat quietly, patiently waiting for her to digest what he had said. She realised that he had told her something important but had left big gaps, yet to be filled. What choice was it that she would have to make that would affect both of them. Erysah sighed and pulled her hand away from his. She slid it up his muscular chest, feeling every ripped muscle beneath the fabric. She wanted to explore him, with her hands, with her mouth and with her body. Erotic images flashed in her mind. Erysah both heard and felt the moan come out of Dayton's mouth, she also felt the stirring in his groin. She didn't stop until her hand was in his amazing black wavy *hair, it was soft and silky, she tugged at it slightly. He released another moan his head moving down towards her as she raised her mouth to his. At this moment she didn't have words. As their mouths collided electricity seemed to arc between them. The evidence of his arousal was now pressed against her thigh, which in turn heated her whole body. When they parted Dayton said in a breathy whisper.*

"See you tomorrow, my love."

"No . . . !" she yelled.

Erysah found herself awake screaming with frustration, she could still feel the warmth where his body had been pressed against hers. The imprint of his arousal still on her thigh. Laying back on her pillow she clenched her hands into fists either side of her and thumped the mattress. Taking a deep breath she released her hands and shook them to get the blood back into them. Her left hand was still tingling, well not her whole hand, just the tattoo. Erysah rubbed it as she rolled over and looked at the clock, it was nearly eight. Sitting up she swung her legs over the side of the bed. Putting her elbows on her knees she put her head in her hands. It was then that she realised that she was wearing the same night dress in her dream. Erysah bet that if she checked the laundry hamper she would find her pink one in there from the previous night. That gave her an idea, she was not leaving her dream tonight frustrated, especially if the dreams were as real as Dayton said they were. Erysah smiled to herself as she formulated her plan.

Confession

A couple of hours later Erysah was standing outside Greg's house. Well, it was Greg's now, after Violet had transferred the deeds over to him last year. Erysah thought that Violet had to know her time was running out. She guessed she was trying to put her life in order, before the inevitable. The thought made her shudder, mortality could be a strange thing. When you're young you think you have forever, then as you get older you realise time is ticking away faster than expected. When you reach your twilight years, you know there is little time and there are things you need to do if you don't want to leave a mess behind. Violet seemed to be in that final stage. Erysah supposed that having her heart attack, had changed the way she looked at life. Suddenly the sensation of someone walking over her grave made Erysah shiver. For some inexplicable reason she felt that this would not be a normal visit. Erysah had a feeling she was going to find out something. A secret perhaps that had been hidden from her for far too long. Looking up at the house Erysah felt another shiver run down her spine. The house was nothing spectacular, just a normal red brick building with a grey slate roof and white framed windows. It was set back off the road which gave it a reasonable size front garden, Neat flower beds bordered the lawns, the whole thing was guarded on three sides by a tall thick hedge. The house wasn't attached to any other building, it stood proud and alone. It reminded her so much of Violet who had lost her husband many, many years ago. Although she never really talked about him, it was a subject that just never came up. Even Greg never mentioned his father, all that she knew was Greg had been five years old when his father died. Erysah found it strange that no one had ever mentioned his name, but she never questioned it. Obviously they had their reasons and it was none of her business, so she didn't know it.

The only thing she did know was that Violet had had Greg late in life, from what she was told Erysah surmised Violet had been in her late thirties, early forties. Greg didn't actually know his mother's age and she never willingly spoke about it. Violet had had a difficult time, it had taken fifteen years of trying and losing several children before she managed to succeed. Some had been still births and the rest were lost during gestation. During her final pregnancy it was decided not to let her go to term in case she had another still birth. Greg was brought into the world a month early. It had been a difficult first three months for him, spending most of that time in an incubator. But he survived and that was all that mattered to Violet and her husband. He had died suddenly of a brain haemorrhage when Greg was five leaving Violet to bring up him by herself. She had been surprised that she had been quite open about it. Violet had told her Greg's story on a number of occasions and Erysah let her because she knew it was necessary for Violet to offload sometimes. Erysah normally looked forward to seeing Violet but today . . . Erysah took a deep breath and knocked on the door, her hand trembling slightly. Greg opened the door on the second knock, as if he had been waiting for her.

"Heard you pull up," he grinned. "Isn't it about time you got that exhaust fixed?" Erysah smiled and nodded. She was relieved to see he was looking much better than the last time. "Come in Erysah, mum has been itching to see you all morning." That so didn't help her feeling of anxiety.

"It wasn't that long ago we saw each other. She was only in hospital for two days." She said trying to shake off the nervousness pulsating through her.

"I know but she seems more eager than normal, as if it is really important. She is even sending me away so she can talk to you on her own". Erysah frowned. "I am going to the bar for a few hours. It will give me time to do a stock take and reorder what's needed. Nice flowers by the way." Erysah gave him a quizzical look, he seemed overly chipper and why would he need to re-order stock if the bar was going to be closed for a while. Erysah shrugged her shoulders, perhaps now he knew his mother was okay he was reopening it. She waved goodbye to him as he walked down the steps before closing the door. Greg didn't seem to realise that Violet was acting out of character, but there again, so was he. Perhaps it was just the strain of everything that had happened and the relief that his mother back home. From the living room she heard Violet call.

"Erysah is that you?" Erysah laughed.

"Who else were you expecting Violet, your fancy man!" she chuckled, as she walked into the living room.

"Don't be so flippant, it doesn't become you, young lady." She chided. Erysah unrepentant entered the room carrying a huge bunch of Carnations in just about every colour there was. Violet's eyes went wide and sparkled with delight. Erysah always knew how to take the wind out of her sails. "Erysah, what on earth, where on earth am I supposed to put all those!" she laughed getting out of her chair. Erysah twisted her face slightly and Violet gave her a look that said, DON'T EVEN GO THERE. They both walked into the kitchen. Violet was a small woman, much smaller than Erysah. Her short grey hair was cropped close to her skull. She was slender and spritely, or she had been before the heart attack. Now she walked doggedly. "I'll make tea, while you find homes for all those beautiful flowers. I hope I have enough vases, if not we'll use jugs." Erysah knew better than to argue. By the time Erysah had finished with the flowers, she had filled three vases and two jugs. "Leave the jugs in the kitchen, put one on the table and one in the window. Bring one vase into the living room, put one in the hall and the last can go into my bedroom. Oh! And while you're up there bring down the large blue tin box with the flowers on it. It is on the shelf in the wardrobe." Whilst Erysah followed Violet's orders, the uneasy feeling increased. Especially after the last instruction. She wondered what was in that box as she picked it up. It was nothing special, although it did look old. It was about a foot square and six inches deep, pink and yellow roses decorated the lid surrounded by a pale blue which covered the rest of it including the bottom. She knew she wouldn't have to wait long. By the time she had come back down Violet was sitting back in her chair. When Erysah handed her the box, Violet took it with shaky hands.

"Will you bring the tea in, it should be brewed by now." Violet didn't even look at her she kept her eyes on the box. Erysah said nothing and went to get the tea tray, her nerves were now getting the better of her and tried not to let it show as she brought in the tray. When Erysah came through the door Violet was looking intently through the box that was now on her lap. Her eyes were screwed up in concentration. Suddenly she sighed with relief as she pulled out a large brown padded envelope.

"Sit down Erysah, please. It's time you learned a few important things that I have been keeping secret from you for a quite some time." She looked at Erysah so seriously. "Not even Greg knows about this." Erysah sat down warily on the chair opposite her, unable to speak. Her skin chilled as a shiver ran down her spine as she poured the tea.

"Funny," she said, her voice tight with strain. "I had a feeling something was going to happen today as I came up to the house."

"Really? I'm not surprised, considering . . ." Violet stopped herself before she blurted something out that Erysah wasn't ready to hear.

"Considering what?" Erysah was curious, Violet was usually very careful when she spoke, as if thinking through every word and every sentence before uttering them. It was the first time she had known her to slip up.

"Never mind, I need you to listen without interruption. Time is of the essence and my time is short." Violet seemed a little testy. Strange this was the second time in twenty-four hours someone had said that to her.

"Short, what do you mean? You are fine, it was just a . . ." Violet held her hand up to silence her. "Okay, okay" Erysah sighed and held her hands up in defeat. She was just about to take a sip of tea when Violet hit her with a bombshell.

"In this envelope is a letter from your mother and a key to a post office box, in Southampton." As Erysah put her cup down it rattled briefly, she was about to say something when Violet shook her head. She sighed and sat back in the chair, she had a feeling it was going to be a long explanation. Erysah began to rub the tattoo on her hand, she had a habit of doing it when she was nervous or whenever her mother was mentioned. She could of had it removed but she didn't have the heart. After all it was all she really had of her mother. "Before I give these to you there is something you should know." Violet took a deep breath and began. "Your mother was my estranged niece." Erysah's eyes widened in surprise, she bit her lower lip to prevent her from saying anything. "My husband John was your Grandpa Joe's brother. John and Joe fell out over fifty years ago and never spoke to each other again. However, just under twenty years ago your mother found out about John and I and made contact. Obviously, it was too late for John as he had already passed away several years earlier. Secretly your mother and I wrote to each other, every year. She wrote to me each year on your birthday, sent me pictures. I watched you grow up, I also saw how your mother deteriorated. Three years ago your mother and I managed to get you into a position where I could watch over you." Violet's voice saddened. "I received this a couple of weeks before she and your Grandparents died. There was a covering letter with it, your mother asked me to give it to you on your twenty first birthday. Unfortunately, I had the heart attack, so this is a bit late." Violet carried on without pause, not giving Erysah a single chance to question or digest anything. The desperation of needing to get the words out seemed to overwhelm her and once she had opened the gates, nothing or no one was going to stop her. "Greg is actually your cousin, but he has no idea. His life is simple Erysah, you know that and I want it kept that way. I trust you will keep this to yourself. We have known each other only for a short time and I would hope that you would forgive an old woman. But if Greg ever found out that I kept this secret from him, it would destroy him." Violet seemed to age another ten years right in front of her and the pain that crossed the old woman's face touched her heart. Erysah couldn't find the words to express how she was feeling right now. All this new information washed over her in a tidal wave. She wondered how hard had it been for Violet watching her grow up from a distance, having to keep her mother's secret and then having to step in after her death and the death of her grandparents. Violet leaned forward holding the envelope. Erysah's hands shook as she took it from her now fragile hands.

"Do you mind if I take this home and read it?" Her voice was as shaky as her hands.

"Erysah I never expected you to read it here." Violet felt as though part of the weight she had been carrying over the years had been lifted and she felt some semblance of relief. She wonder if she would be able to relieve herself of the rest of her burden, only time would tell. Erysah shook Violet out of her thoughts.

"I've always found it strange how you always felt like family to me," she laughed nervously. "Now I know it's because you are," Erysah smiled but her eyes held unshed tears. She clasped the envelope to her chest as if it was the most precious gift she had ever been given. Today she had been given more than one gift. She couldn't hate Violet, it wasn't in her but it made things a little strained. She loved the old woman and Greg, who she now knew to be her cousin. That thought made her smile. They finished their tea and talked a little more about the letters that had been written to each other over the years. Violet showed her the photos that her mother had sent documenting Erysah as she grew up. She could remember when some of them had been taken, but not others. She managed to hold back the tears but not the pain that was growing in her chest. When she left Greg had not come back, Erysah presumed he was still at the bar. She decided to put what had happened on the back burner for now because there was another matter to take care of. Something that was of great importance to her. The past could wait a little longer, she wanted to know now if she had a future.

By the time Erysah got home it was quite late. She had stopped off at a fast food restaurant and eaten there, because she really couldn't be bothered to cook. Erysah put the large padded envelope down on the coffee table and just stared at it. She was afraid of what it contained and what the key would unlock. For some strange reason her thoughts turned to Dayton. She wished he was here with her now, so she could melt into his arms and feel safe. Tomorrow, she thought. I have had enough revelations for today. I just want to dream and be with Dayton. A smile spread across her face as she picked up the innocuous white plastic bag from the couch and headed for the bedroom. After showering she got out her surprise. What would Dayton think when he saw her in it and where would they meet. Would it be at his home or would she find herself in hers. Erysah's mind raced at all the possibilities. It was amazing how she felt so positive that they would meet. For some unknown reason she had no doubt in her mind, not anymore. Laying on her bed she smiled to herself. Erysah had taken great care that she hid Dayton's surprise. She didn't want to push him to quickly as she waited anxiously for sleep to take her.

Erysah found herself back in the room where they had been the previous night. She was sitting in his favourite chair, how did she know that? Erysah puzzled. At first she thought that she was alone, disappointment hit her. How could she be alone in their dream. Then she felt a breath on the top of her head,

Dayton whispered her name into her hair and then bent down and kissed the top of her head. Erysah smiled as one of his hands slid onto her shoulder and down her arm as he walked from behind the chair. When he reached her hand he tugged her to her feet. As Erysah's eyes met his she couldn't hide the joy she felt. She had left her hair loose, so that her unruly curls bounced around her body. Helping to disguise the fact that she was dressed differently. Dayton swallowed hard he found himself wondering what her tresses would feel like against his skin. His groin began to twitch in anticipation. Would tonight be too soon for them, was she ready to go that far. The thread was much stronger than even he had thought possible and the other threads were starting to take hold, beginning to mesh together. Mind, heart, soul, body then blood, but that was for the Ritual of Transcendence. Mind was secure. Heart was stronger. Soul was connected. Everything had moved quicker than he had anticipated and it overwhelmed him. However he did not want to push too hard and frighten her away. He had already committed so much, even Erysah had committed more than he had expected her to at this stage. Dayton just held her for a moment. He felt blessed when he saw the look in her eyes. He knew his emotions were getting the better of him. Erysah lifted her head as she stroked his face tenderly.

"What's wrong Dayton?" He looked down at her, his heart in his eyes. He could not help himself. He could not speak at that moment, he just found her mouth with his and kissed her with reverence. The kiss was so sweet and gentle. Erysah responded and teased his lips with her teeth causing Dayton to moan. He was trying to be restrained but she did not help. When they came up for air Erysah spoke. "Any chance of having a look at this wonderful house of yours?" Dayton was surprised by her request and disappointed that he had not thought of it first.

"Why yes of course! Where are my manners." Dayton release her body temporarily and clasped her hand as he led her through the library door into a dark panelled hallway. The floor was a dark wood with a plush red carpet that ran down the centre. He briefly showed her the kitchen, which was surprisingly quite modern. The living room and dining room both were dressed in the period of the house. It reminded Erysah of a stately home you would visit on a day trip. She also noticed that the rooms didn't seemed to be used. It was as if they had been frozen in time. At one end of the hall was a wide staircase that led up to the next level. The second floor held four bedrooms, each decorated *in a different colour scheme and two quite modern bathrooms, which again surprised Erysah given the rest of the house. In every room there were heavy curtains and tapestries lining the walls and disguising windows. Erysah felt as though Dayton was giving her a whistle stop tour, prattling on briefly about each room in turn. Not once did he mentioned which room was his. Suddenly Erysah stopped, causing Dayton's arm to snap back. As he turned round he knew what question was on her lips and for some reason he had been dreading it. He could have pretended that his room was one of the four upstairs, but he knew that she would know he was lying. He would not want to do that to her. He suddenly found himself looking at her attire and was puzzled. Previously she had been in knee length silk nightdresses but tonight she was wrapped up in a long ankle length coat of some sort. She was hiding her sensuality. 'Why?' He puzzled.*

"What?" *he queried, knowing full well what she was going to say next.*

"Which room is yours Dayton?" *He struggled with that question, she could see it in his face.*

"Why are you dressed like that?" *he said, trying to parry the question. Erysah smiled coyly and colour began to rise in her cheeks. Despite her reaction she was determined to hold her ground.*

"Don't try and avoid my question, Dayton." *She wasn't going to be swayed, not tonight. She was determined to have her way.*

"You have not answered mine." *He said coolly. She pulled her hand from his.*

"That's not fair! I asked you first!" *She stopped short. Crikey! All that was missing was her stamping her foot and she would be behaving like a spoilt brat.*

"So we both have unanswered questions, how are we to solve this dilemma?" *He could not hide the sound of amusement in his voice.*

"Hmm . . . how about if you show me your room . . . then I will let you see my new nightdress." *There was a hint of mischief in her tone which shocked even her. But it was said now and there was no taking it back.*

"And what is so special about your nightdress?" Dayton asked intrigued, trying not to let his mind run riot. If he was not careful he would lose what little self control he had left, as it was, walking had become a tad uncomfortable. Smiling mischievously Erysah reached up to his ear and whispered into it, her hot breath hitting him straight in his nether regions. He was finding it difficult to breathe.

"Because . . ." she whispered seductively. "I brought it especially for you." Dayton's mind nearly went into meltdown. Here he was worrying if things were going too fast and if she was ready for the next stage. And here she was buying him a special gift, something that she had wrapped herself in. He was beginning to wonder if he would survive this night. "Well . . ." Erysah raised her eyebrows and put her hands on her hips. 'To hell with it', he thought, she would find out sooner or later.

"I actually have a room downstairs that I use. I only use a small amount of the house, just a couple of rooms." Erysah had already guessed that, so it came as no surprise. With that Dayton took her hand again and led her downstairs back into the library. Erysah was slightly confused, but said nothing. Reaching into the bookcase to the right of the fire place Dayton found the secret button that released the door mechanism. To Erysah's surprise a bookcase situated behind the large oak desk started to move, revealing another small room. She knew these houses sometimes held secret rooms and passageways but she had never in a million years dreamt that she would see one. Once they entered the room the door closed and Erysah had the strange sensation of movement. Suddenly the movement stopped and another door opened behind them to reveal the most opulent room she had ever seen. Lush velvet cascaded from everywhere in greens and reds. In the centre was a huge four poster bed, draped in black satin sheets and quilts matching the rest of the room. As Erysah stepped into the room she felt the deep plush carpet beneath her feet, it was so deep and soft her toes disappeared. Off to the left she saw another door, Dayton noticed her eyes move to it so he guided her to it. Inside was a huge sunken bath as big as a small swimming pool, made of marble it was dressed with gold taps in the shape of dolphins. It reminded her of a private roman bath. Erysah was speechless and her mouth gaped in surprise. Dayton could not resist the invitation and claimed her hot delicious mouth. Their tongues wrestled and their teeth nipped. Dayton forgot the fact that she might find out his secret but she never touched his teeth. Before long they were both gasping for air. Dayton looked at Erysah smiling, his face lit up. "I have shown you my room, now what about your end of the bargain?" Erysah laughed.

"Okay but one quick question . . . was that a lift we were in?" Dayton nodded. "So we're are in a secret part of the house?" He nodded again. "Did we go up or down?"

"Down." He had no intention of lying. "And that was three questions." He chuckled at the wonder and excitement of her expression. Erysah took a deep breath to steady herself.

"Oh . . . okay. Would you like to unwrap your present now." She was nervous but her mind was set. She wanted this man with a fervour she never knew she had. Her emerald eyes sparkled as her cheeks held the warm pink glow of her blush, he found that just as enticing. As she spoke his jeans became far too tight. Dayton nodded with a silly looked on his face. All of a sudden he was the one that was nervous. Erysah, his Erysah was giving him another gift. One of the most important gifts, herself. If she lay with him now she would surely lay with him in the physical world. She was entrusting herself to him. Slowly with unsteady hands he pulled at the belt around her middle until it loosened. Dayton looked into Erysah's eyes almost afraid to look anywhere else. Slowly, very slowly he opened the robe to find a deep green chiffon at her shoulders. As the robe dropped to the floor he followed it. He was not looking at the robes journey Dayton was following the flow of green chiffon that started at the shoulders and travelled over her body to the floor. It was pleated from the curve of the neckline with another layer of fitted chiffon underneath. It was held in at the waist by a thin plaited gold belt. His eyes continued to travel down over her hips and thighs down to her ankles. Erysah shook her head which caused her red hair to cascade around her body. Dayton's breath caught in his throat. He stared breathlessly at this vision of beauty. He stepped back so he could drink all of her in. Erysah was beginning to wonder if it was too much, her body trembling with . . . what? Fear? Anticipation? Excitement? She hadn't got a clue, her emotions were all of a jumble as he stared at her with a look of awe.

"Are you okay? Dayton?" Dayton nodded like an imbecile. "Do you like it?" He nodded again. "Is it too much?" She was starting to doubt herself, had she pushed him too far? Dayton shook his head, if he had been an animal he would most likely be drooling. Perhaps he was, taking a deep breath to steady himself, he found his voice.

"I am sorry Erysah," he eventually managed to say, "you leave me speechless. There are no words to describe the vision I see before me." Erysah started towards him and as she did the gossamer material moved, it was then he realised she wore nothing beneath the gown. Dayton groaned loudly and put a hand through his hair squeezing it tightly at the back. "You are driving me insane, Erysah. I am trying to be a gentleman here and think of your virtue." He paused for what seemed like an eternity. "But I find myself having lustful thoughts about you. And now this gift, this vision." He gestured towards her with both hands. "What am I to do?" He clenched his fists by his sides to stop himself from grabbing her and taking her there on the floor. Erysah had wanted to surprised him but she had no idea that he would have such a reaction. It pleased her in more ways than she could imagine. Erysah's smile lit up her face.

"Stay still for me." Dayton nodded in response because at that particular moment he did not think he could move anyway. She didn't need to move any closer, as she was just a step away from him. Erysah reached out her hands and put them on Dayton's chest. He squeezed his fists even tighter as she slowly began to unbutton the black shirt he was wearing. When she tugged at the material to pull it out of his jeans it rubbed against his erection making him moan. Eventually his shirt landed on the floor and she caressed and kissed his ribbed muscles. Paying attention to his nipples which were as hard as hers. Dayton groaned with pleasure and moved his hands to her hair. It felt like silk between his fingers. Erysah stood on tiptoes and nipped his chin waking him from his stupor. Pulling her head back he looked down at her questioningly.

"Carry me to the bed," her eyes were dark with desire. He slid one hand behind her back and the other went to the back of her thighs. The feel of the material sent electric shocks across his skin. Erysah couldn't believe how sexy she felt, her body was on fire and the heat from Dayton's skin only increased the flames. Dayton lay her on the bed, gazing into her eyes with heat and passion glowing in his.

"I want to devour you," he said his voice hoarse with lust. Erysah laughed nervously but she wanted to tease him.

"I hoped you would be hungry." Erysah giggled briefly, she couldn't believe what she had just said and covered her mouth with her hand.

"You are asking for trouble, Erysah." He growled. Trying to warn her that once he had begun nothing was going to stop him until both of them were completely sated. Taking her hand away from her mouth he leaned in to kiss her, she shook her head to stop him. He was surprised by her action.

"No, Dayton," she said seductively. "I am begging for it." That was it, Dayton lost all sense of propriety. Before she could blink he was laying naked on the bed next to her. The evidence of his arousal pressing hard against her thigh.

"Are you sure you know what you are asking?" Dayton could not help himself, it was in his genetic makeup to ask. Erysah looked at him and nodded the flames of passion in her eyes. He didn't say anything else, he let his body do the talking. His hand hovered over her body without making contact. The gesture was so erotic Erysah squirmed in anticipation, despite that fact that he had yet to touch her. She felt as though she had been caressed all over. Erysah moaned.

"Dayton, please! Don't torture me." she implored. Dayton's eyes flashed in a myriad of shades of blue. Making her gasp. Dayton took that breath into his mouth as his hand started to slide down one side of her body the two layers of material causing her body to tingle. He could have suckled her breast through the fine fabric but he wanted to see and feel everything tonight. He would leave those kinds of games for another time and Dayton knew there would be plenty of those after tonight. Dayton worked his way from her mouth to her ear, nibbling gently. Down the side of her neck, he continued to travel down to her shoulder, tasting her skin. The sweet seductive taste of her was all consuming. The sounds of her soft moaning spurring him on. Eventually after what had seemed forever he reach the soft curve of her breast. Erysah's breaths were coming in short gasps, she hadn't realised that he had already exposed one perfectly formed creamy mound, peaked with a tight rose bud. Her nipple was so hard it was very sensitive as he blew over it before taking it into his mouth.' Oh, God!' Erysah thought as she closed her eyes fisting the bed cover, it seemed to intensify the feel of his deliciously hot mouth. She arched against him wanting more contact. Some moments later he was giving her other breast the same attention, her hands threaded through his long black hair holding him to her. Lifting his head she moaned at the absence, but he leaned up and took her mouth once more before speaking.

"Erysah, I need to get this gown off you because I do not want to damage it. I have future plans for this." His voice was so husky he could hardly get the words out. Erysah moved her body to enable him to remove the night dress leaving her blushed body free for him to see. His own body seemed to swell even more at the sight of her, she made the mistake of looking at him as he returned to the bed after carefully placing the garment over a chair. The sight of his erect manhood, begging for attention made her eyes widen. He was much bigger than she realised.

Dayton crawled up the bed. Using both hands one on each of her feet and slid his way up. Gliding his hands from her feet to her ankles, then her calves made her breathless. She felt the burn of his hands as they travelled up her legs. By the time he got to her knees she was already starting to open up for him. His palms stroked the insides of her thighs. It was hard for her to focus, she was drowning in pure pleasure. Her feelings were swamped by the awareness that her body was alive and screaming. Dayton's lips followed his hands making her squirm the higher he got. She panted, trying to gain some control over her body. Her juices flowed and she was glistening in more ways than one. When Dayton reached the junction of her legs he could smell the heady aroma of her arousal. It smelt like honey and orange blossom. He was unable to resist, he had to have just a little taste before finding the haven of her body. Ducking his head he only meant to have a small taste, a little lick. But when his tongue touched her Erysah almost lifted her whole body off the bed as the electricity of the orgasm hit her. More of her sweet nectar spilled into Dayton's mouth, making him moan in ecstasy. The vibration coursed through Erysah's body like a freight train. He feasted on, her helping her through her orgasm which left her whimpering for more.

"Please, Dayton I need you, all of you!" she said in desperation. Dayton knew he could hold out no longer, his restraint gone. However, he did not intend to be rushed. Tonight it would be all about enjoying each other. He placed the head of his erection which was already weeping in eagerness at her entrance. The heat between them was almost unbearable, he rocked gently forwards and backwards penetrating her a little more each time. Giving her the time she needed to adjust to him and giving him time to steady himself with the *tightness of her. Sensations bombarded him and he almost lost control as Erysah moans asked for more each time. Eventually she had all of him, filling and stretching her impossibly. He had to stop a moment the pressure causing him to almost lose control. "Please, don't stop." She begged. Dayton began to thrust slow and long savouring the feel of her, like a velvet glove gliding over his already sensitive length. His thrusts became more urgent and faster as the passion took over him and engulfed them both. He felt Erysah's orgasm and was unable to hold the roar inside as his own release came.*

Erysah woke to find herself naked on the bed feeling well and truly sated. However, she felt bereft by the fact she was alone. She knew she had been thoroughly made love to. The evidence was obvious as she stood shakily. The junction of her thighs still pulsated from her orgasm, as did the tattoo on her hand. '*How* strange', she thought. Then she remembered back to another dream where Dayton had been stroking it, only it wasn't there. Erysah remembered she was naked and wondered where her nightgown was. As she looked around the room she spotted it draped over the chair in the corner. It made her smile as she remembered him laying it on the chair in his room and the look of him as he walked back to the bed. Bold, proud and unashamed. What she couldn't understand was that it was still night time. Normally she woke in the morning. Although nothing was normal about the situation. Erysah cast her mind back to the other dreams and realised that perhaps the extreme emotion must have ended it. Erysah was now in no doubt that the dreams were very real and nothing would convince her otherwise. She would be looking forward to the nights instead of dreading them, no more nightmares. Although she did have doubts, would he keep his promise and find her in the real world? She hoped so, but at the moment she didn't care. It was the happiest she had been since she didn't know when. Erysah decided she would make it easier for him. She could tell him where she lived, then he would have no excuse. Her plan had worked tonight, maybe it could again. All she had to do was to be subtle about it. Then again, why be subtle, she could just tell him and force the issue. God she was so confused, she had no idea which was the best way to go about bringing it up. Dayton had already told her that he loved her and she definitely felt well and truly loved, in more ways than one. She laughed to herself, feeling giddy by the whole experience. She felt like dancing around the room even though she was still naked. Dayton had already invaded her mind and now her body, well in the dreams anyway. Erysah blushed at that thought. He was also starting to invade her heart and soul, soon she would be totally lost to him. Did she care? Erysah didn't know. All she knew was that whenever she was with him her life felt complete.

Dayton lay on his bed covered in Erysah's sweet smell from their lovemaking. He had ended the dream not because of their climax but the roar. He did not want to explain it to her just yet. Not that he was scared, actually that was not true. He was terrified of revealing his true identity to her. He was terrified of her denying him, as Kaspir's Solelil had. No, he was definitely not going to dwell on that. Things were different with Erysah, he felt it in his heart. He decided to put it to the test tomorrow night. As hard as it would be he would not initiate the dream, he would wait an extra night. It would kill him to do so, especially after what had just happened between them. With the memories of their intimacy Dayton went into the bathing room to cleanse himself. Not that he wanted to wash away her smell. On the contrary, her smell was ingrained into his memory. He could now find her in the real world and soon he would. Then the dreams would become reality, in every sense of the word. Little did Erysah know that very soon his hunt for her would begin in earnest.

The Letter

The previous night had been quite a revelation, in many ways. She had tried to go back to sleep, but she had found herself thinking about what had happened between her and Dayton. Eventually, Erysah decided to get up. After showering and dressing she thought it was time to 'bite the bullet' and open the letter from her mother. She had no clue as to what was in it, even Violet had no idea either and her mother's letters to Violet gave no indication. After breakfast she went and sat on the sofa, cradling a mug of coffee Erysah stared at the envelope on the table. She couldn't make up her mind about it. It was nothing special and the only thing written on it, was her name. Sighing she put the mug down and picked up the manila envelope. Turning the envelope over in her hands she deliberated and squeezed it once or twice. It was a large rectangular envelope just like any other, she couldn't feel the key through the packaging but she wasn't surprised the envelope was padded after all. Ripping the thing open Erysah emptied the contents onto the small oval glass topped coffee table in front of her. The key came out first, clinking as it landed. There was nothing attached to it and it was nothing special, just a typical locker or cash box style key. It was followed by a pile of what looked like photos wrapped in a plain piece of paper held together with a rubber band. Lastly she dug out several sheets of hand written paper. The paper was handmade, the kind you can buy in craft shops. A lump came to Erysah's throat and a single tear fell on her arm. She knew this wasn't going to be easy. In fact it was going to hurt like hell. Her heart was already aching, she missed her family so much. Two years wasn't a long time in the great scheme of things. Her wounds were still very fresh and the nightmares hadn't helped. Erysah stared at the contents scattered in front of her for a long time, unable to decide where to start.

Lifting the sheets of paper she looked at the words on them but saw nothing but blurry lines. It took a while before she could focus Erysah's eyes kept filling with tears. Every time she tried blinking them away, they kept coming back. Eventually taking a deep breath, she wiped her eyes with the cuff of her tee shirt and began to read:

25th May 2018

To my darling daughter Erysah,

I am so very sorry for this. I wish I had the strength to tell you what you need to know to your face. But, I'm a coward. I find I can't bear to live any longer with this feeling of emptiness. I am but a hollow shell. I tried desperately to carry on for nearly twenty years with these feelings, but I can't. The guilt of what I have done haunts me every day, without pause. Why do I feel guilty?

It's because I could never give you the love you deserved. The real love, that came from your grandparents. Guilt, because of my mother and father's suffering, as they watched me die a little more each day and I couldn't tell them why. But I will remedy that very soon, first I needed to tell you, have to tell you, even if it's only in this letter. As I said before I am too much of a coward to tell you to your face. I could not bear to see the look of condemnation that would be on it, after keeping this from you your whole life. Hopefully you will understand and maybe my conscious will be clear, at last.

I know I told you that your father was a one night stand. That's not exactly true, we were together for almost a week. The most amazing week of my life. I am also the reason he died. He died because I wasn't brave enough, wasn't strong enough, didn't love him enough or have the courage enough to do what was needed. I can't explain the details to you, it's not my place.

We met at the bar I was working at. There was an instant connection as soon as he walked through the door. Although, it had been a chance meeting, he said he had been looking for me for a very long time. We spent a very passionate five days together. He sort of asked me to marry him, but it would have to be in his religion. I was okay with that, what I didn't realise was that it wasn't just a religion. It was a way of life. A way of life I would have to follow, leaving everyone and everything behind. I know I am going round the houses with this. But I am finding it difficult trying to express myself. I have held on to this for so long, it's really difficult and some of the things I am unable to tell you, mainly because I didn't understand them myself.

Let me start by telling you about your father, his name was Kaspir. He was tall, looked like an eighties rock star with long blonde curly hair and amazing eyes. He had a body to die for and the sex was out of this world. And before you think I should not be saying these things to you because I am your mother. By now you will be more than old enough to know about sex and relationships. I have enclosed some photos of the two of us that were taken when we were together. People say that you looked like me but you got your curls and your height from your father.

I have enclosed a key, if you are wondering what it is for, it is for a post office box at the main collection centre in Southampton. In the locker are some things that your father left us. It explains everything that he never told me, that he should have before the ceremony. Sometimes you find out things are not always what they seem Erysah and life has many unusual surprises.

I have put the box in your name, so all you have to do is ask for it. I am very grateful to Violet for all the years she and I wrote to each other and I hoped she looked after you well after I left you. Please don't be too hard on her, it's not her fault. The secrecy was at my request.

I would suggest that you leave it a few days before collecting what's at the post office. I am sending this letter to Violet now. It will be sealed so she won't know what it contains. But I will write my final letter to her with this giving her instructions on what to do. Once I have done this I am going to tell your grandparents the truth that I have been hiding for so long. I do not know what their reaction will be, but I have set a date and a time.

We've planned a little trip, it will be good to tell them away from home. Telling them in a neutral place may help, I hope. I did love you in my own way, but you were a constant reminder of what I threw away.

Eventually it became too much for me to bear. Again Erysah, I am sorry, so very sorry for everything.

Remember one thing for me, if nothing else. Please do not ever blame yourself. It was never your fault.

Your mother.

Anya.

Erysah sat there clutching the letter as silent tears streamed down her face. When she had managed to gather enough strength she put it down and picked up the pile of photos off the table. Unwrapping them she found that there were only half a dozen of them. As she slowly flicked through them her heart felt as though it had been torn from her again. It was almost the same feeling she had when she had been told about the accident two years ago. Pain and anguish raged in her chest, she began to hyperventilate finding it difficult to breathe. Anger rose to the surface and all she wanted to do was scream and rip her mother's letter and the photos to shreds, so she would never have to feel this way again. But Erysah knew that wouldn't solve anything. There were unanswered questions and despite the pain, she wanted, even needed the answers to them. Taking a some deep breaths she tried to calm herself. She could see the attraction her mother must have had to Kaspir. He reminded her a bit of Dayton in his stature. And yes, she could see where she got her curly hair from. Her mother looked so happy in the pictures, but her father, as she now knew him to be, looked as though he had a lot going on in his head. She spread the photos over the table so she could see them all. They all seemed to display the same two emotions, joy and hope. Although she could see a kind of desperation in her father face. Picking up the key she turned it around in the palm of her hand, it was nothing special.

Erysah felt numb, her feelings so jumbled they seemed to be cancelling each other out, until there was nothing. She had read the words but not digested them. Erysah felt her stomach rumble. When she looked at the clock it was nearly four in the afternoon. Where had the day gone? How many times had she read the letter and looked at the photos? How long had she sat there without feeling? How long had she sat there crying? And how long had her anger lasted? Erysah couldn't answer any of these questions. She thought that she had read the letter only once, but maybe not. Feeling stiff she got up and went into the kitchen area. Looking in the fridge for food, she found some eggs and cheese. 'Omelette', she thought. Her brain couldn't think of anything else at that particular moment. Simple was good and probably the best for now. As she ate, her thoughts turned to Dayton and how she wished he was here, so she could share this with him. It was then that she realised what the letter had told her. It told her why her mother and grandparents had died on that day two years earlier. Erysah gagged on the food that was in her mouth. Spitting it out she put her plate down on the counter and went back over to the coffee table picking up the letter again. It was dated two days before the crash. They had been travelling to the coast at the time. Her mother must have told her parents whilst her grandfather was driving. Was it an accident or had she deliberately caused their deaths? No, she had said that she was leaving her.

"Oh, God! Mother! No!" Erysah screamed as she tossed her head back fists clenched against her temples. Her whole body shook with the intensity of emotions flooding through her, eventually she collapsed onto the sofa. Erysah cried for what seemed like forever. Grief overwhelming her again and again, sweeping over her in what seemed like never ending waves. When she was able to focus she realised night had come. She was too emotional to sleep, she desperately needed Dayton. Erysah wept pathetically calling to him as she drifted off into a tormented sleep. Her mind was in so much turmoil, would he reach out to her tonight. She had no clue, she could only hope he would hear her call.

Dayton had not long got back in. He had deliberately stayed out longer because he knew that if he was at home he would travel down the thread to Erysah. For some inexplicable reason he was feeling very restless and he could not understand why. Unless it was the urge to see Erysah. He always felt calm after a good feed and he had fed very well. He had gone to a town on the other side of Aberdeen and fed on a couple who were in the throes of passion. It had made for a powerful boost. Thinking about the couple made him yearn for Erysah, but he had made a vow to himself. One he intended to keep, even though it was agony. He went to the bookcase and pick one of his favourite books. It was an original copy of Edgar Allan Poe's collection of short stories. Sitting down in his brown leather chair he began to read one of his favourites . . . Shortly after he began to relax.

The next second he found himself in a strange room. It was nowhere he recognised. He was sitting on a sofa and someone was with him curdled in a ball. They were weeping and there were papers strewn all over a low table. Dayton turned his head to the huddled form and recognised who it was. He reached out and placed his hand on her back, as he spoke.

"Erysah?" Suddenly the form seemed to stop shaking as if holding their breath.

"Dayton?" she said turning round her face all red and puffy, tears streaming down her cheeks. The pain that he saw in her eyes tore at his heart. "Oh God, Dayton!" Her voice hitched as she threw herself at him. Dayton automatically put his arms around her while he tried to understand what had happened. He held her close and tried to soothe her as best he could. He wondered if he was the cause of her distress because he had stayed away, guilt gnawed at him. How could he have been so cruel to her, his beloved. It had been agony for him but he had given no thought to how she would feel. Eventually, he spoke.

"Whatever is the matter Erysah? Where am I?" He was so confused.

"In my apartment." This was not possible, was it? "I was given a letter from my mother." Her voice shaky. He could not understand why? But he felt on a small relief but his guilt still clung to him.

"Why would this upset you, Solelil?"

"Because . . ." The words seem to stick in her throat. "She's dead." But before her asked the where's and the why fors, she continued. "She had been dead for two years." She looked up at him. "Why after all this time when my life was . . ." Erysah didn't know how to finish that because she didn't know what her life was at the moment. She was in limbo. Dayton kissed her tear stained cheeks and brushed them with his thumbs. He could almost sense her pain through the mesh. Dayton could only surmise that she had subconsciously found the thread and travelled down it and called him to her. Was the thread that strong that it work both ways already. It was the only explanation. It was certainly a shock for Dayton but Erysah seemed to be relieved that he was with her. Erysah twisted round on his lap where she had thrown herself and reached for the letter and gave it to Dayton. As she did one of the photos of Kaspir was revealed. Dayton froze and stared at it. With trembling fingers he picked it up. Erysah looked at him puzzled. His face had paled and he looked as though he had just seen a ghost.

"Dayton?" she shook him slightly. Surprised by his reaction. "Dayton, do you know him?" He nodded numbly. Still holding the photo he began to read the letter. When he came to his name, his eyes went again to the photo. His eyes blurred, Erysah saw the unshed tears in his deeply sad eyes. "Who was he Dayton? Can you tell me?" He didn't finish reading the letter. He put both the letter and the photo down and stared at her. Yes, he could see some of his friend in her. Was it possible? It had to be, the proof was laying all over the small table in front of them. Dayton picked up another photo, this one had two people in it. Erysah's parents, one being his lost friend, the other Erysah's mother. Erysah had her eyes and hair colour. "Dayton, please talk to me." Instead he dropped the photo and kissed her, she didn't complain. The taste in their mouths was bitter sweet coated in salty tears from both of them. He did not want to talk right now, he desperately wanted Erysah, needed her.

"I love you, my beloved. Erysah, lay with me now, let me make love to you. As I cannot yet find the words or the courage I need to tell you what you wish to know." He whispered against her lips. She understood his feelings and needs because they were her own. Without speaking Erysah stood up and taking hold of Dayton's hand she led him into her bedroom. The room was plain and simple, cream coloured walls were accentuated with artwork, some modern and some not. There was a basic bed with an ornate metal headboard and a dressing table with stool and a chair, on which lay the green chiffon gown she had worn the night before. A brief smile lifted his face. But he was still feeling numb from the revelations of this night and so was Erysah. They needed each other like never before, a basic primal need encompassed them both. There was no erotic foreplay, they just undressed leaving their clothes where they fell and lay on the bed, holding each other. Kissing and caressing each other with tender strokes until the need overtook them and nature took hold. As he entered Erysah both of them started to feel alive again. He was not gentle, thrusting deep and hard like a man possessed. Erysah didn't care and responded likewise, arching her body to meet his thrusts with a desperation of her own. When they were finished they both were covered in the sweat their frenzied lovemaking had caused. As he held her in his arms, she held him in her velvet sheath, which was still clenching from the after affects of her orgasm. Erysah was the first to speak.

"We are connected, aren't we?" He nodded.

"Yes. It seems in more ways than one."

"Did you finish reading the letter?" Dayton shook his head. "Apparently my father left some thing, my mother locked it away in a post office box." Dayton looked at her face then.

"Have you retrieved it yet?" Erysah shook her head.

"My mother advised waiting a few days before getting it. Whatever it is must be either shocking or revealing, perhaps even both." Dayton had a very good idea of what it might contain. The truth about who and what they were. Dayton had no choice now but to tell her before she had the truth revealed by a piece of paper.

"A very good idea. We have both had a shock tonight and we need to talk about what we have found out." Erysah nodded. Dayton eased himself from her tender folds. "I suggest we bathe and then return to the other room." Erysah led him into her en suite bathroom. She turned on the shower. Dayton seemed to be amazed by what he was seeing. Rain inside the small room.

"Have you never had a shower before?" she asked quizzically, raising an eyebrow. Dayton just shook his head. "Come on," she said as she pulled him towards the cubicle. It was only just big enough for the two of them, their bodies only inches apart. Reaching for the shower gel she squeezed some onto her hand and turned to face him. Erysah raised her other hand and using her index finger made a circular motion. Dayton understood and nodded turning round for her.

Her soft warm hands massaged the gel into his shoulders, back and his arms. She put some more on her hands to wash the backs of his legs and buttocks. She seem to take more relish washing that area and his body reacted. Once she had finished with his back she turned him round and applied more gel to his arms and torso. Dayton concentrated on her face whilst he revelled in the texture of her hands running over his body lubricated with soap and water was itself stimulating and his erection stood between them. Although, Erysah avoided contact with it while she washed his body. He did not fail to see the mischievous grin on her face. As her hands continued her ministrations down the front of his legs, she deliberately blew over the bulbous head of his shaft and watched him shudder. A moan passed over his lips. She looked up and smiled at him. She was saving what she considered the best for last. Next she made sure his shaft was extremely clean, soaping the length of him. Dayton staggered back, leaning against the wall of the cubicle, whilst Erysah continued her cleansing routine on him. Dayton had closed his eyes savouring the feel of what she was doing to him. Suddenly the sensation changed. The head of his erection was covered by something hot and moist, it was not until he felt the scrape of teeth he realised it was her mouth. Dayton gasped and looked down to see her crouched, her red hair running like fire over her shoulders, back and down his legs. He could not believe what she was doing. The feel of her hot wet mouth on his steel shaft was unlike anything he had ever experienced. Seconds later she had his sac in her hands as she worked her mouth on his erection. Vibrations coursed through his body as she moaned at her own pleasure. Eventually he pulled her up before he lost complete control of himself.

He kissed her deeply then held his hand out for the gel. It was his turn to use his hands on Erysah, making sure she was also clean. It would also give him time to gather himself together again. As he applied the gel to Erysah's body he took the same reverence with her as she did with him. Starting with her back he lathered her shoulders, arms and back. Then he moved down over her pert bottom and down her legs. As he came back up her legs he could not resist slipping a hand between them, rubbing against her folds. It was Erysah's turn to moan. Dayton could not resist also planting a kiss on each buttock before standing up and turning her round to face him. Applying more gel on his hand he washed her neck, shoulders and arms. Moving to her glistening breasts, as he washed and rinsed them he took the opportunity to suckle each in turn. Erysah began to gyrate under his hands and he travelled lower avoiding the triangle of curls that led to her secret haven that he wanted to own. His hands travelled over her legs in slow long movements until his hands were at her junction, this time he cupped her. Pressing the heal of his hands against her pubic bone, he rubbed backwards and forwards. The friction making her moan, he sucked that moan into his own mouth, while he continued to rub the heel of his hand against her. Erysah rubbed against his hand in rhythm with him. Dayton slipped a finger in and then another and then a third stretching her so wide. Erysah's gasps came in short breaths and she had to hang onto his shoulder as her legs turned into jelly. She was swamped by the fire he had lit. Swapping positions so that her back would be against the wall he lifted her. She automatically put her legs around his waist and her arms around his neck, he positioned her directly above his erection.

As he lowered her down slowly their eyes met, it was almost as if he could see the threads forming into a mesh, binding them irrevocably together. Dayton took his time with their lovemaking. Watching her every reaction. The lust. The passion. The love. He stopped for a moment. Although, she had never said the words, he could see it. Another gift, how blessed he felt. They still had a few hurdles to get over before their journey would be complete. And some of it she might find distasteful. They would cross those bridges when they came to them. When Erysah leant forward and kissed him he realised he had been still for longer than a few seconds. The kiss spurred him on as nothing else could. They both climaxed together and after rinsing themselves off they returned to the bedroom and got dressed. They had spent more time together than he had realised and the sky was starting to lighten.

"Erysah, I have to go but I will be back tonight". She knew it was coming and nodded. He kissed her gently as they slowly faded away from each other.

When Dayton was back home he had a lot on his mind. All of it to do with Erysah. The fact that Kaspir his best friend had fathered her. Her mother killing herself and her parents, perhaps by accident, perhaps not. More than anything, how on earth had Erysah been able to invoke the dream. Was it because of who her father was . . . Dayton pondered. He just hoped she would heed both her mother's advice and his own and wait before collecting whatever was in that box. It was too late to speak to anyone now, it would have to wait until tomorrow. With a heavy heart he entered his chamber wondering how he was going to tell her what he had been hiding from her all long.

Revelations

Erysah had been really tired after Dayton had gone back to his home wherever it was, even though he hadn't really been there. She realised that she hadn't got the energy for anything at all. So she catnapped most of the day away. It was the phone ringing that brought her back to reality. She rolled over to answer it, as she had brought that handset into the bedroom. She had started to do that after the incident where Greg was trying to ring her and couldn't get hold of her.

"Hello." Her mouth was claggy and tasted foul, she needed to brush her teeth to take away the feeling. That's what she got for being lazy and sleeping the day away.

"Erysah? Are you alright?" the voice sounded muffled at first, but that could have been because she was still groggy.

"Yes, sorry. Is that you Violet?" her throat felt dry and brittle.

"Of, course. Who else would be ringing you?"

"Greg." She replied simply. "Only you or Greg ever ring me unless I get telesales people bugging the hell out of me wanting me to buy something."

"Sorry Erysah, I was just concerned after our conversation the other day and when I didn't hear from you. Well I was worried."

"Stop!" she snapped, surprised at her own reaction. "You'll put yourself back in hospital. And I don't want that responsibility." For a long moment there was silence from the other end. Erysah sighed. "I'm sorry Violet I didn't mean to snap at you but I've had quite a couple of days."

"I know Erysah," Violet replied. "It's going to take time for you to adjust to this new information."

"You know this will change things between us." As much as she didn't want it to, that's exactly what would happen. It saddened her.

"Yes, I know." Violet sighed. "But I hope we can build back the trust."

"I don't know, Violet. How can I face Greg knowing what I know. You asked me to keep this from him, he's been like an uncle to me and then I find out that he is my cousin." God she didn't know if she would be able to ever face him again and if she did he would know something was different. Despite the fact that he is a quiet, simple man, he was not stupid.

"I understand Erysah, you need time. Time to get your head around things. Why don't you take a holiday, you haven't had any time off since you first started at the bar." Erysah considered the suggestion for a minute. Yes, it would be good to have some time to herself to sort things out, but she also had to find out some other things. There was also the matter of Dayton. They had a connection in more ways than she could comprehend. And she kept wondering about her tattoo, the way it didn't appear in the dreams but tingled afterward. What did that mean?

"Yes, I think that might be a good idea. Will you tell Greg for me I don't think I could face him right now."

"Yes, of course I will. Will you keep in contact?" She could hear the worry in Violet's tone and it tugged at her.

"I don't know. I may decide to go away somewhere. Get a fresh perspective on things." She had thoughts in the back of her mind of finding Dayton and staying with him.

"Yes I understand, be safe and take care of yourself, Erysah. I will miss you. Let me know when you're ready to come back."

"I will," but she felt as if she was only giving Violet lip service. She didn't actually know if she would be back. It would depend on what happened between her and Dayton. "Bye, Violet look after yourself and tell Greg not to worry." But she knew she would, that was part of who she was.

"Bye Erysah, we love you." Those words were like a knife twisting in her heart. But behind those words had been secrets. Secrets that made her feel betrayed.

Dayton woke earlier than normal he had to contact Sollest and ask her advice. Would Erysah being the daughter of one of their kind make things easier or more difficult during the ritual. How would it affect her transcendence? Dayton went to the end of the bed and pressed the hidden button just under the finial it began to move back against the wall, as it did the stone floor moved and steps were revealed that led to an underground corridor. The walls lit by torches that sat in sconces guided him into the earth below the manor house. The corridor sloped gradually and continued in a wide spiral as he travelled below the ground. Eventually he came to a large cavern, the walls glittered with pyrite as the flames from the torches reflected off it. Although, there were no priests in his culture Dayton was one of the few protectors of the sacred temples and also a guardian of' the veil'. Only he and the other guardians were allowed the privilege of seeking out Sollest and the other priestesses for questions their race had. Everything came through them. There was one guardian and one temple for every clan, except for the phoenix clan because they lived beyond the veil. Kaspir had been the Dragon Clan's guardian before him and after they lost him it had been passed on to Dayton. There was more at stake than just his life. Who would guard Sollest if he failed. No one was allowed to know. She chose her own guardian and they were selected on the day of the current guardian's journey into the black.

Dayton went to the ceremonial pedestal and pressed a series of symbols. The veil appeared and began to shimmer. From behind it a solitary figure stood. Dayton approached the veil, neither he nor the other passed through it.

"Dearest Sollest." Dayton said as he went down on one knee, paying tribute to her.

"What troubles you, guardian?" Sollest never addressed him by name. Always remaining aloof until required to perform the rituals of their people. That was the only time he knew that she and the other priestesses ever passed through the veil.

"I have found my 'Solelil'." He confessed.

"This is good, when will the ritual be held?" Her monotone voice echoed through the temple. There was no joy in it, no relief.

"There are some concerns.". He was unsure how to tell her what he had gleaned.

"Concerns?" He could not see her face, but from the tone of her voice, he knew she was puzzled. Dayton took a deep breath before parting with the information.

"Yes, she is not fully human." His voice quivered as he told her.

"How and in what way?" Dayton noticed there was a lack of surprise in her voice.

"She is the daughter of Kaspir."

"Ah yes, poor Kaspir. You have proof?" She tried to sound saddened, but she couldn't quite pull it off.

"Yes, a written confession from her mother and pictures of both of them together. He raised a picture he had taken from Erysah's flat."

"Then the prophecy has come to pass." There was a hint of relief in her voice, which confused him.

"Apologies dearest Sollest, prophecy?" Dayton was more confused than ever by her admission.

"Yes, millennia ago before I became your High Priestess. I heard of a prophecy amongst many other things. The old High Priestess passed on much information before entering the black."

"May I ask what was the prophecy?"

"No, but I will tell you this much. If she completes the transcendence ritual. It will begin a new era for our race." Dayton was not one to judge the High Priestess, but he had a feeling he would leave the temple with more questions, than answers.

"If she completes the ritual will I be allowed to know?"

"If she completes the ritual, all who are in attendance will know. It will then passed on and eventually all will know. Now go and prepare your 'Solelil' and make sure she accepts. We need her to be with us." With that the veil and Sollest faded. There had been no inflection in her tone. He almost felt as though he had been scolded by a teacher for asking too many questions. But why was it so important to the Vardesh? Dayton was completely confused by the whole conversation he had had with her. Where did that leave him now? With a sigh he went back to his chambers, he was desperate to see Erysah.

Erysah felt as though she was being stroked very gently. She turned round to see Dayton laying on her bed, his hand supporting his head as he smiled down at her.

"We have much to discuss you and I," he said rubbing a few strands of her hair between his fingers. *Erysah agreed she was eager for the conversation, but she was even more eager to arrange to meet him.*

"Yes, and I have taken a leave of absence." She said emphatically. *Dayton looked puzzled. "It means I will not be going to work and I can do . . ."*

"Other things?" Dayton finished the sentence for her, raising his eyebrows.

"Yes, other things!" she said smiled, her eyes hiding her intentions but the slow curve of her mouth was giving her away.

"Like what?" Why were they playing this game, he wondered. He did not really care, he was with his Solelil. He could not help but return her smile.

"Like . . . you." He was curious as to what she meant by him. Erysah placed a finger on his chest and started to draw squiggles on it.

"Oh!" He thought she meant finding out about her father Kaspir. "What about Kaspir?"

"That to . . . but . . ." she hesitated but her chest was filled to bursting and she had to release the pressure there. "Oh, Dayton we don't know each other at all really and I should not be saying this, but . . . it's how I feel." She was stuttering and stammering and blurting her words out like a child. Suddenly, she went all shy and coy, lowering her head. Dayton lifted her chin with one finger and asked her.

"How do you feel, Erysah." His heart was in his mouth, whatever she had to tell him, he would have to except, good or bad. "You know you can tell me, I will not judge your words." His smile seemed to light up the whole room, but deep down he was worried. Erysah needed some distance between them so she was able to speak. If she was too close to him she became overwhelmed and the words would be trapped in her throat. She abruptly stood up and walked to the other side of the room, when she had reached the wall she turned. Dayton was about to follow but she held up her hand and shook her head. For a long moment they just stared at each other. Dayton was getting worried when she did not speak. He tried to moved again, still she prevented him. "Please, Erysah. Tell me what is wrong?" Dayton was really confused, he thought everything was going really well between them. Now he was concerned that he had gone too fast and that it was all falling apart. He sat on the edge of the bed waiting for his world to collapse. Erysah looked at him her eyes glistening with tears. To stop herself from wringing her hands she put them behind her and began rubbing the place where the tattoo was.

"Nothing's wrong. That's the problem." She said shaking her head.

"I do not understand?" Dayton looked at her bemused. Erysah closed her eyes and took a deep breath to steady herself. As she exhaled the words that she had been holding in came out in a rush.

"I love you, Dayton. I love you, okay. I shouldn't, but I do." Dayton was stunned, it was not what he was expecting at all. She was right, how can this be . . . . They did not know each other, but he had already fallen deeply in love with her. And now she had fallen in love with him. As Dayton just sat there and stared at her, Erysah felt foolish. "I shouldn't of said anything," she closed her eyes to hide the tears that threatened to fall. Suddenly she felt claustrophobic, as she slowly opened her eyes she realised that Dayton had caged her in against the wall. She was staring straight at his chest. Slowly Erysah raised her head to look at his face, she was terrified by what she might see there. As their eyes met she could see an intensity in his. Cautiously he lowered his mouth to hers. The sensation was exquisite, soft, hot and wet and as she moaned into his mouth, her lips parted. Dayton took the daring step of putting his tongue in her mouth again. Would she find the hidden teeth that were concealed behind his smile. Despite all his fears and the battle of their tongues, she never went near them. When he released them from their kiss, Erysah asked.

"What was that for?" Dayton smiled his eyes shining so brightly they were almost blinding.

"For your gift," he said simply.

"Gift! What gift?" Dayton got her very confused about all the gifts she had supposedly given him. As far as she was concerned the only 'gift' was when she bought the nightdress. It was the night she had virtually seduced him.

"You have given me many gifts in such a short space of time, Erysah. I do not know how to repay you."

"You're being so silly Dayton." She laughed at him. She didn't mean to but he seemed to be talking nonsense. Dayton scowled at her and she stopped abruptly. She had never seen him like this, he was so serious. Immediately she apologised. "I'm sorry, Dayton but what you're saying doesn't make any sense to me." Dayton grabbed her hand and led her to the sofa in the living area. Sitting her opposite him and holding both her hands, he looked at her. His face was calm and a little frightening. Dayton could see the anxious look on her face, he smiled slightly to try and reassure her.

"I will not hurt you Erysah . . . I would never hurt you but I will not have you make light of things, things that mean so much to me." Erysah bent her head in shame, *'what did I do?'* She wondered. *"Look at me, Erysah. I want to see your face and I want you to see mine, when I tell you what I have to say."* Erysah shook her head and kept it down, unable to see the hurt in his eyes that she had put there. *"Erysah . . . please . . . this is important to me."* She slowly raised her head, his face was calm and his eyes had softened. *"Erysah, you are right we have not known each other as we perhaps should and there are things that you still need to know. You already know I love you."* Erysah nodded. *"You have given me several important things that represent everything in my culture."* Erysah was confused but stayed silent, she had a feeling that Dayton had some serious things to say. And she desperately wanted to know, as much as she could about him.

"Firstly your mind . . . our minds are connected by what we call a thread and that is how we can meet in these dreams. But they are not the kind of dreams as you know. These are more real, physical. In them we can touch, feel and remember every sensation. The more we connect the stronger the thread and . . . and you have shown that you can use the thread yourself to contact me. That should not have been able to happen, not yet anyway. It may have something to do with your father, I am not sure." She was just about to say something when he continued. *"I will get to Kaspir later."*

"But . . ." Dayton put a finger to her lips. She couldn't resist giving it a quick kiss. Dayton gave her a scolding look, which was meant to tell her to behave. Erysah smiled at him unrepentantly. Dayton shook his head, trying not to smile.

"Second you have given me your heart, a most precious gift because it is attached to your soul. And where your heart goes your soul will eventually follow and then you will have given me that too. That will be the third gift. Your body is another gift, although we have only shared our bodies in these dreams, we will I have no doubt share them in the real world. When that happens well . . ." Erysah took a deep calming breath as her heart started to beat faster. Dayton spoke with such awe and reverence, it was hard to think straight. *"You want to ask me something?"* He could see it in her face and more strangely in his head. Erysah nodded.

"When . . . when will we meet? If you don't come for me soon I am going to come looking for you Dayton." He could see she meant it by the intense look in her eyes and the determination in her voice.

"Soon, my beloved. Very soon." He was finding it difficult not to begin his own travels to find her.

"How will you find me? You don't know where I am. I haven't told you. I need to tell you." She was beginning to sound desperate. Dayton smiled, he stroked a finger down the side of her face. The sensation sent ripples through her body.

"Let me finish telling you everything you need to know about me first. It will also tell you about your father Kaspir. And make no bones about it. What I am about to tell you will test your love for me, beyond anything you could imagine. Are you ready to prove the strength of your love Erysah? Are you strong enough? Are we strong together?" Erysah's heart threatened to jump out of her chest, she didn't know if it was out of fear or excitement. Erysah took a deep breath to steady herself.

"Yes Dayton, I'm ready. My love for you is so immense it seems to overwhelm me. Please let's just get this over with so that we can move on . . . to better things." Dayton could see a sure and steady look in her eyes as she lifted her chin proudly. He could not resist, he had to have a small taste before he committed himself to telling her, his biggest secret. Their lips barely touched, but it was enough to send fireworks through both their bodies.

"Just remember Erysah you are my heart and I would spare you anymore hurt. But I need to reveal to you my true self and by doing so I will also reveal who and what your father was." Erysah thought that was rather a strange statement to make. 'True self' he made it sound as though he were some sort of alien. However, she nodded just once wanting to get it over with.

"Kaspir and I come from a place that was known as The Plains, our line, our race if you like is called the Vardesh. We are not quite as we appear. We travel during the hours that most humans sleep. We live longer than humans, much longer." Erysah realised she was holding her breath waiting for his next words, was he going to tell her he was some sort of vampire. "Yes, Erysah, that is exactly what I am telling you." Erysah couldn't believe he had actually heard her thoughts. "Ask your questions Erysah and I will answer them truthfully. I will hide nothing.

"This isn't a joke, is it?" She shook her head trying to make sense of things.

"No Erysah, I would not jest about a thing like this." This was not a joking matter, he was terrified.

"If you are a vampire, do you drink blood?"

"Yes."

"Do you kill people?"

"No! Never." The thought of that horrified him and Erysah could see it written all over his face.

"Sorry, preconceived ideas. Do you have fangs?"

"Yes."

"Can I see them?"

"No." Disappointment ran through her for some unearthly reason and she couldn't understand why.

"Why not? If you say you have them, surely I would be able to see them." Why did that make her feel cross.

"You cannot see them because they only extend on the onset of feeding. But I can let you feel them."

"How?" This really intrigued her and she stared at him intently. Her eyes were of excited child opening an unexpected gift. Dayton was still waiting for her to react negatively, but so far everything was okay. She had asked her questions and he had answered them. Now came the final test.

"There are two ways, One is with your fingers, the other is with your tongue." There seemed to be a bit of a challenge in that last statement. Hmm, she thought. Considering what to do. She had forgotten that he still had her hands in his. As she pulled them away he reluctantly let them go. Erysah shunted forward slightly so she did not have to stretch, whatever she decided to do. Dayton was surprised that she had not recoiled away from him. She seemed more curious than anything.

"You will have to open your mouth for me Dayton." Dayton did as she asked and closed his eyes, he did not want to see the look of revulsion on her face.' Perfect,' Erysah thought, now he won't be able to tell what she was going to do. As of yet she hadn't quite made up her mind, but she felt a sense of devilment creep through her. Even after everything he had told her and she had listened, disbelieving at first but she knew he wasn't lying. Dayton never lied about anything. He tended to leave information out, rather than lie. Erysah went up on her knees using the back of the sofa to steady herself. She wedged Dayton between the sofa and herself and straddled him. Putting one hand on his shoulder and the other on his face, she brushed his lips with her fingers. He was tempted to snap at them but he held himself very still. Dayton had hoped that she would have chosen the latter option. However, it looked like that was not what she intended to do. Erysah saw his face drop, that made her smile. It had also made her mind up for her. Suddenly and without warning Erysah fused her mouth to his. Shocked and stunned Dayton froze. The hand that was on his shoulder slid down his arm and she urged him to put it round her. Erysah kissed his lips which made his mouth respond and his other arm encircled her. Finally her tongue entered his mouth in such a sexy way it made him groan. Erysah shuddered as her tongue began to seek out his elusive fangs. Slowly as her tongue explored his teeth she found them. He had two sets, the lower ones were blunt but the top ones seemed very sharp. Thankfully because they were retracted they did not cut her. After the full exploration of his mouth, she retreated back so she could see his face. His eyes were open and there was a looked of amazement and wonder on it. She began to laugh then. Not because she thought him silly but because she thought him wonderful. The warmth that spread through her seemed to make her skin glow slightly. Dayton was mesmerized by it. Erysah put both her arms around his neck and then kicked back on the back of his calf to get his attention.

"What?" he asked, stunned.

"Carry me," her demand was almost petulant.

"Where do you want to go?" He had a feeling he knew, but he was enjoying playing this game with her and he was not about to spoil it. Smiling she kissed him again, this one had more meaning and he got the message. Dayton cupped her bottom as he stood up and headed for the bedroom. Erysah wrapped her legs round his waist. He lay her on the bed and slid next to her. This time he was going to make sure he pleasured her thoroughly.

"Dayton, just one question," she asked while he was unbuttoning her blouse and kissing his way down her body. The delicious feel of his lips making her body burn. *"If my father was a vampire, what does that make me and why don't I need blood?"* Dayton looked up from her midriff.

"Hmm, I am not sure. Even Sollest does not know how or why you are alive. Normally procreation only takes place after the transcendence ritual." Erysah grabbed his head and pulled it back up before he could resume his previous task.

"Transcendence Ritual?" Dayton groaned and put his head on her stomach. *"What aren't you telling me Dayton?"* crossing her arms over her breasts. *"I want to know everything and now before we go any further."* Dayton was already feeling uncomfortable as his erection was straining in his jeans as he sat up.

"Okay." He knew he was not going to get away with fobbing her off anymore. *"Here is how it works for my kind. When we reach maturity, we have one year to find our 'Solelil' (our soul mate) so to speak. The hope is that we find them early enough and if everything goes as planned, a mesh is formed connecting mind, heart, soul, body and blood . . .* Erysah interrupted him.

"How old are you when you reach maturity?" He knew that question would come up, he was trying to avoid that one until after the ritual. She saw him wince briefly. *"Dayton, you have already told me that you live much longer than humans."*

"We look for our soul mates during our 'year of yearning,' which is when we reach five hundred years of age." Erysah's eyes almost popped out of her head,

she gasped and sat up making her breasts bounce. Dayton swallowed hard as his trousers tightened even more.

"Really? No way! You don't look more than about twenty eight."

"We do not age as fast because of the blood, it affects our chemistry and has a rejuvenating effect. Anyway once the most of the mesh is formed the ritual of transcendence can take place. It is like a marriage. There are five stages, we have completed almost three. Mind, heart and the soul is almost finished, there is just the body and blood to complete. The body we can complete when we meet in the real world. Erysah could not resist smiling at that thought and Dayton did not miss it either.

"And the final part, the blood?"

"That is part of the ritual of transcendence. And will complete us."

"What happens if the ritual is not . . ." she gulped as the word stuck, "completed?"

"Then we have what happened to your mother and Kaspir. She lived for a number of years but would have felt empty and unfulfilled."

"And Kaspir?" she already knew as it had been in her mother's letter. She just didn't want to hear it out loud.

"He went into the black." Dayton felt the emotion well up inside him as he said those words.

"The black?" Then realisation set in. "Oh . . . My . . . God . . . Yes, I remember, he died!"

"Yes, he was my best friend. I never had a chance to say goodbye because I wasn't allowed to go to the ritual. Only those who have already been through the ritual can attend. So I cannot tell you what happens there." Which was true. It was the one thing that even the guardian was not privy to.

"Dayton I am so sorry." She reached for him and pulled him to her. She held his head to her heart.

"At the time he was the guardian of the veil, now that has been passed onto another." He did not want to tell her it was him, he had already given her so much information. He worried it might be too much for her. Erysah suddenly got up and paced across the room restlessly.

"Would the same thing happen to us? Dayton?" He stayed where he was staring at Erysah pacing back and forth, thinking it would be easier for both of them if he let her do her own thing.

"Only if the mesh was weak and you refused to complete the ritual."

"What happens to me if I complete it? Would I become like you?"

"Yes, normally you would, but because you have Vardesh blood in you already, it is hard to predict."

"Would I survive?" Erysah had some concerns on that score, because she was already part Vardesh. Erysah kept stopping and looked at him every time she asked a question.

"Yes, of that I have no doubt." Dayton was emphatic in his statement. Erysah felt relieved on that score.

"Where are these plains? I have never heard of them." Dayton was beginning to get nauseated watching her pace from side to side, but said nothing. It was obvious her way of dealing with somethings.

"In your world it is known as something completely different but I am not allowed to reveal where I am yet." She accepted that, understood it even. If people knew about them, well she dreaded to think what would happen. Suddenly she turned round and dived at him throwing him back on the bed landing right on top of him. Her eyes sparkling and her smile wide. Dayton was taken completely by surprise.

"Can we compromise?" She asked, hardly able to contain herself.

"Compromise?" Dayton did not understand what they could possibly compromise on.

"Yes."

"How?" This woman he had fallen in love with was sometimes extremely unpredictable, life would certainly not be boring he was certain of that.

"By finding the middle ground." Erysah was getting more and more excited at the prospect of travelling towards him in some way. Making the time and distance shorter for both of them.

"And where would that be?" He was intrigued by her suggestion. Yes, it could work and it would mean they could be together sooner. She was as eager as he was for that.

"You know where you live and I know where I live, so what if I told you where I live. You could work out where the middle was. I could make my way there and so could you. What do you think." Erysah's mouth was running away with her again. So he stopped her with a kiss, a long slow drugging kiss. That made even his toes curl. When he came up for air her looked at her flushed face.

"Slow down, Erysah. I think it is a great idea. But I do not live on the plains anymore. I moved away hundreds of years ago. I live in Scotland now."

"Scotland!" she exclaimed. "That's not that far from me. I live just outside Southampton, we could be together in just a few days. When can we start?" She was bouncing on top of him which was making very uncomfortable, as he still had a raging hard on.

"Erysah! Please stop! You are not helping me at the moment." Erysah realised what she was doing and stopped bouncing on him. She looked a bit sheepish. "You still have to collect what Kaspir left you and I must confess I am curious as to know what it is." Dayton was hoping he had not done something to jeopardise the race.

"Yes, you're right I have to finish this first. If I don't I won't be happy." Dayton was relieved for a number of reasons. The main one being she was not trying *to snap him in half anymore with her bouncing. He rolled over taking her with him.*

"Now where was I?" Erysah laughed as Dayton resumed applying his lips to as much of her body as he could. That would give him some time to regain some sensation back into his crushed manhood.

Kaspir's Tale

When she woke up the next afternoon, Erysah had never felt so happy. She had just about forgiven Violet for keeping secrets, because she knew it wasn't her fault. Anya had made her swear not to say anything. Despite her being dead these last two years, it was now Anya that was bringing everything out into the open. Erysah stopped herself short . . . Why the hell was she referring to her mother as Anya all of a sudden. Perhaps it was the secret that she had kept all those years or maybe the betrayal for killing herself and her grandparents. No wonder Papa Joe had a heart attack when she told them the truth. It had been fanciful to her ears when Dayton had explained about himself and Kaspir, her father That was now really surreal thinking about her father, the man she had never known. A man who was not really a man, well he was a man but not human, a vampire. Now she was going to find out what he had to say to Anya before he died. She couldn't believe what Dayton had said about that. What if . . . no she wasn't going to think about it. Everything was going to be fine for her and Dayton, she would rather die first than go through that. Erysah sat there for a moment thinking about those thoughts. Perhaps that was how her mother was feeling. Maybe, the fact that she was pregnant stopped her from doing it earlier. If she were in the same position as her mother, she wondered, what would she do?

The journey to the post office and back took almost three hours. Erysah had been stuck in traffic for nearly two hours all told, due to road works on the main street of the city. She should have remembered, because it had been that way for the last few weeks. They were redoing all the water mains in the centre of the city. As she walked into her flat Erysah began to feel uneasy. There seemed to be a presence in the place, not physical as such but something more . . . what she couldn't put her finger on it. She would have said ethereal or something like a ghost or spirit, but that was ridiculous. She didn't believe in those things. Mind you up until yesterday she didn't believe in vampires either. That thought made her smile for some strange reason.

She put the package on the coffee table next to the letter and photos from her mother and headed into the kitchen. Erysah had promised Dayton that she wouldn't open it until they were together. While she waited for the evening to set in she fixed herself something to eat and drink. She realised that she hadn't been eating very much just lately. Maybe one meal a day and usually in the evening. Was it because she had been sleeping late or was she just losing her appetite. The last few days had been quite stressful. After about an hour in the kitchen, raiding the cupboards for whatever she could find to eat. Erysah eventually made her way back to the sofa. She tried not to look at what was on the table as she sat down. Laying her head on the back of the sofa and looking up at the ceiling, she wished Dayton would hurry up and come.

The next thing she felt was a soft pressure against her lips. Warm and spicy, she responded to the sensation automatically and when she opened her eyes she was looking into two pools of the deepest blue that were Dayton's eyes. She flung her arms around him and he picked her up and sat her on his lap. Her eyes glistened with tears and Dayton wondered what was wrong.

"Nothing's wrong, Dayton I'm just so happy you are here."

"Are you reading my thoughts now?"

"I heard your question." Erysah looked puzzled, she could have sworn he had spoken.

"But I did not speak, the question was in my head but I never said the words." Dayton was beginning to wonder what was happening. Things were occurring that should only happen after transcendence. "It must have something to do with the fact that you are part Vardesh." It seemed the only plausible explanation.

"Oh, It must be that then." Erysah said. Dayton did not want to dwell on it, at the moment. They had more pressing things to deal with. Like what was in the package on the table.

"May I?" he asked indicating to the package. Erysah nodded. She felt safe in his arms and the feeling that she had earlier seemed to have disappeared. She thought about telling him about it, but it seemed silly now. Dayton picked up the package and put it on Erysah's lap. With shaky hands she began to open it. Unlike her mother's this package contained a black velvet pouch with something heavy and round in it. It also contained two rolls of parchment, one of which the seal had been broken, the other untouched. As she put the items on the coffee table, Erysah had that strange feeling of uneasiness creep over her again. She shivered and Dayton hugged her even closer.

"Are you alright Erysah?" he asked her, feeling a slight shift in the ether.

"I'm not sure, but it's the second time since I've brought the package home, that I have felt uneasy."

"In what way?" He was intrigued to know if she had felt the shift too.

"I know this will sound ridiculous, but it's like there is a presence, a ghost or spirit or something like that here in the room." She had felt it and Dayton wondered if his suspicions were right about what the pouch held. It would make sense that Kaspir would have one, considering he used to be Sollest's guardian. It should have been in the temple, why give it to Anya? And why are there two scrolls? And why was one still sealed? Dayton felt off kilter something was not quite right, there were too many questions and that worried Dayton. "What shall we look at first?" Erysah's voice made him focus back on her.

"The open scroll I think, it may give a clue as to what is in the other scroll and the pouch." Erysah nodded in agreement.

"Makes sense," she said as she leaned forward to pick it up. As of yet Dayton was unable to bring himself to touch the contents, because he knew he would feel the psychic vibrations of Kaspir on them. One thing he did know was that once a guardian was chosen, Sollest had to enhance their abilities in order for them to be able to communicate with her. Slowly Erysah unrolled the first scroll, she held it so they could both read it at the same time.

My beloved Anya,

These will be my final words to you.

I had to beg Sollest to be able to do this. I did not want to leave you with nothing. And after what Sollest has told me I leave you with more than anyone could have hoped for. But you will learn about that soon enough.

I am very sorry my love. It was my fault, I was too late. In my joy at finding you I forgot the rules. I forgot the mesh. Being her guardian I should have known better, but I was rushed by time, of which there was so little. I should have done better. I am so very sorry Solelil.

There are two things in a bag with this scroll. In this bag is a black velvet pouch. You may looked at what is inside, this is to go with the other scroll, which I implore you not to read. It is not for your eyes, but for the future. You will know all too soon, who it is for.

In putting these items with yours. I have taken advantage of Sollest's kindness, may she forgive me. I should have not but I could not help myself.

I hope my friend will also forgive me. I would have liked to say my farewells to him. But I know too much to speak anymore.

Farewell my love.

Kaspir.

Dayton could not believe Kaspir had referred to him in the letter to his Solelil. What on earth had he done. Dayton's mind was racing with the possibilities.

"Dayton are you okay? Why did he mention you?" Her words shook him from his meditations.

"I do not know but I am intrigued as to what is contained in the pouch and other scroll." He was not just intrigued he was worried.

"Scroll or pouch?" Erysah asked, raising her eyebrows.

"Scroll, I think. It may refer to the pouch."

"Okay." She nodded as she swapped scrolls. Carefully she broke the seal and they started to read the second scroll.

> To my beloved daughter, Solelil to my friend, Dayton.
>
> I know you are both going to be very surprised when you read this.
>
> Sollest made the mistake of telling me that Anya was somehow with child. Perhaps it was because there was little or no mesh, who knows.
>
> She also told me who she has chosen to replace me. Perhaps she did not think I would have time to write to you. Sometimes things are not always as they seem. However, she forgot or maybe she did not forget about the channeller, which is in the pouch. It allowed me a little extra time to write this.
>
> Dayton your Solelil is very special, she is a rarity. One of a kind and the future for our race. Nobody knows their destiny, but I can tell you this yours is together.
>
> Speak with Sollest and return the channeller to the temple. Ask her to forgive me.
>
> Kaspir.

Dayton picked up the pouch with a shaky hand and opened the draw string. Inside there was a large gold disc, about five centimetres in diameter. On one side was an impression of a dragon and on the other was an impression of a phoenix. He dropped it into Erysah's palm. As she held it in her hand she felt a strange warmth course through her body. Then the channeller began to glow, the glow started to spread engulfing both of them. The light wasn't painful, it caused their bodies to pulsate. From the light surrounding them, two dark figures started to take form growing in size and strength. After what seemed an age there were two people standing in front of them, hand in hand.

Dayton and Erysah looked at each other in disbelief. Standing before them were Kaspir and Anya and they both were smiling at them.

"Greetings old friend." Kaspir's voice was just more than a whisper.

"How?" was all Dayton could say.

"You can thank your Solelil." Anya looked at Kaspir.

"Her name is Erysah." Anya's chided her voice sounding like chimes in the wind.

"Sorry, beloved. You can thank our daughter, Erysah." Erysah just stared at them both. She was sure her mouth was gaping in astonishment. "She can enhance the power of the channeller."

"But we are not in the real world! We are only connected by the thread, in dream state." Dayton was desperately trying to comprehend what was happening and why.

"We know and so does Sollest."

"What has Sollest got to do with all this." Dayton had already had a conversation with her about Erysah being different. She had mentioned a prophecy. "What have you done Kaspir?"

"It is not what I have done exactly, it is what we have done." As he said this he looked at Anya. Suddenly, Erysah spoke, diverting everyone's attention on her. It was like she had been in a trance, except she had been listening to everything that was being said. She was processing the information before speaking. For the first time she really looked at her mother.

"Are you happy?" she suddenly asked her mother.

"Yes." The chime in her voice lowered slightly.

"Did you deliberately cause your death?"

"Yes, I could not live without Kaspir any longer." She looked at her Solelae with adoration in her eyes.

"Why did Nana Jean and Papa Joe have to die?"

"It was their choice, I was going to jump out of the car after telling them, but they stopped me. They said if they returned without me, they would have to tell you everything. They thought it better for you if you did not know the truth. I never told them that I had already arranged for you to find out when you turned twenty-one."

"What about Nana Jean and Papa Joe, where are they?" Erysah's voice was toneless as if there were no feeling as she spoke.

"They are not here. They are human."

"So were you." Erysah replied. It was Kaspir who spoke to her then.

"Sollest made an exception, because of you. Although, your mother is not Vardesh she has been allowed to be with me, in the black because she is my Solelil." Erysah knew now what had happened.

"Why because of me?" Erysah felt as though she was in a dream within a dream at that particular moment and perhaps she was.

"As I said in the scroll, you are very special."

"Sollest, she has the answer then." Dayton needed to speak to her as soon as possible.

"No!" Erysah said and turned to Dayton and held his face in her hands to look him straight in the eyes. "She has done this, Sollest has made this happen."

"How?" Dayton was really confused. Erysah seemed to understand more than he did.

"Ask Kaspir, he knows more than he is telling. Isn't that right mother!" Erysah's tone was accusing as she glared at them both. Her mother nodded and nudged Kaspir with her elbow.

"You know Sollest will never reveal everything. Tell them what you know. Please Kaspir." Kaspir hung his head sadly and nodded. They had sacrificed themselves for this, as she had planned from the start. It was justified. He had already broken rules, one more would not make any difference and they had little time left he could feel the pull of the black calling them back.

"Sollest, she is the reason. Ever since she has known about the prophecy she has been trying to find a way to make it happen. When I became guardian in my two hundredth year, it gave her the time to set things in motion. I do not know how she managed to do it. Anya and I had to be sacrificed for it to happen. We did not know at the time, however I suspected as much. Hence the scrolls and the channeller."

"We have to go now Kaspir, the black pulls us greatly. Goodbye Erysah. Be who you are supposed to be." Anya smiled as she started to fade.

"Farewell old friend." Kaspir's voice faded, as did he.

Erysah dropped the disc on the coffee table and it landed with a loud clank. Sagging into Dayton her tears came fast and furious as she sobbed into his shoulder. The encounter had left him numb and he did not know what to do, so he just held her. He held her for a very long time, until she was all cried out.

Whilst he was trying to comfort Erysah he kept going over the conversation they had had with Anya and Kaspir until his head ache. He did not understand any of it. He had only been Sollest's guardian for just over twenty years, but he could not believe that it would be possible for her to manipulate things in such a way. Kaspir had been her guardian for almost three centuries and would have spoken to Sollest many times over the years. Speaking on behalf of others, at their behest. If he thought about it he had never actually seen Sollest. They *communicated through the veil and she only came through for the rituals. He had not been allowed to attend a transcendence ritual, because he had not gone through one. However, he knew that was definitely about to change.*

Erysah began to straighten herself up, her eyes were all red and puffy. Dayton kissed each eye, softly soothing the pain away. He kissed her cheeks, drying her tears with his lips. Then he reached her mouth and took it with unbinding love. Erysah felt a tug on her heart and at that very moment she knew she had lost her soul to him. Dayton's body jerked slightly as he felt the connection take hold.

"The mesh is getting stronger, isn't it?" Since she had held the channeller Erysah could feel the connections. Things were definitely not what they seemed. She had been able to do things she shouldn't have been able to. Like reaching down the thread and bringing Dayton to her and reading his mind, even if it had been the once. There was also the enhancing of the channeller. What would happen when things became real, as if they didn't feel real enough already.

"Yes, the first three parts of the mesh are now complete." Dayton sounded down, as though he wasn't happy. But after what had happened neither one of them seemed overjoyed. They had both suffered again tonight, feeling the loss of their loved ones, for a second time. The only consolation was that they had been able to say goodbye.

"Now what?" Erysah looked at Dayton contemplating their next move. There was no going back, things had gone too far. Not that either one of them intended to do that.

"We move on." Dayton knew she was thinking the same thing, it was not difficult their minds were so strongly connected now. Thoughts could be sent and picked up easily from either one of them. They would soon be at the stage where they would not need to speak to each other to communicate.

"To what? To where?" Erysah needed to shake off this feeling. She didn't want to feel sad and depressed anymore. Kaspir and her mother had moved on and so should they. Dayton managed to pick up on her thoughts and agreed with her. He stood up lifting her with him. Erysah looked at Dayton and noticed a twinkle in his eye. She started to wriggle. He just held her tighter.

"Put me down Dayton." She tried to sound stern but wasn't having any luck.

"No." He said whispering the word into her ear making her shiver and sending heat through her blood.

"Where are you taking me?" As if she hadn't already got a very good idea. She desperately tried not to laugh, but he could hear the smile in her voice.

"You my love, need a shower." Dayton smiled at the thought of how erotic he had found his first experience of showering with Erysah.

"Are you saying I smell!" She tried to sound disgusted but it didn't work, even her shocked expression held a hidden smile.

"Yes," he teased. "You smell of tears and salt and sadness and I intend to wash them all away." Erysah secretly loved the way he was bossing her about. As they entered the bathroom he turned on the shower and sat on the toilet seat with her. Very slowly he began to take off Erysah's clothes. Slipping off her shoes and socks, he rubbed her feet gently making her kick out as he tickled them.

"Stop!" She squealed. I have very ticklish feet. Dayton began to wonder if she were ticklish anywhere else. He undid the button on her jeans and pulled down the zip. Lifting her up with one arm he tugged them past her bottom. Erysah hadn't realised just how strong he actually was. Dayton continued to pull her jeans down her legs exposing her smooth flesh to both his eyes and his hands. Once her legs were free of the material he caressed her thighs with the merest of touches. It felt like being stroked with a feather. Erysah leaned into him and moaned, she could get used to being looked after like this.

He toyed with the top of her panties making her gasp. Then moved under her tee shirt, splaying his hand as wide so he could touch as much of her skin as possible. Erysah sighed the feeling of his large warm hand on her tummy was delicious. As his hand slid higher, so did the tee shirt. Then he found the edge of her bra, Erysah began to mumble something he could not quite hear. But then again he knew what was in her mind and he had no intention of rushing anything. He was going to wash away her sadness both inside and out. Erysah raised her arms so he could remove her top, she now sat on his knee in just her green lacy underwear. Dayton dipped his head and pressed a kiss to the mound of each of her breasts, although he was dying to lick and taste them properly. But he restrained himself he wanted to savour that pleasure for the real flesh of her body. Erysah's arms encircled his head as he continued his affection on her breasts. As he slid the cups down exposing her, she arched her back and offered him more. Her inner sanctum was wet with anticipation and hot with desire. Erysah was beyond thinking, just feeling was enough.

Dayton got up and placed Erysah on the toilet seat then stood before her. Her eyes were level with the bulge of his erection straining at his jeans. She wanted to touch him but knew that he didn't want that right at this moment. He wanted to undress for her. To display himself for her like a proud peacock. He stepped back as far as he could, so she could get a better view of him. She could then watch him as he gazed at her body, as he had left it. Her breasts spilling over her bra a feast for him to devour with his eyes and her lace panties that barely hid the triangle of curls nestling at the apex of her thighs. Erysah concentrated on Dayton's hands and nothing else. She watched every movement they made. Watched every button pop open. Watched as every inch of chest was revealed. Watched as his shirt floated to the floor. Erysah clamped her knees together and tried not to squirm with the desire that was electrifying her body. His hands moved to take off his silver tipped cowboy boots. She watched him until his feet were bare. Then his hands moved again to his waistband, unclipping his belt which held a golden buckle with the initials DG on it. Erysah watched as it slowly slid through every loop until it was laying on top of his shirt. Her breath was coming in short gasps as he reached for the first button on his jeans. She licked her lips wondering if he had anything else on under there or if he had gone commando. One button popped, then another, then another. Oh, my, she thought biting on her lower lip as another button popped. When the final button was undone she held her breath, he had managed to hide his erection from her so far. However she knew that would be short lived. As he started to push down his jeans, he bent in the middle. All this time he had been watching her. Her whole body was flush with desire. The way her eyes widen, the way she licked her lips and then bit the lower one. And now the way her lips parted slightly in readiness for something . . .

Removing his jeans he stood revealing all of himself to her, she stood and unclasped her bra, letting it fall to the floor, then slid down her very wet panties. Gone were all thoughts of before, there was just Dayton in all his glory. What she really wanted to do was to cover every inch of him with her mouth.

Dayton could see it in her eyes, but what she did was to turn round and get in the shower. A soft moan escaped as the water hit her already sensitive skin. Dayton could not believe it, within seconds he was in the shower with her. His erection pressing into the small of her back, whilst hands moved round to cup her breasts, teasing her already budded nipples with his thumbs as the water cascaded over them. Erysah rubbed herself over him, causing him to groan into her shoulder. He could feel the roar building inside him and he would not be able to stop himself. Erysah slipped her hands behind her back and clasped his erection in her palms, urging him on.

One hand released a breast and slid down to the slit that lay at the bottom of her body. With one finger he travelled to where he found the most sacred part of her. Erysah gasped with pleasure as she exploded from his touch. He released her other breast moving his hand onto her shoulder. Dayton nibbled her lobe and whispered for her to lean forward. As she did his hand slid down her back. Erysah rested her head on her hands that were pressed on the far wall. Dayton moved his hands to her hips, crouching down he nipped at her bottom. Taking the hint she spread her legs. As he stood the head of his erection knocking at her door only once, before he slammed himself home with a roar. Erysah screamed with surprise. Dayton held still for a minute waiting for Erysah's reaction. He did not have to wait long as she started to pull away from him and then slammed herself back to him. Dayton more than got the message. He then took over, thrusting deep and hard, so hard sometimes he lifted her off her feet. By the time they were finished they barely had the strength to make it to the bed. They hadn't even dried themselves. The both lay naked on the bed on their fronts heads resting on their arms facing each other. Eventually Erysah managed to get her breathing under control so she could speak.

"What was that?" she asked him.

"What was what? He had a feeling he knew what she was going to ask but wanted her to be specific in her question.

"I thought I heard you roar. But it was not the kind of roar I've ever heard before."

"You did and you would have never heard this type of roar." Why did things have to be so difficult for him. He would love to be able to just tell her everything

and get it over and done with, but she needed time to assimilate things and adjust to the knowledge. She smiled at him.

"I'm intrigued, go on." Her smile was all the encouragement he needed.

"The Vardesh are made up of five clans. Eagle, Cat, Wolf, Dragon and Phoenix." He watched her face carefully for any reaction. All she did was raise her eyebrows and nod. I am from the Dragon clan. Legend has it that we are descended from dragons and at one time could assume their form. However, over the centuries the bloodline has weakened and although, we still have dragon blood in our veins we can no longer transform. But we still have our inner dragon, which comes out during extreme emotion."

"I have never heard you roar before?"

"No, but I did the first time we joined our bodies. I ended the dream on climax because of it. I did not want to scare you." Erysah laughed and then kept on laughing until tears came streaming down her cheeks. "What is wrong, why are you crying again." Dayton was at a loss. Eventually Erysah gained enough control to speak.

"I'm not upset, Dayton. I just think it's so funny. I thought that the strong emotion had cut short our dreams. And you left me in quite a state on more than one occasion." She stroked his back following the sleek muscles that lay just under the surface, while Dayton gloried in the sensation he admired the view of Erysah's statuesque form. "Now I find out it was you ending the dreams because you were afraid of scaring me."

"It is almost dawn," he said changing the subject. Erysah stopped laughing and hiccuped at the realisation of his words. "We have ran out of time again. Erysah nodded knowing what was coming next. She kissed him on the end of his nose.

"See you tomorrow," she said and smiled.

Plans

When Erysah woke up the next afternoon she had already got in mind what she planned to do. She wouldn't leave without telling Greg or Violet that she was going away. While she hadn't talked to Dayton about it, she had a feeling that once she had gone through the ritual she might not be able to return to her old life anyway. Not that it mattered, all that mattered to her anymore, was Dayton. She couldn't believe how fast things had progressed. Although now, they were not progressing fast enough. She was sure that Dayton felt the same. She hadn't even asked him how much time was left before the ritual had to be performed. Dayton didn't seem to be worried, but she was. She had loads of questions going through her head.

Had he found her straight away? How long had he been looking for her?. When did he first make the connection between them? Wait she knew this one, rushing into her bedroom she found her dream diary. When she opened it she found it strange, she hadn't written any of her recent dreams in it. The ones where her and Dayton had . . . Well there was too much to write and some of it was extremely personal. Hell, it had been sex on a plate most of the time. The thought made her smile and feel warm inside. She flicked through the diary to find the entry. Yes here it was the 12th April 2021. How long ago was that? She wondered. Carrying the diary with her she went into the kitchen area where she'd hung a calendar. Nearly seven months had passed. How long did that leave? It depended on the first question, which she didn't know the answer to. 'Wait a minute', she thought. 'Didn't Dayton mention a 'year of yearning'? That gave them about five months, didn't it.

Erysah wondered could she travel the thread and ask him. It was an interesting thought. Perhaps she could use the channeller. Excited by the idea she almost ran to the coffee table which still had everything spread across it. They hadn't even put the gold disc back in its pouch. Sitting on the sofa she looked at the clock it said 4pm. The sky was beginning to darken so maybe it would work, she would never know if she didn't try.

A wave of excitement coursed through her veins as she picked up the disc she and held it dragon side pressed to her heart. She took a deep breath and focussed on her target. Looking deep inside herself she found the mesh. Somehow she knew it was the route to take. Erysah wondered which part to use. Did it matter? She didn't think so, so she used the three strongest ones as the fourth was barely a link. Travelling through the mesh she concentrated on connecting with Dayton. When she finally found him he was still sleeping, she knew this because his conscious mind wasn't aware of her. Erysah whispered his name in his head like a kiss between lovers.

Dayton was sleeping peacefully, his brain just functioning enough to keep his body alive. No memories ran through his head, no dreams. Nothing at all. Suddenly he felt a strange sensation creep through him. A feeling of warmth, of love and a kiss. His eyes shot open as he became aware, sitting up he looked around the room. Then he heard the whisper of his name. He bolted off the bed searching his sleeping chamber looking for the source of the voice, panic held him in a vice, but he was alone. No one knew of his private chamber, except of course Erysah. In fact he could have sworn he had heard her voice calling him. Then he heard his name again which was followed by a chuckle.

"Erysah?" he whispered. As if she was going to answer him. Like she was an invisible spirit haunting him. However, she did answer but not in the way he anticipated. "*I'm in your mind silly.*" She could sense his confusion and wanted to ease him.

"How?" This time he sat down on the end of the bed and spoke only into his mind. '*How is this happening, we are in the real world, not our dreams*'.

'*I know, good isn't it*'. There was delight in her voice and his heart swelled with love for her. '*I love you too*', she said.

'*But I did not say anything*'. Dayton was severely at a loss as to what, how or why this was happening.

'I felt it in the mesh. Did you know there are actually four threads? Although the fourth one is very fine at the moment but it's there'. Dayton gasped, no that was impossible, he thought. *'Obviously, nothing is impossible between us. And to answer the how, I am using the channeller'.*

'How do you know how to use it?' He was totally perplexed.

'Your guess is as good as mine, but it worked and to me that's all that matters'.

'What was so important for you to risk such a feat?' His fear for her at this moment was off the scale. He was helpless and could do nothing. She had tied up the link in the physical world, so he could not use the dream world to go to her.

'I wanted to know how long it took you to find me? So I could work out how much time is left.'. Dayton may not think it didn't matter, but to her it did, a great deal.

'Erysah please stop this. Break the link so I can come to you'. Erysah heard the pain in his voice. *'I cannot come to you while we communicate like this'.* Dayton felt Erysah sigh.

'Okay, I'll see you soon'. With that she broke the connection. Dayton was aghast. He needed to go and see Sollest. She had to know the answers to the questions he had. Getting off the bed he pushed the button to move it back to reveal the entrance to the temple. He had a feeling that Sollest knew he was coming.

Erysah placed the channeller back in its pouch and gathered everything together that was strewn across the coffee table. As she piled everything up Erysah realised she needed a box of some sort to put it all in. There was no way she was going to leave this lot behind. It was too valuable and it was also her secret heritage. Something no one should find. Getting up Erysah headed into the spare room where she kept her clothes and shoes that were out of season. Surely she would have an empty shoe box somewhere. If not she would just have to empty one. As she looked through her things Erysah contemplated what her life would be like with Dayton.

What sort of adventures would she have. How would she change after the transcendence ritual. What would she be like. She already knew she was different. But was that because of who her father was. Did that mean she had never been just an ordinary human being.

Erysah also thought about what her life might have been like if she had never met Dayton. Not that she wished she hadn't, he had got under her skin so deep that he burrowed his way into her soul and yet she still wondered. Would she still be working for Greg at the bar or would she have moved on to better things. Surely she wouldn't have spent her life stuck behind a bar. She had ambitions, didn't she? Maybe she would have found a man and got married and have kids.

"You still can," came a voice from the doorway. As Dayton stood there smiling at her.

"Dayton, what how? Oh, damn I must have nodded off."

"That's a fine greeting." He huffed as he turned away, walking back into the living area. 'Shit,' Erysah thought as she dove after him, except she hadn't noticed that he had stopped and turned back to face her. She ran straight into his open arms. "Now that is a better greeting." He laughed with satisfaction scooping her up as she landed in his arms. "Although, I do not hold with that kind of language. Whether thought or spoken." His mock scolding did not hide his smile which was in his eyes too.

"You can be an awful tease, do you know that?" Erysah said laughing as she thumped his chest. "now put me down. Dayton dropped her on her feet but kept his arms on her hips.

"Tease, tease, what is this thing you accuse me of?" Dayton was straining not to fall into conniptions of laughter, as he teased her mercilessly. He realised for the first time he was playing with her. He had never really laughed, although the Vardesh were capable of emotions, they were just more subdued. Perhaps it was not until they had found their other halves that their emotions awakened fully, coming alive. Erysah scowled at him and she opened her mouth to give him a piece of her mind, he pulled her back up and kissed her into silence. When he had finished devouring her mouth he put her back on her feet. Erysah felt *slightly giddy from the lack of oxygen. She glared at him, even though she was not angry with him.*

"I see you're prepared to fight dirty." *She said, still holding the box in her hand so she pulled away from Dayton and went over to the coffee table, making sure she swished her hips in the most provocative way she could. Two could play at that game and yes she could feel Dayton's eyes were locked on her derriere. She could hear him groaning in her head. She smiled at him over her shoulder and blew him a kiss. Dayton just shook his head and followed her to the sofa.*

"What is the box for?" *As he watched her put it on the table. He noticed that she had tidied everything up that was scattered there.*

"You do ask silly questions, at times Dayton." *Okay he had to agree this time. It was sort of obvious she was packing everything into the box for transportation. As he watched her place things in carefully he was reminded of what had happened earlier. The last thing she picked up was the little black velvet pouch. He grabbed her wrist to stop her for a moment. She turned towards him.* "What?" *He nodded to what she had in her hand.* "Oh, you want to know about this afternoon." *He nodded again unable to speak.* "Would you like me to tell you or show you?" *He gently took the bag from her hand as his throat closed just at the thought of it.*

"Just tell me Erysah. I do not think my heart could take another episode of you with the channeller." *He said as he placed the pouch in the box and put the lid on. She laughed at him and nodded.*

"Okay. I didn't do much really. I picked up the channeller turned it so the dragon was facing me and pressed it to my heart. I took a deep breath and searched into myself looking for a thread. However, I saw four threads. Like I told you, three of them were really strong. But the fourth was extremely fine, like it was just beginning." *Dayton interrupted her for a moment.*

"That fourth thread should not even exist yet. That is the thread of the body which only takes form when we join our bodies in the physical world." *Erysah started to giggle lifting her hands to mouth to try and stifle the roaring laughter that was bubbling up in her chest. Dayton was not impressed with her, his face contorting in disapproval.*

"I'm sorry Dayton, but sometimes you say things in the strangest of ways." She said through her hands." I presume you're talking about sex."

"No!" he snapped, which totally shocked Erysah. She had never heard him so angry before. Dayton took a deep breath to calm himself." I am talking about the union of our bodies in a sensual and reverent way." That was it, Erysah lost it. She let rip big style. Dayton's mouthed dropped opened in astonishment. He did nothing more than pick her up, slinging her over his shoulder. Erysah kicked her feet trying to wriggle free, so he slapped her rump, which shocked her into stopping her laughter. She thumped at his back and screamed at him to put her down. He did nothing more than dump her on her bed and sat across her thighs. Pinning her arms above her head with one hand he leaned over her, his head a mere inches away from hers. She tried to look demure but she was still suffering the effects of her laughing fit. "You!" he said sternly. "You, need to learn some respect." Erysah wasn't sure what he planned to do, but she started to squirm, trying to get free. Dayton sat back and waved his index finger of his free hand, as if to say, oh, no you don't.

Erysah froze . . . her eyes wide in shock. It was the first time she was worried at what he might do. His face was a mask, it was devoid of all emotion. Even his eyes seemed cold, Erysah shivered. She watched that finger as he brought it to the side of her body just below her ribs. Her mind ran riot, would his hand turn into a claw and cut through her skin. Had she brought the dragon out of him, for the first time she was actually scared. Dayton could see the terror in her eyes, he did not mean to scare her but she over stepped the boundary and she had to pay. Gently he poked her, it made her flinch a little. Then he rubbed his finger in that soft area, she wriggled. Dayton's eyes began to sparkle with mischief and the corners of his mouth twitched. If she liked to giggle and laugh then he would tickle her into submission. He could see the relief wash over her and she did not look happy about it.

"You . . . you . . ." she tried to get her words out but she was so cross with him for scaring her like that she couldn't. It wasn't until the real tickling started that she realised what he had planned. He released her hands and started in earnest. After about ten minutes she was begging him to stop. She had been screaming, laughing, crying and now she could hardly breathe. Gasping for breath she tried to say 'stop', except she couldn't form the word properly. Dayton stopped then. "When we meet in the real world Erysah, you will see what

I mean. I have not made love to you as I will when we are really together. What we do in our dream will be nothing compared to when I really have you to myself. Do you understand?" Erysah nodded slowly, still trying to regain her breath. Dayton bent down towards her and kissed her gently. *"I love you deeply, my beloved Solelil. You are my life, my heart, my soul, my everything."* He then he broke into a huge grin. *"Also please remember that I am able to tease and torment you too."*

"You b . . ." But she didn't get to finish what she was going to say, because Dayton kissed the word out of her mouth. When he had finished he rolled off her and they both started laughing. When they had calmed down Erysah asked the all important question. *"Where are we going to meet?"*

"Ah, good question, but before we can decide that. Where do you live?"

"I live in a small town called Bittern, near Southampton." Erysah wondered if he would tell her where he lived but she doubted it. She wondered if he even knew where Southampton was. *"Have you any idea where I need to travel to?"* Dayton was quiet for a few minutes, his eyes closed as if trying to plan a route in his head. In fact if she tried hard enough she would be able to . . .

"Please do not do that. Until the ritual has been completed you are not allowed to know. Unlike what your fantasy writers say, we cannot remove memories. It would be detrimental for our race to have someone who knew our true identity and where our sacred temple lay."

"I'm sorry Dayton, it just gets a little tempting to try out things. I'm nothing if not adventurous." She smiled, even though he couldn't see her face, he could feel it through the mesh.

"Do you know the north of England?" Dayton eventually asked her.

"No, I've never really left Southampton." How sad was she, she had led such an insular life. No wonder she was eager to experience new things. Dayton had unleashed a side of her she hadn't realised existed.

"There is a small market town called Barnard Castle, near Darlington. It would take me two nights to get there. I estimate that you could get there in

the same amount of time. It would be better than trying to get there in one journey. There is a place called Derby which is about halfway you could find a place to stay overnight."

"Okay, I'll make arrangements for places to stay in both Derby and Barnard Castle. I presume we will be staying there for a short time?" Dayton nodded as confirmation. "Will we be able to get together during that time?" She had a feeling the answer might be no.

"I will make contact with you briefly at the end of my first nights travelling. Because I will be unable not to." His confession made Erysah feel a little better. She would be able to travel during the day but Dayton couldn't do that. Thankfully it was November and the nights were longer. "I will start my journey tomorrow night, be safe my love."

"I will and from what you have told me I presume we will be heading to somewhere in Scotland." She couldn't resist saying what she thought. With a sigh Dayton nodded.

"You know we are." He should have known better, but there was no way to avoid it. As long as she did not know the final destination until she got there, it would be fine.

"Time to set things in motion." He said as he kissed her goodbye.

Erysah went on the internet almost as soon as she woke, looking for places to stay in the destinations Dayton had mentioned. Derby was easy, it was a fairly big city and there were plenty of hotels to choose from. She chose a place that was near a large car park, where she could park over night. It was right in the centre of town, so she could do a little exploring without getting lost. Barnard Castle was a different story, it was a small market town. Despite this she found a quaint little hotel in the centre of the town. She had been grateful that it wasn't the holiday season, otherwise she might not have been able to get anywhere to stay. Thank goodness for the internet and the phone.

Speaking of the phone, she thought to herself she had better ring Violet. If she gave her some idea of what she was doing, then perhaps they wouldn't worry so much. Erysah found she was really nervous about ringing them. It was so bad her hand was shaking as she punched in the number. The phone seemed to ring for a long time, then the answer phone kicked in. She tried not to contemplate that Violet might be back in hospital. More than likely Greg had taken her out for some fresh air. Erysah didn't have time to try again later, she still had to pack. So she left a message.

"Hi, this is Erysah. I just thought you should know that I have decided to go up to Scotland for a while. I thought I might as well drive up there and have a look at a few sites on the way up. I haven't decided how long I will be away yet, but I will try and ring again when I get there. Take care both of you. Bye." When Erysah put down the phone, she didn't know if she would make that call. But she hoped so. Picking up the shoe box that was still sitting on the coffee table, Erysah walked into her bedroom and started packing. By the time she had finished it was lunchtime. After grabbing a bite to eat, she packed her car and said goodbye to her apartment. Erysah had a feeling she wasn't going to see it again anytime soon, if at all.

The Journey

By the time Erysah left her flat it was nearly three in the afternoon. She hadn't had a return call from Violet or Greg, but she wasn't surprised. She didn't suppose Greg was very happy with her at the moment. And things had become strained between her and Violet. She didn't have time to worry about it now, she had to get on the road. Although she had planned the route carefully, there was always something to cause delays. She had planned in a couple of breaks so she wouldn't get over tired with driving. If she wanted to drive nonstop she could get to Derby in about four hours but that was a long time to drive without a break. So Erysah had planned to stop in Oxford first, she would arrive there in a couple of hours. Perhaps she could grab some food at a cafe before continuing on. Her last stop before Derby would be in Solihull. She could grab a coffee or something else to keep her going. She estimated that she would reach Derby by about nine. Enough time to get something to eat before going to her room. Or she just might have something in her room. It just depended on how tired she was when she got there.

She had flung her duffel bag in the boot of her car. Thankfully she had gotten the exhaust fixed as soon as Greg had mentioned it. The last thing she needed was to be pulled over by the police, as her schedule had no room for delays. As she got in a thought crossed her mind to nip over to Greg's house. She didn't know why perhaps it was guilt but she really didn't have the time. If she did they would probably delay her with too many questions she wouldn't be able to answer. She needed to continue on her journey or she wouldn't get to the hotel in time. The pull towards Dayton was irrefutable. Things had been set in motion that couldn't be stopped, even if she wanted to. And she so didn't want to. Erysah chuckled to herself at the thought.

Dayton rose just as the sun had set, he was so grateful for the long nights and up here they started even earlier. He already had everything he needed packed in a small valise, he had been ready now for a few days. After the last conversation with Sollest he had been angry at what she had told him. He would tell Erysah but he wanted to do it face to face, not in a dream. As he looked at the clock in the library he realised he had to get moving. He would need to get a taxi from Stone Edge to Aberdeen, so he could catch the late train to Edinburgh. That still meant a good forty minute walk from the manor house. The moon was waning which meant the road to Stone Edge would be very dark. They did not have street lights, but Dayton had no real need for them as he had perfect night vision. His heart was beating faster than normal and his nerves jangled with anticipation, as he made his way along the narrow road that led to Stone Edge.

Dayton reached Stone Edge just a little after six. The train was due to depart at eight. The taxi ride would take about an hour or so, he would still arrive at the station in plenty of time to catch it. People knew Dayton in Stone Edge, even though they did not know exactly where he lived and that was the way he preferred it. He was a frequent visitor for many reasons, one being it was his main source of nourishment. Sometimes he would travel to Aberdeen or another village near there for a change. Not wanting to cause too many problems within the town. Town that was a bit of an over statement, it was little more than an overgrown village and only supported him at the moment. Of course, that would change when Erysah arrived, but that still would not cause any great problem.

Going to a phone box that was situated near the church he rang the local taxi firm and waited for it to arrive. It turned up five minutes later, as Dayton put his valise in the boot and climbed in the back of the car the driver spoke.

"Braw nicht," his accent laced with Doric. Thankfully Dayton had lived there long enough that he understood them without difficulty.

"Yes," he said as he nodded in agreement. He was not really paying much attention as his mind was elsewhere.

"Wo tae?" The driver asked.

"Aberdeen train station." The man's eyes lit up in excitement, from his reaction you would have thought he had just won the lottery. The driver was very happy, a trip to Aberdeen was a good fare. Because of the distance he could make almost ten times what he would normally make in a night, plus he knew his passenger was a very good tipper. Dayton just stared out of the rear passenger side window his mind on other things rather than the inane chatter of the cab driver. He was wondering where Erysah was on her part of the journey. 'Soon, very soon my love'. He smiled to himself at the thought. Before he realised it the car had stopped they were parked outside the train station. Focussing on his surroundings again Dayton paid the man, giving an extra large tip tonight. He did not care his heart was filling with joy and anticipation. Suddenly the driver caught him by surprised. The man cleared his throat. Dayton looked at him for the first time. He could not tell his height but he was a balding man and what little remained of his dark hair circled around his head in a two inch band. He looked at Dayton with his deep set brown eyes that were hooded by heavy lids, showing concern.

"Yes?" he queried.

"Whit's adae?" Dayton smiled, he actually smiled at the man.

"Nothing," he said shaking his head. "I am on my way to meet my future wife." He could not resist telling the man for some reason. And it would be good for the town to know that there would be a new face about. Dayton did not know why he had used that phrase but it felt right. To all intent and purpose that is what she would be to him.

"Braw," said the man returning Dayton smile. Dayton thanked the driver and gave him at least twice the fare then headed into the station. It was an old red brick building, with a clock tower above the entrance. The evening was cold, but on the platform it was even colder as the breeze tunnelled down the tracks. The ticket office was closed, so he had to get his ticket on the platform. It was cold and austere as he went to the ticket machine. Oh, how he longed to be on the train, travelling towards Erysah. Dayton expected to reach the Dragon Clan homes around midnight. He would then be able to speak to Erysah and make sure she was okay. Dayton was not happy that she was driving but it would come in handy later. It would

Dream Lover

be easier to travel back by car they could complete the trip in a little over five hours. He did feel a little guilty because it would fall on Erysah to do all the driving. They could stop again in Edinburgh but it would have to be at a hotel. He could not risk taking her to a clan house. Not until after the ritual had been completed.

By the time Erysah reached Oxford at was half past five. The journey had been long and tedious she was in desperate need of some air and a stretch of her legs. Deciding to stick to her plan to stop for an hour Erysah found a car park and headed down the high street to find a cafe where she could get something to eat and drink. As Erysah walked past the shops looking in the windows, she realized that it was well after six when she had actually hit the high street. Finding a small bistro that was just opening its doors she asked if she could get a meal. The waiter nodded and guided her to a seat near the window.

"You are lucky our main trade doesn't start until about seven thirty." He said. "What would you like?" Erysah ordered Tuna Pasta Bake and a black coffee. She would need the caffeine to keep her alert for the rest of the journey. As she ate she watched people pass by. Some seemed to be going home after a long day at work, others just starting to go out for the evening. The bistro started to fill at about seven. Erysah realised she couldn't risk stopping at Solihull, because she would reach Derby too late. By the time she got back to the car, it was nearly eight. It would be at least ten at least before she got to Derby, an hour later than she had planned.

The train had pulled out on time and he was now on his way to Edinburgh. As Dayton watched the world rush by, he mulled over the brief conversation he had had with the taxi driver. Thinking about his eagerness to announce that he was to be married, what would Erysah think about that? Would she understand that the ritual was a form of marriage. Would she recognise it as one? What if she did not? What would his clan think if he wanted to marry Erysah in the human way. It was the twenty-first century after all, for too long they had dragged their heels in the past. It was time to move with the times and perhaps make some new traditions.

By the time the train had pulled into Edinburgh station, Dayton had made his mind up. He was going to ask Erysah to marry him. In Stone

Edge there was a wonderful little church which would be perfect and it could be done just before the ritual. There would be plenty of time, as the ritual would be held at midnight. Yes, he thought to himself. He would make the arrangements as soon as he could, after asked Erysah to marry him. But his main problem was the purchase of a ring. He could not propose to her without one. He had had many years to study humans and their traditions, so he knew it was required. As he weaved his way through the ancient streets of Edinburgh he thought about it. He would ask his clansman for help in this matter. He was sure they would be of assistance. Before long he found himself outside their property. A simple and innocuous town house at the end of a terrace, which sat next to a wide expanse of green, some sort of park. As he mounted the steps, the door of the property opened, it was obvious he had been watching out for him. The man standing in the entrance way swept his arm from the doorway into the house, in a please enter motion. As soon as he was over the threshold the door closed behind him.

"Welcome guardian," the man greeted him. Everyone knew who he was but there were few who actually knew his true name, because when they gained such a position they were always called by their title.

"Thank you Garroch. I am happy to be here. How is Melindra?" He knew that Garroch had found his Solelil some fifty years ago and that they were expecting their second child. Their first had been a son who was now in his twenty-fourth human year and attending the local university. Luckily for the Vardesh until a child reached the age of ascension at the end of their of twenty fifth human year, they could tolerate daylight. Until then Vardesh children aged mentally twice as fast as a human but physically they aged the same. The Vardesh had no problem bringing up their offspring because until the human age of eleven they were home schooled, in reality mentally they were actually twenty-two. When they moved into public or private education. They were independent individuals and able to take care of themselves. From the age of six they would adapt to the being awake in the daylight hours. This gave them great independence and responsibility within the household.

"Come into the living room and meet my family." Garroch walked past him and headed down the hallway. Opening the second door on the left he entered a spacious but cosy room, followed by Dayton. The room was typical of the era and looked as though it had not changed over the centuries. Dayton knew that they had only lived there a relatively short time. As with all properties that belonged to the clan they passed from one family to another on a regular basis. This was to give the illusion that people died or moved on. It helped allay any suspicion about who they were. As Dayton entered the room he was greeted by Melindra who sat in a chair with her feet on a low stool. Her belly was already rounded, even though she was only half way through her pregnancy. Giving that Vardesh woman are pregnant for eighteen months that meant she still had nine to go.

"Welcome guardian." She smiled. "We are pleased to be of service to you. I apologise for not standing but I am feeling rather tired tonight." Dayton nodded.

"There is no need to stand on ceremony." Jarro could not resist the opportunity to take advantage of such a statement.

"What brings you to our abode?" came a voice from a table in front of the window. Melindra gasped and Garroch cleared his throat. "What?" said the voice again as he raised his nose out of the book he was reading. Despite Melindra and Garroch's discomfort, Dayton found it amusing but hid his smile anyway. It would not do for him to be encouraging the boy and his parents would not be happy either.

"Jarro!" Garroch scolded. "You cannot speak to the guardian like that." His eyes showing his disapproval at his son's forwardness. Dayton felt that Jarro had been justified in asking such a question and was prepared to answer him. Turning to the boy's father he said.

"No, Garroch do not scold your son. He has a valid question and one I would take pleasure in answering." This got everyone's attention.

"Pray do tell," Melindra's curiosity spiked. She gestured to the sofa opposite her.

"Please sit," he said to Garroch, "and come join us young Jarro." He winced at the condescension. Once everyone was seated he began. "I journey to meet my Solelil." Both Garroch and Melindra looked at each other unable to hide their delight.

"Oh, how wonderful," Melindra exclaimed.

"When will you get to her?" Garroch asked.

"One more nights travelling, will see us together. But I have had thoughts of having a human marriage performed before the Transcendence Ritual." Now Garroch and Melindra gasped but Jarro smiled.

"That would be a wonderful idea. If she commits to that she would commit to anything." Jarro stated. Dayton approved of Jarro. His was the sort of progressive view that they needed to bring them into the present.

"Yes, my problem is that I want to ask her to marry me tomorrow, but I do not have a ring. Can you recommend a reputable jewellers that will still be open tomorrow after sunset?" Dayton felt a little awkward asking the question but he would not be thwarted over this.

"Oh, guardian," Melindra almost squealed. "We can do much better than that." Within minutes she had rose out of her chair with unexpected vigour disappearing and returning with a small beautifully engraved black enamelled box. Dayton looked at Garroch confused.

"Guardian, my Solelil loves to make jewellery and we have quite a good business. Most items are commissioned or are sold over the internet." Dayton nodded and understood Melindra's excitement. Melindra handed Dayton the box.

"If it would not offend, guardian I would take great pleasure in providing this ring for your Solelil." Dayton was about to speak when she added. "As a wedding present." Garroch nodded in agreement. He felt honoured that this family would do this for him. With bated breath they waited for him to open the small box and view the ring. Dayton did not want to disappoint them. As he opened the box and looked at the ring his eyes widened, it was exquisite. Made from gold and platinum that surrounded a cluster of rubies and emeralds in a twisted knot formation which travel along the top third of the ring. Dayton was almost lost for words.

"Surely you do not expect me to except this."

"Yes, we do." Said Garroch. "We hope your Solelil will love it as much as you seem to."

"I am sure she will. I would be honoured if you would attend the marriage ceremony with Jarro and of course the ritual. Obviously, Jarro will be unable to attend the ritual, but I would be honoured if you both of you would. They nodded in delight and said together.

"But of course Guardian." Dayton smiled and nodded.

"Now I wish to retire, so I can contact Erysah before it gets too late. I need to know she has travelled safely."

"Is that her name? It is beautiful. I hope you find her well." Melindra then looked at her son. "We have a safe room for guests. Jarro would you please show the guardian the way?" Jarro nodded and led Dayton through the house to his room. The safe room was originally the dining room which was situated in the middle of the house and there were no windows as the building was attached to another.

By the time Erysah made it to Derby it was gone ten, she went straight to the hotel. Once she was in the room it was all she could do not to collapse into bed. She needed a shower first she felt dirty and achy from all the driving. Before her shower she called room service and ordered a sandwich and a hot chocolate. Erysah had just got out of the shower when the room service waiter knocked on the door. She thanked him and gave him a tip before sitting down at the little table that he had set the tray on. It was almost midnight before she climbed into bed, she was a little less achy but very tired. Within minutes she was asleep, as she was drifting off, she wondered where they would meet in the dream. She had no idea where he was and he only knew the name of the place she was at.

Erysah felt warm all over as a breath of air blew passed her ear. She smiled to herself. Dayton she thought, 'who else' came the reply in her mind. She twisted herself round as his grip loosened slightly so she could move. She realised she was laying on his bed the one that was in his chambers. She didn't question it because she knew he could choose to meet her anywhere. Dayton's eyes glistened with unshed tears, he realised that she was just one more day away. He was overwhelmed by the depth of his emotions, as he blinked a tear escaped. Erysah raised her hand to his face and brushed it away with her thumb.

"I love you." She said simply, smiling, her heart bursting. Then she moved forward to kiss him and he was lost. Everything he was did not mean anything anymore, not unless she was in his life. Whether for another five hundred years or five hours he did not care. She was his life and he did not want to live without her. When she released him he saw her heart and soul in her eyes and they were shining for him.

"I love you, Solelil," his reply just as heartfelt. "I cannot wait until tomorrow, when we truly meet." She looked a little worried about the mention of tomorrow. She thought about the tattoo that was one her hand which amazingly never appeared in the dreams. What if he didn't like it, what would she do? "What is the matter Erysah?" He crushed some of her curls in his hand savouring the feel of them.

"What if you don't like the real me?" Her face creased with worry. People in dreams are never what they seem. It was Dayton's turn to laugh at her this time.

"Erysah, oh my sweet, darling Solelil. I am sure you will more than live up to my expectations. I could say the same to you, I may not be as you expect."

"I want this day to end so we can get this over with. The waiting is killing me Dayton. I just want to be with you, the real you. Not this facsimile."

"Believe me when I say this neither one of us is a facsimile, as you call it. And tomorrow I have something important to ask you." Erysah's heart began to flutter as did the butterflies in her stomach.

"What?" Erysah's curiosity sparked. "Can't you ask me now?" Dayton shook his head.

"No, this must be done in person." Erysah looked a little disappointed but she did not press. He was keeping something very close to his chest and nothing was coming through the thread. *"See you tomorrow, beloved."* He said as he kissed her and faded away.

The contact had been so brief but Dayton could not stay any longer he was getting far too close to asking the question. He wanted to get down on one knee and do the full proposal, how human of him, he mused. He felt as Erysah did, he found himself wishing the day away, so he could continue his journey to her. He took out the little black box that was in his pocket. He held it in his hands and pressed it to his heart. When had he become such a sap, having a Solelil had turned his life upside down. But when he thought of Erysah, he knew he did not care. He loved her with all his heart and she was all that mattered to him.

After Dayton left Erysah woke up her mind going into overdrive, what on earth did he want to ask? It couldn't be anything to do with their relationship because he was just as desperate to meet. So what was so damned important that he had to say it in person. Had he got another secret, something like hers that didn't appear in the dream? She kept thinking about the name he called her 'Solelil' and wondered what it really meant. She missed him terribly her chest hurt. There contact had been so brief, but he did tell her it would be. She craved more much more and now she was less than twenty-four hours away from him. Erysah wondered how Violet and Greg were. She made a mental note to try and ring them in the morning. She thought about the stress that Violet's confession could have had on her heart. She really didn't want to think about it, if anything happened . . .

"No," she said shaking her head, she wasn't going to think about that. It wasn't her fault, she hadn't been the one keeping secrets. Perhaps Violet was trying to clear the books before. 'Urrghh! Erysah, stop taunting yourself,' she reprimanded herself. She couldn't be responsible for other peoples actions only her own. Erysah cast her mind back to Dayton's visit. What question did he have for her and why would it have to wait until they met. Was it about the ritual. She knew the ritual would include blood, well it would wouldn't it. After all, he's a vampire. Would he have to bite her? If so what would it feel like? After tossing and turning for a while Erysah finally went back to sleep.

When Erysah woke it was almost two in the afternoon, she couldn't believe she had slept so late. She was going to have to grab a bite to eat in the town and then hit the road straight after. She was eager to be on her way. Tonight was the night she would finally meet the man she had fallen in love with. The man in her dreams, he was the man of her dreams. 'What a cliché,' she smiled to herself. Erysah still didn't know how it had happened. Not exactly love at first sight but pretty damn close. Taking advantage of the shops she went and picked up a few items that she thought she might come in handy. Then she grabbed something to eat in the food court on the upper level of the shopping centre. Then trying to calm herself down she made her way back to the car. The car park where she had parked her car was attached to it, so it made her life easier. By four that afternoon she was heading up the A38 towards the M1 which would take her to her beloved Dayton.

Dayton was grateful to Garroch and his family for allowing him to stay with them until he started the next leg of his journey

"Thank you once again for the amazing gift. I will be in contact with you soon about the arrangements."

"We will see you soon, Guardian." Nodding slightly. After the farewells Dayton made his way back to Edinburgh train station. Descending the steps onto the platform, reminded him of his private entrance to the temple. Only this time he felt like he was being swallowed by a huge beast. The feeling of claustrophobia was overwhelming, his chest tightened and his breath caught in his throat. He laughed at himself, he was actually feeling nervous.

The train bound for Darlington was leaving at seven and due to arrive at nine. By the time he got a taxi from there to Barnard Castle it would be gone ten. Looking up at the clock on the platform he estimated they would be together in approximately four hours The thought made him smile. The thing that was causing his nervousness was asking that very important question which had been on his lips since last night. Who would have thought such a human thing would invoke such a response in him.

As he boarded the train his heart beat with anticipation. Just a few more hours. What would it be like meeting her in the flesh. To run his fingers through her lush flame red curly hair would it feel the same as in the dreams. And her alabaster skin so pale and creamy, soft to the touch. He sat back and thought about Erysah in every way possible. His gut clenched anxiously as he waited for the train to move. Slowly the train began to pull out of the station, the gentle rocking motion made him feel sick. The clanking of the wheels on the tracks adding to his tension. Gradually the train gathered speed and the clanking became less noticeable. The sway of the coach reminded him so much of the rocking motion of a tall ship. His last great journey. He had been a stowaway on one, nearly three hundred years ago. He was travelling from his family home in Europe. His parents had encouraged him to come to Britain, to find his own way. Many offspring were encouraged to move away from their parents. It was a lot easier to stay hidden in smaller groups. There would be no more than two or three families in any town and perhaps only one in a village. The Vardesh had to spread out to enable them to seek out their other halves. This was due to the relatively small time frame they had to find them, many died, both male and female. Vardesh women only conceived every twenty to twenty-five years, most of the time they were single births. However, twins occasionally did occur, unfortunately, in many cases neither mother or babies survived. Any that did were classed as wonders and were revered by all. Pairs usually had many children in order to give their people the best chance of survival. In their mating prime, usually the first three hundred years together. Pairs could have as many as ten offspring, in the hope that one or two of them found their soul mates. Once they left home, they knew that they would never see their parents again. Parents would never know if their children survived and found their soul mates or raised a family. It was a hard choice but a necessary one. Most left home about fifty to a hundred years after they had ascended so that the family groups did not get to large which would sooner or later compromise them all.

Dayton hardly noticed the scenery, as it flashed by the window in the darkness. His thoughts were many miles ahead of him, wondering if she had got to the hotel yet. Before he realised it they were calling the stop for Darlington. He had to laugh at himself as he got up with all his thoughts centred around Erysah, carnal and otherwise he had an erection straining in his trousers. Dayton was glad he had a long coat on because he did not know who would be more embarrassed him or the on lookers. No jeans tonight, he had dressed up for her. He wanted to look his very best, tonight was going to be the beginning of a new chapter in both their lives. Stepping from the train he hailed a taxi, his nerves were starting to get the better of him. He wondered if Erysah felt the same. They were so close now he could almost taste her. He hoped the taxi driver was not slow and that he would get there in good time. Just then he heard a whisper in his mind. He knew she had arrived at the meeting place. Dayton was more eager than ever to arrive.

Erysah had arrived at the hotel around nine, there had been some road works on the A1(M) which had slowed her down. When she got to the hotel she found it was more like a quaint pub that also rented rooms. She guessed that it must have been at least a hundred years old maybe more. When the landlord greeted her he was not what she had anticipated. He was certainly not a typical Yorkshire man. His hair was long and grey as was his beard, in fact he looked like a reject from ZZ Top. But he was polite and never questioned her when she informed him that she was meeting her fiancé there and that he would be arriving soon. Why she had said that Dayton was her fiancé she didn't know, but she had to say something that didn't seem seedy. As if she was really going to turn round and say that she was going to meet a man that she had been having an affair with in her dreams, yeah right. He'd have her committed.

Once in the room she unpacked the things she would need for the night. While she was in Derby she had taken advantage of a certain lingerie shop there and purchased another slightly seductive outfit. She was determined to make tonight ultra special, even though she was as nervous as hell. She hadn't made the mistake this time of wearing a long towelling dressing gown. This outfit came with its own over gown. Erysah sat down on the bed and smiled, in her mind she said over and over again. 'I'm here Dayton, come to me. I'm waiting'. Her hand automatically rubbing over the dragon tattoo for comfort.

TOGETHER AT LAST

Dayton arrived at the small hotel Erysah had booked for them. The landlord who was a tall thin man with long grey hair and a red face greeted him, directed him to the room his fiancée was in. He could not resist letting this unknown person in on his secret. He showed the landlord the ring and told him that he was actually going to propose to her tonight. The landlord smiled, tapping his nose as if he was in cahoots with Dayton and nodded his approval, when he saw the ring his eyes popped out of his head. Dayton was surprised that she had chosen to say that he was her fiancé. Because after tonight that is exactly what she would be, if she said 'yes'. If she said 'no', he had no idea what he would do, would it affect the ritual?

By the time Dayton got to the door of their room he was extremely nervous. His collar felt too tight, even though the top button was open and his palms were sweaty. Now that was a surreal thought, their room. This room was for them. Dayton's hand shook as he reached for the door handle, he looked at it in surprise. Taking a deep breath he turned the handle and walked into the room, trying not to automatically look for her. Keeping his eyes down he turned and gently closed the door, turning the key in its keep locking them in together. When he finally turned round to look into the room, he saw her. She had her back to him, there sitting on the bed with hair of flame flowing down her back in a river of red, was Erysah. His breath stilled in his throat and he could not move. Slowly she stood and walked over to the window and opened one of the curtains. She could see both of them reflected in the blackness of the window, he was just as she knew he would be. Her reflection smiled back at her. Closing the curtains again she turned to face him, making sure that the hand with the tattoo was hidden. He wasn't dressed in his usual jeans and boots he was all gussied up in trousers, shoes, a long dark coat and a white shirt open at the neck. She looked him up and down and smiled at him, not yet having the nerve to meet his gaze which was travelling over her body making her feel hot to her core. Trying to hold herself together, she spoke her voice trembling slightly.

"I'm sorry I didn't realise we were going out. I feel a little under dressed," she said teasingly. Her voice had faded to a whisper but he heard every sweet sound it made. He groaned as he took in the vision of her. If he thought he was hard before, it was nothing compared to how he felt now. "Are you just going to stand there all night and stare at me. Dayton, say something, please!" Unfortunately his voice had taken a holiday. Erysah couldn't believe that this man before her, a vampire at that was frozen to the spot and struck dumb. So she did the only thing she could think of, with one hand she undid the wrap covering the negligee she wore and dropped it to the floor. Dayton's eyes nearly exploded out of his head when he saw what she was wearing.

This time he did move, well his hands anyway. He dropped his valise that was still in his hand, undid his long coat and dropped it on the floor behind him. Erysah eyes nearly did the same as Dayton's when she saw his erection straining desperately for release. Erysah's eyes started to sparkle with mischief then. She decided to take full advantage of the situation. "You look as though you need some help Dayton," she said licking her lower lip then she slowly clamped her tongue between her teeth and drew it back into her mouth. The gesture made Dayton's body jerked. Erysah stepped forward her eyes were now on his. He had a look of utter awe, she didn't think he'd moved even if lightening struck.

Dayton watched every little movement her body made under that very short blood red silk nightdress with the black lacy material that covered her luscious breasts. She was everything that had been in those dreams and more. If he did not get a grip on himself he was going to lose it big style. He would make Mount Vesuvius look like a burp. Erysah crossed the floor to him and pressed herself against him. She could feel his desire hot and needy pressing into her stomach. Forgetting about the tattoo she cupped his face and brought it down towards hers. He was like putty in her hands. Hers to mould, hers to do with as she pleased. The sensation of her hands on his face were glorious. But when their lips met, it was like and explosion of feeling, Dayton suddenly woke up from his stupor. He had managed not to lose his control, in fact somehow he had managed to regain control of himself. He thought that things would be the other way round, but oh, how wrong had he been. Suddenly he had Erysah in his arms, they were still kissing when he managed to get them to the bed. But now he had a decision to make, did he ask before he made love to her or after. Would he be capable after, could he hold on to his urges long enough to do it properly. Erysah seemed to understand he had a dilemma and she realised it was to do with the question. Although, she wasn't sure what the question was, she made the choice for him. She pulled him down on the bed and looked him straight in the eye and said.

"Later." He looked at her and knew she was right, this had been building between them for far too long. It had to be completed, the thread that had miraculously begun had to be completed. Erysah slowly began to undo his shirt buttons and smooth it away from him so she could get at his skin. He did not think that there had not been an inch of chest that she had not explored with her hands or her mouth. Eventually he lost the shirt completely, then she made her way down to his shoes and socks and removed them. This left her one final task and that was to get rid of his trousers. She grabbed his hands and made him stand in front of her. All the while his eyes never left hers. Erysah was glad he didn't have a belt on tonight. She undid the clasp and then the zip, very slowly releasing the pressure of the material that had been constricting his hot, hard swollen length. It was Erysah's turned to groan as it released and jutted out toward her face. The head of it weeping with anticipation of what was to come. Erysah couldn't resist the temptation of licking the drop of fluid oozing from the head. Dayton jumped back his trousers round his ankles and stepped out of them. He waved a finger at her.

"Oh, no, Erysah. It is my turn." His face was deadly serious which made her shuffle back on the bed. He had yet to find out her other little secret. Dayton walked back over to the bed and grabbed both Erysah's hands and placed them on the wooden head of the bed. He placed her fingers round the turned slatted pieces. "Keep them there, please." Erysah nodded and thought that if the hem of the night dress crept up any further her secret would be revealed. He then straddled her upper thighs, she could feel the weight and coolness of his naked balls on her bare skin. His erection pointing at her in warning to behave or else. He had been waiting for this moment for so long, finally now he was going to have a true taste of her.

He kissed her ear, the side of her neck and then licked her from throat to ear. Erysah gasped in astonishment, the sensation of his tongue was indescribable. It was like being stroke with wet velvet, warm and silky. He then did the same on the other side.

"You've been keeping secrets," she managed to croak out in between gasps. As he moved down to the lace covered mounds of her breasts. He scraped his teeth gently over the already erect buds then took them one by one into his hot insatiable mouth. Erysah was desperately trying not to scream in ecstasy. One minute she was biting her lower lip the next minute her top. While his mouth was concentrating on her breasts. His hands were caressing her arms and the length of him was pressing into her belly. Her body was getting hotter and wetter by the second. Dayton stopped the attention he was giving her breasts and moved down her body, dragging himself over her legs. Her knuckles were turning white from gripping the wooden struts so hard. When he slid off her he gently brushed his middle fingers up the inside of her feet which made her move them apart. It was then that he found her secret out, his eyes began to sparkle.

"Erryssah," he drew her name out almost seductively. She lifted her head to look at him. As she saw his expression she knew she had been busted. "Someone has been a very naughty girl and naughty girls have to pay a price." Erysah's head flew back on her pillow. She had no idea what he had in mind but she knew that she was in for something torturous. What she had no clue but Dayton had a very wicked look in his eyes. She didn't have to wait long. Grabbing one ankle in his hand and leaning his back against her other leg he proceeded to lick his way up the inside of her thigh with that velvet tongue of his. She felt as though he was trying to lick her into submission. He held her fast as she squirmed and groaned in sheer pleasure. Before he reached her apex he turned and repeated the same treatment of the other leg. Erysah couldn't believe that a tongue could create so much pleasure. She honestly didn't know how much more torment she could take.

Suddenly he grabbed both ankles and raised her feet until they were resting on his shoulders. Erysah's eyes went wide pleading with him to have mercy. Her body was already mush, if he touched her where she thought he was heading with that tongue of his, she didn't think she would survive. And that's exactly where he was going. As soon as his tongue stroked over her bud, she shattered. But he didn't stop, he continued through her orgasm as her body relinquished her nectar. Just as she thought she had died and gone to heaven he dropped her legs. Dayton positioned himself at her entrance. And nudged. She was so hot that she thought that she might go up in flames. He pushed in slowly trying to give Erysah time to adjust. Even he was worried about the size of him. In the dreams their bodies were able to accommodate each other easily but this was not a dream this was the real thing.

"Dayton you're bigger than I realised. You can't possible fit in me." She was starting to tense slightly. It wasn't the fact that she hadn't had sex before, because she had. She had been a bit rebellious at university and had a lover or two. So she wasn't worried about losing her virginity, it was just the size of him. Dayton was almost twice the size of a normal man. It made her eyes water just to think about it.

"Relax Erysah please, it will be okay. I will take my time, I promise." Erysah nodded and breathed deeply calming herself and with each breath he nudged in a little further until she was full to the brim with him. He had not yet hit home but he did not want to scare her. "Are you okay?" She nodded. "I will go slow, okay." She nodded again, her eyes were almost glazed over with the sensations. Dayton began to move slowly, at little at a time lengthening the strokes until he had a rhythm going. Soon Erysah matched his stride.

"More." She managed to gasp out.

"Are you sure? I do not want to hurt you."

"Yes, I want all of you, Dayton." With that he plunged himself into her, right up to the hilt, so that his balls slapped against her bottom. She made a whimpering sound and he almost stopped. Erysah felt his hesitation. "I'm okay Dayton, please, don't stop." He kept going until they were both on a precipice, one more thrust took them over. Erysah screamed and Dayton roared. He collapsed rolling them both over on their sides. He did not think he could swell up anymore but he had and Erysah seemed to have him in a death grip. There was no chance of him pulling out of her anytime soon. "Dayton, is it my imagination or do we seem to be stuck together at the moment?" He nodded looking just as confused. "I guess the fourth thread is complete then, but I didn't think it would be so physical." She said unable to hold back the grin that was spreading all over her face. Looking at her beautiful face he had to agree then burst out laughing and so did she. After the laughter had died away they managed to disengaged from each other. "By the way what was this important question you were so eager to ask me.?" Erysah asked as she managed to sit up. If she thought that she had be sore before she had been sadly misled. Dayton walked over to his valise and grabbed a pair of sweat pants out of it to put on. "Don't," she said. "I like looking at you." Dayton laughed.

"I cannot ask you this question while I am naked, Erysah."

"Why not?" she pouted.

"Because it would be unseemly." He retorted.

"Okay, I'll make it easier for you," and she took off her night dress.

"That does not make it easier, Erysah. It only makes it harder." Erysah started to smile.

"So I see," she said, looking at his rejuvenating body.

"That is not fair," he said trying not to smile. He went over to his trousers and retrieved the box out of his pocket and placed them on the chair. He turned round to find her sitting on the edge of the bed one leg crossed over the other and leaning back on her arms. She looked like a renaissance picture. That made his shaft twitch some more. By the time he had got back to Erysah he was fully erect again. Dayton groaned. "I wanted to do this properly," he said, as he dropped down in front of her on both knees. Erysah sat forward feeling slightly confused.

"If it's about the ritual and the blood, I'll be fine with it. I'm not squeamish." She said with determination.

"No, this has nothing to do with the ritual." Dayton wished now he had done this first, before making amazing love to her.

"Then what is it Dayton?" Her forehead creased as her eyebrows came together. He had got her completely confused.

"Erysah . . ." He stared into the depths of those emerald green eyes knowing he was lost. "I want you to . . ." The pauses between the words were causing more anguish for her and then he finished the question. "Erysah, will you marry me?" and he produced the little black box with the ring inside of it. Erysah was stunned into silence. "I love you Erysah and I know that after the ritual we will be as man and wife in our world. But before that I wanted to marry you in your world first. Will you marry me in the human way? Erysah." His mouth had gone onto auto pilot so he just stopped and opened the box. Erysah gasped and stared at him.

"You mean it?" Dayton nodded unable to say anything else, just waiting for Erysah to speak. "Oh Dayton I love you with all my heart and if that's what you truly want then yes Dayton. Yes, I will marry you." And she slid off the bed and kissed him with everything she had. When she came up for air, he took the opportunity to place the ring on the third finger of her left hand. It was then he noticed the dragon tattoo. Erysah became really nervous and started to hyperventilate. She didn't know what to say or do. Dayton seemed not to notice as he just stared at it. It wasn't until Erysah tried to pull her hand away he spoke.

"How long have you had this? He asked as he stroked his thumb over it.

"About three years." Dayton looked up at her then, she wanted to turn her head away terrified of his expression, but when he looked at her his face held wonder and it confused the hell out of her.

"Why?" He seemed just as confused. Erysah sighed. "Why did it not appear on your skin in the dreams?" His thumb continued to stroke over the tattoo and now it was beginning to tingle. She tried to pull her hand away again but he held it firm.

"Please Dayton let go." She asked pulling at her hand again, this time he did let go. Erysah got up and put the robe back on, leaving Dayton still on his knees. His eyes followed her as she paced. He knew she was upset and went to hold her. At first she resisted twisting in his arms but he had trapped her arms as she had hugged them to herself. Eventually she melted into him her eyes tearing up. "I don't know why it didn't appear in the dreams. I didn't think about it much, although I did worry about what you would think when you saw it." She mumbled into his chest. Dayton stepped back from Erysah holding her by her shoulders.

"Erysah." He said in a voice so soft it was a caress. "Please look at me." She didn't respond, so he cupped her chin and raised her head. As their eyes met she could see no condemnation in them, just love. He found her left hand again and lifted it to his mouth and placed a kiss on the tattoo and then the ring that he had put there. "Will you tell its story?" he asked. He knew there had to be one, most humans did not get tattoos like that for nothing. They always represented something, having a significant meaning behind them. He dragged Erysah back to the bed and took off her robe, she didn't complain as he climbed into bed pulling her with him. Snuggling up with her he rested her left hand on his abdomen so he could see both the ring and the tattoo. Kissing the top of her head he said. "Now we are comfortable, will you tell me about it?" The warmth of Dayton's body seeped into hers and she could feel his love pulsating through the mesh. She nodded against his chest and began. By the time she had finished telling about the only day she could really remember spending with her mother he could understand why she felt the way she did. He lifted her hand and stroked the tattoo once more. Touching the ring they both looked at it, then looked at each other.

"It feels right there," she said to him smiling. Her smile lightened his heart after seeing her so upset.

"It looks right there," was his reply. "Now I am sorry to have to say this but we need to prepare the room for the daylight hours for me. We cannot let any light in the room." Erysah just nodded and got up and went into her duffle bag pulling out a piece of black material and some drawing pins. "What else did you buy on your way here?" Erysah just shrugged her shoulders. After about ten minutes the room was light proof. Despite the fact Dayton could have made love to Erysah again he wanted them both to get some sleep. They would have a long trip back to Stone Edge and he planned on doing it in one trip. "Erysah?"

"Hmm," she replied as she looked for her toothbrush.

"Tomorrow we will need to make the journey to my home in one trip. That means you driving all the way. Will you be alright with that?" He was concerned he did not want to over tax her, especially after all the travelling she had already done.

"Yes, of course. If that's what we need to do then that's what we'll do." Dayton grabbed her hand and led her to the bed. Erysah smiled even though she worried, she didn't know if she would be able to sleep.

"Do not even think it, Erysah we are going to sleep."

"I don't know what you are talking about." Although the sparkle that was in her eyes and the raised corner of her mouth were a dead give away to her thoughts, even if he could not get anything through the mesh.

"Sleep, no argument."

"Okay," she sighed, as they both got under the covers. Dayton spooned himself around her. Erysah couldn't resist wriggling against him, so Dayton slapped her rump, making her squeal. She glared at him over her shoulder but there was no animosity in her eyes, far from it. Dayton shook his head.

"Sleep!" he insisted. She gave in and snuggled in. '*No more dreams*', she thought to him.

"No, no more dreams, just the real thing." He whispered into her ear.

"Shame," she said disappointed. "I could have the best of both worlds then." Dayton kissed her on the shoulder. She could feel the smile under his lips.

"You are incorrigible," he said against her skin, making her shudder. "Go to sleep, Erysah. You have a lot of driving to do tomorrow, you need the rest." Erysah nodded and sighed. Dayton knew he had finally got through to her.

"I do have one question, before we go to sleep." Dayton relaxed into her body.

"What?" he sighed, would they ever get to sleep.

"Well . . . we were not exactly quiet earlier. How come no one came knocking on the door?"

"Ah . . ." Dayton had hoped that she would miss that little trick.

"What do you mean, ah!"

"Well . . ."

"Never mind well! I'm not going to sleep until you tell me." She tried to turn around to face him, but he clamped his arms around her.

"Okay, Erysah. If I tell you, will you please go to sleep?" Erysah nodded. "I am able to muffle sounds that are in close proximity to me. So, when we were in the throes of passion, no one could hear us."

"Handy, any more hidden talents?"

"Not telling, now go to sleep!" Erysah yawned and nodded sleepily. Within minutes she had drifted off and Dayton felt at last that he had come home. He was complete, whole for the first time.

Onwards to Scotland

When they woke it was early evening. Erysah didn't think that she was that tired. But there again the previous night she'd been driving nonstop to get here and then there was the love making. Dayton hadn't been kidding when he said that it would be . . . what were the words he had used? She knew she had made him cross and he had made her suffer in a most unusual way. Oh yes, now she remembered plucking the words from the dream. *"When we meet in the real world Erysah, you will see what I mean. I have not made love to you as I will when we are really together. What we do in our dream will be nothing compared to when I really have you to myself."* Boy, he had certainly kept his promise. She didn't think there wasn't any part of her body that hadn't been touched, in one way or another. In fact just the thought of it was making her hot and bothered again and she began to squirm against him.

"Erysah, will you stop that please. You are projecting images into my head that will lead to trouble. It is bad enough that you are rubbing against me and I am having a reaction." Erysah chuckled to herself she knew what he meant because she could feel his shaft twitching and swelling at her back. Erysah couldn't resist another wriggle against him. That got her another slap on her rump, before Dayton got out of bed. Erysah rolled over to watch him, hoping he would turn round so she could feast her eyes on him. Dayton looked over his shoulder and shook his head. "Not going to happen, get up and get dressed." Erysah stuck her tongue out at him and wrinkled her nose.

"Spoilt sport!" she pouted. Dayton just laughed as he put on his trousers before turning round. Erysah could still see the evidence of his arousal pressing against the material. Erysah wanted to play and tease, so she slid down the covers to slowly reveal her naked body. But all that got her was her clothes being thrown at her. Huffing she grabbed them and scowled. "You're no fun."

Dayton sighed and came over to the bed and sat next to her naked body. He gently stroke and cupped her right breast with his hand, rubbing the nipple between his finger and thumb. Erysah moaned and pressed into him and he bent to take her mouth. Erysah went to reach for the zip on his trousers but he stopped her. Pulling away he laughed. "Get dressed, Erysah! We have to eat and get on the road. It will take a good six or seven hours to get to . . ." He had almost told her where they were going.

"Get to where, exactly?" Dayton shook his head.

"I will tell you this much, we need to go through Edinburgh to get to our destination., okay." Erysah nodded, she knew he wouldn't tell her everything, not yet.

"At least I know which direction to go in and I won't have you telling me every five minutes the way to go." She laughed and gathered her clothes up which she had scattered all over the bed. After dressing, they uncovered the window and door which they had blacked out. They packed their bags and headed down to the bar. The landlord nodded to Dayton in a knowing sort of way, which made Erysah look at them both. He just smiled and nodded back.

"Landlord is there any chance of something to eat and drink before we leave? We have to be in Edinburgh later." He asked him.

"I'm afraid it will only be sandwiches at this time of day. Oh, and by the way congratulations." He said looking at the ring on her finger.

"Thank you." Erysah blushed and turned to Dayton glaring at him. '*How did he know?*' Dayton, just shrugged and smiled that brilliant smile of his, causing Erysah to go all warm inside. They were interrupted by coughing coming from the man standing with them.

"If you go into the lounge out back I will bring you something." The landlord nodded in the direction.

"Erysah you go through, if you give me your keys and tell me where you are parked, I can put the bags in the car ready. That way we can leave straight after eating." Erysah nodded and gave him the keys and directions to the car. She had a sneaking suspicion that he was going to do more than just pack the car, but said nothing. As if reading her mind he kissed her cheek and whispered a confirmation in her ear, which caused heat to pool at her core.

"I will not be long," he said giving her a knowing look. Erysah just nodded. Fifteen minutes later the landlord returned with a large plate of sandwiches and a pot of coffee. Erysah thanked him and as he turned to go out the door, he bumped into Dayton who had returned with a single white carnation in his hand. The landlord turned back and smiled at Erysah but she only had eyes for Dayton.

"I will bring your bill in shortly," he said. Not even questioning how Dayton had managed to get a flower at this hour. Dayton just nodded and went and sat opposite Erysah and handed her the bloom.

"Pour vous, Solelil," he said smiling. Erysah took the flower and smelled it's sweet fragrance. "Now eat you will need the energy." He was being bossy but she really didn't mind, she just wanted to get to wherever it was they were going.

"What about you, have you got enough energy?" Her eyebrows raised as she poured herself a coffee. Dayton nodded and smiled.

"Do not even go there, Erysah." She looked at him innocently. Dayton just shook his head and laughed stroking a finger down her cheek, after tapping the end of her nose he pointed at the food. Erysah got the message and picked up a sandwich.

Thirty minutes later Dayton had paid the bill and they left the hotel. Once on the road they headed for the A66 north towards Scotland. Dayton spent most of the journey staring at Erysah, either her face or her hand on which she wore his ring. It gave him a strange sense of pride. A quite unfamiliar feeling for him. Now and then Erysah would glance over to him and see the smug look on his face. It made Erysah smile and she glanced down at her own hand. She couldn't believe that he had taken the step of asking her to marry him. She loved him and for her that was enough, but obviously Dayton wanted more. Erysah was more than happy to give it to him. Every time she looked at the ring resting there on her finger, she felt her body shiver and was grateful he didn't mind the tattoo that was there. The ring and the tattoo actually complimented each other, neither one taking from the other. She had no idea what to expect when they got to . . . wherever it was they were going. She also didn't know if she was going to meet anyone when she got there. Did he have family living there with him or any of the clan? She knew that in the dreams there had only been the two of them but as Dayton guided most of the dreams he could have done it deliberately. Erysah had only known Dayton a short time and had only really met him about twenty-four hours ago. But she would follow him to the ends of the earth, if she had to. As long as they were together, she didn't really care.

It was nearly midnight when they got to Edinburgh. Dayton knew Erysah needed to rest for a while. He desperately wanted them to reach his home tonight, but perhaps he was being selfish? Now Dayton had a choice to make hotel or go back to Garroch's. How would Erysah feel meeting others like him. Garroch's home would be safer for him, but going to a hotel would be easier for her. As if she could sense him mulling something over in his mind, Erysah pulled over and stopped. She turned to him and inquired.

"What's the problem Dayton?" he looked at her and saw the fatigue in her eyes.

"The problem is you are tired and need to rest." She was going to interrupt him but he shook his head. "It would have been nice to have made it home tonight. You need to have at least a couple of hours break and some refreshments an we still have at least three maybe four hours travelling left. My dilemma is, do we go to another hotel and prepare the room as before, supposing you have enough material in that bag of yours. Or . . ." Dayton hesitated.

"Or . . ." Erysah prompted.

"Or, we stay where I stayed last night at a house of one of my clan. I would not want you to feel uncomfortable or scared." Erysah raised her eyebrows at him when he said that.

"There is only one question you have to ask yourself Dayton," she said wearily. "Will I be safe?" She looked straight into his eyes.

"Yes, yes. Of that I have no doubt." He answered honestly.

"Will we be imposing on them if we just turn up on their door step?"

"No, I er . . ." he hesitated once again. Erysah was losing patience with him. Her tiredness showing.

"You er . . . what?"

"Well, they do not call me by my name. The call me by my title." Erysah looked at him questioningly. "They call me, guardian."

"Guardian?" Dayton nodded. "I presume from this title you guard something."

"Yes, something and . . ."

"Annd?" Erysah reiterated.

"And someone." He confessed, he could not and would not lie to her. Erysah's face showed only slight surprise. "It is difficult for me to explain right now. Will you trust me? Erysah?" Dayton's spine was stiff with tension.

"Yes, Dayton. I trust you." Dayton's shoulders drooped as he visibly relaxed. "Now will you please direct me to this house, before I collapse." Dayton nodded and smiled, slightly embarrassed by his behaviour. It took them another twenty-five minutes to there. Dayton seemed to be really nervous about their arrival. Erysah wanted to ask the obvious question. 'Is there something that you're not telling me?' but she already knew that he hadn't told her everything. So she tried to reassure him instead. "I'm sure it will be fine Dayton," she said smiling. Dayton nodded and got out of the car and went to the boot to retrieve their luggage. By the time he had shut the boot, Erysah was standing next to him. Tucking his valise under the arm that held her duffel bag, he grabbed Erysah's hand with the other. As they approached the door Dayton looked at Erysah and asked.

"Are you sure about this?" Erysah's answer was unexpected.

"No, but let's do it anyway." She said as she used the knocker to knock on the door. "Too late, now." She turned and smiled at him. The door opened and the man who answered it was just about to speak when he stopped, mouth open. He stared at Dayton with a look of astonishment on his face. Dayton nodded feeling slightly uncomfortable.

"Guardian, you honour us again with your presence and you bring with you your Solelil. Please come in both of you." Erysah didn't know if she was allowed to speak or not. So she just followed the man and Dayton into the house. After closing the door he led them into the room that Dayton had already been in before. Erysah surmised it was the living room. It was very grand and opulent compared to Erysah's flat. The last time Dayton had been in the room, it was not devoid of occupants. Erysah was still looking around the room when then door opened and three people in walked. The man who had opened the door to them, a pregnant woman and a man who looked just a little older than herself. She looked at Dayton and he held her hand and mouthed 'it is okay.' Erysah nodded.

"Guardian, we have never been so honoured." The woman said as she seated herself in the chair she had previously occupied the last time Dayton was there. The man who had opened the door stood behind her chair and the other one stood next to him.

"Thank you for extending your home to me once more." Erysah thought that the way they spoke was so formal, even reverent. "May I be allowed to introduce my Solelil? All three of them bowed their heads, when they raised them Erysah was surprised to see them smiling, no not smiling, their faces were beaming with joy. Erysah was taken aback by their reaction. Dayton then spoke to them individually. First addressing the man who had opened the door to them. "Garroch, may I introduce my Solelil, Erysah."

"I am honoured to meet you Erysah." And he bowed his head briefly once again. "Erysah, may I introduce my Solelil Melindra and our son Jarro."

Dream Lover

"Pleased to meet you and thank you for letting us stay." She felt really awkward because she was unused to communicating with these kind of people. Just then Dayton brushed her mind, 'you are doing fine, relax.' Erysah smiled. Just then she noticed Melindra looking at her hand. Melindra then looked up at her 'husband' for want of a better word. She indicated towards Erysah and when he saw the ring on her hand he smiled down at his Solelil. Dayton had seen them look at Erysah's hand. Suddenly Melindra spoke.

"Does it fit Erysah?" Erysah found this a rather strange question and Dayton seemed to have an odd reaction to it.

"Yes, it is a perfect fit. I don't know how Dayton managed to find such a wonderful ring, considering we only really met yesterday." Erysah hadn't really thought about it until now.

"I am so pleased it is one of my favourite pieces. I knew it would be perfect for you." Melindra's statement made Erysah look at Dayton for and explanation. He almost groaned out loud. It was Garroch that spoke then, saving Dayton from the situation.

"My Solelil makes jewellery, which she sells over the internet. People have also commissioned specific pieces from her. The guardian explained to us his intention and Melindra was more than happy to provide."

"It is our gift to both of you, a wedding gift." Melindra added. Erysah understood and smiled and turned Dayton. Who for some reason had his head down. She raised her hand to his face and touched his cheek with one finger. He lifted his head and gazed into her eyes. He looked so awkward, she thought it endearing. *'It's okay,'* she said into his mind. Erysah wanted to lift the tension that was in the room and be damned with the consequences, so she addressed the couple directly.

"Garroch and Melindra I'm new to this but I have to be me, so I apologise in advance if I offend anyone." Dayton was about to speak but she put her finger on his lips to stop him. "I know your background, when I say background. I mean, I know you're not human." No one showed surprise in that statement. "Please all of you do me a big favour and sit down, you're making me feel uncomfortable. I'm not used to formality. It would be nice to have a conversation and get to know you, if that's okay." Jarro was the first to speak.

"Thank goodness for that, my legs were beginning to ache," he said with a smile, as he went and dragged a chair from the table and sat where he could converse with everybody. Erysah started laughing. Garroch sat in the other chair opposite Melindra and Dayton sighed with relief. Which made her laugh even more. Eventually getting control of herself she managed to speak.

"I'm so sorry for that, but if you could have seen it from my point of view, you all looked so stiff. I thought that I would be the one who found it difficult to be around you all. It seems to me, it is the other way round." Everyone laughed at the absurdity of the situation.

"I must apologise for my parents Erysah." Jarro said. "They are not used to human interaction. The Vardesh usually only mix with each other. Only I have had the opportunity to mix with humans."

"How?" Erysah was really curious. "Do you attend night school?" It was Jarro's turn to laugh.

"No, I go to Edinburgh University, it is not until I reach the age of ascension that I have to avoid daylight, wicked tattoo by the way." He said nodding towards her hand.

"Thanks it was a present from my mother." She was taken a little by surprise by Jarro, but she liked him. Changing the subject she continued.

"Melindra I notice you're expecting, when are you due?"

"Not for another nine months, we carry our children for a much longer time because of our body chemistry."

"Okay." That made her wonder how long her mother had carried her considering she was part Vardesh. She then turned to Dayton.

"Do they know about my father?" Dayton's eyes went wide and he shook his head. "Can we tell them, are we allowed?"

"I do not know Erysah, this thing has never happened before. Not that we know of. Do you want to?" Garroch and his family looked slightly confused.

"Will you tell them Dayton, please." Erysah noticed the name registered with Garroch and Melindra. Dayton nodded and felt all eyes on him.

"Erysah is not quite as you might think she is. Her mother was human but her father was Vardesh." Shock appeared across their faces, as if it was absolutely impossible. Silence hung in the air for what seemed a lifetime.

"Who could possibly be your father?" Garroch eventually asked after the shock subsided. Erysah said one word.

"Kaspir." Garroch and Melindra stared at them.

"Yes Garroch, Kaspir was my best friend and the previous guardian." Dayton added.

"We knew Kaspir, we were present at his Solelil's Ritual of Transcendence. It was a terrible loss." Both Dayton and Erysah were stunned by that piece of information. It never even crossed Dayton's mind that they might have known Kaspir or even been at his ritual. Erysah would have asked more questions, but suddenly she was overcome with fatigue and she slumped against Dayton.

"Sorry," she said as she yawned, not speaking to anyone in particular.

"Erysah has travelled all the way from Southampton, driving with only short respites. She is exhausted, may we retire?"

"Of course, guardian we apologise for the distraction." Garroch was already picking up their luggage.

"Forgive us, we never intended to . . ." Melindra began to say. Dayton just shook his head.

"It was Erysah and I that detracted from the norm." Dayton was trying to apologise as he picked up a sleeping Erysah in his arms.

"No need, we will talk tomorrow before you leave. I am sure there are questions on both sides that need discussing." Dayton nodded as he followed Garroch up to their room. Once alone he carefully undressed Erysah, so not to wake her and placed her in bed. He then disrobed and joined her. He pulled her body close into his and mulled over what Garroch and Melindra had said.

Garroch joined Melindra back in the living room. Jarro had decided to retire to his room and continue his studies for a while. As Garroch entered Melindra looked up at him.

"What does it mean Garroch?" She remembered the ritual, it had been the last one she had gone to. It was so sad that she had said she did not want to go to another. At the time Garroch had agreed with her. Now the guardian had requested their presence at his own. They had accepted without knowing who his Solelil was. And there was also going to be a wedding ceremony before the ritual. There was no way to get out of it because once accepted it was a binding contract. Garroch could see the concern on her face.

"I do not have an answer for you, Melindra. As far as I have known it has never occurred before." Garroch rubbed his forehead as if it pained him.

"What about the keeper? Would he know? Would he have a record?" Melindra was clutching at straws, in the hope of finding some kind of solution.

"Yes, the keeper. Of course, we could contact him. However, that means I would have to travel to see him before a time was chosen." Melindra understood and nodded. "But I cannot go and see them without the guardian's permission."

"Why? Why must you ask permission?"

"Because we are only allowed to ask about our own line. It would be sacrilege to seek information on another line without permission. Perhaps it may be better to suggest to them that they seek him out and find out what they can, if anything." Garroch held our his hand towards Melindra. "Come Solelil, let us also retire. You look weary." Melindra nodded.

"I am strangely weary and this gestation is much different to my other. I seem to be much larger than before and I tire much quicker. Perhaps I should see the deliverer?" Garroch nodded as he led her to their rooms.

The next evening Erysah sat in the kitchen with Jarro and ate a Spanish omelette, which Jarro had prepared for the both of them.

"I didn't realise that vampires ate?" Erysah was eager to find out more about the Vardesh and it meant to be one.

"Until I reach the age of ascension I am for all intent and purposes just like any human except that I am twice as old." He laughed.

"So if you don't mind me asking, how old are you?" Erysah was really curious.

"In human or Vardesh years?"

"Both, I would like to know the difference?" Jarro could see genuine interest on her face.

"In human years I am twenty-four, in Vardesh years I am forty-eight. My year of ascension is next year. After my Ritual of Ascension I will be a vampire. If you want to know more about it you will have to speak to Garroch."

"Where is everybody anyway? Have they gone to feed?" Erysah asked as if it was a natural thing for a human to say, but there again she wasn't all human, was she.

"Probably, Melindra needs to feed once a week, while she is carrying. Garroch will go with her to make sure she is okay and as for the guardian, well . . ." Jarro shrugged his shoulders.

"Why do you call him guardian and not by his name?" Erysah enquired.

"It has always been so. If a Vardesh has been risen to a higher status like guardian or keeper, they are known by their position in the clan."

"So are there some Vardesh whose names are not known?"

"No, there is always someone who has known them before their change in status."

"Oh, okay." Erysah couldn't think of another question at the moment, so she decided to change the subject slightly. "What are you studying at university?"

"Wow, Erysah! That was a bit random considering what we were talking about." Jarro chuckled, he was secretly pleased that she might be interested in what he was doing. "Celtic and Scottish studies. This country has always fascinated me and I hope to finish my research before my ascension. I am hoping I can discover how the Vardesh came to be here. I would like to take over the keepers position within the clan."

"How would that work?" Erysah was so fascinated by the conversation she was having with Jarro, she never heard Dayton come into the kitchen. It wasn't until Jarro looked up and clammed up that she realised he was there.

"I hope you have been looking after my Solelil, young Jarro." Erysah thought that his comment was unnecessary, especially as Jarro was actually older than her in every way. Erysah threw him a look of disapproval over her shoulder at him.

"Yes he has, which is more than I can say for you. Why didn't you wake me and let me know you were going out?" '*Ouch!*' Thought Dayton. She has bite. "You had better believe it!" She retorted to his thoughts. Jarro started to laugh and Erysah glared at him. He put his hands up in surrender.

"I'm outta here. See you again, Erysah. Have a safe journey." Erysah nodded in reply. Dayton went over to her and dragged her up for a kiss.

"If you think you can get round me like that Dayton, you can think . . ." she never got to finish her sentence. For as soon as his lips made contact with hers, she melted. When he raised his head he had a smug look on his face. "Not fair Dayton, that's cheating." Dayton smiled at her, raising an eyebrow in a 'I have no idea what you mean look.' He then squeezed her tightly and laughed.

"I will use any weapons at my disposal to make sure you are not angry or upset, especially at me." Erysah laughed and slapped his arm.

"There's a saying all's fair in love and war and two can play at that game Dayton." Erysah had a devious twinkle in her eyes.

"Come on, we need to say our farewells and continue on to my home." Home, his home but once they married and she had transcended it would be hers to.

"Our home." Erysah corrected. Dayton smiled his heart missing a beat as she accepted that fact so readily, grabbing her hand he led the way. In the hallway stood Garroch and Melindra, along with their luggage.

"Farewell Erysah, we will see you soon." Garroch was still a little staid but it was better than when they had first arrived.

"Safe journey Erysah," Melindra said and stepped forward to embrace her. As they hugged each other they both felt and odd connection between them. It only lasted a second or two, but it was enough to make them both react. "Oh!" Melindra exclaimed.

"Exactly!" said Erysah. Both men had a looked of concern on their faces, wondering what had just happened. Then both Melindra and Erysah went into a fit of giggling. Garroch was the first to speak.

"What just happened? What is wrong Melindra?" His face showing grave concern for his pregnant Solelil. Dayton just stared at Erysah in disbelief.

"Nothing is wrong, everything is right Garroch. There will be no need to see the deliverer." Melindra then addressed Dayton. "Guardian, it seems that your Solelil already has a special gift." Dayton was confused. "Erysah will you tell them what just happened." Erysah was stilled stunned by the whole incident but she nodded. After a few moments she gathered herself together and explained.

"When Melindra and I touched I saw that she was carrying twins and I automatically gave her the information mentally. It happened so fast I didn't even know what or how it happened." Both Garroch and Dayton stood aghast. Chins on the floor and eyes on stalks. The sight was so funny to the women, they burst into hysterical laughter. It was so loud that Jarro came out to see what all the commotion was about.

"Whatever is the matter?" Jarro asked at the sight before him, even he found it funny but kept himself under control. Both Erysah and Melindra were doubled over, tears in their eyes. As they laughed, their men stood frozen in shock for some unknown reason. Eventually Erysah seemed to gain some semblance of control and stuttered out a strange question to Jarro.

"Would you prefer brothers or sisters?" She was desperately trying to breathe through her hysteria.

"Why on earth would you ask that?" Jarro was totally perplexed by the situation.

"Because," his mother spoke for the first time. "I am having twins." She smiled at him. "Two babies and they are . . ." Garroch seemed to wake up then.

"Are what Melindra?" He wrapped his arms around her shoulders. He was still staring at his Solelil in disbelief. Melindra looked at Erysah.

"Not my decision, Melindra. This information is for you to share as you see fit." Melindra nodded and smiled.

"Well . . . Garroch, you hoped that we would have a girl this time, now we will be doubly blessed." She sighed leaning into him. Dayton was still trying to take in everything that had been said. *'Who was his Solelil, what was she?'* His mind was racing. Erysah dug her elbow into his ribs to bring him out of his thoughts. They were getting a bit too loud and she was getting very annoyed with him.

"What?" he said looking down at her, having no idea why she had poked him.

"I think we should go, don't you?" The tension in the air was palpable. He nodded and with that they said goodbye, loaded the car and got in.

"I am sorry Erysah, my mind was engaged."

"Yes I know, I heard." There was a bitter edge to her words. "Who am I? What am I?" she said sarcastically staring out of the windscreen. Her hands trying to crush the steering wheel into submission.

"I did not ever mean that in a derogatory way. It means you are an unknown, you display traits that are unusual even for a Vardesh. I think Garroch and Melindra were right when they suggested seeing the keeper before the ritual." Dayton's mind was a maze of confusion.

"And when was this discussed?" Venom accompanied her words. "When the three of you were out trawling." She couldn't believe how angry she was with him.

"Erysah please, I am sorry." Dayton felt helpless, he had no idea what to do. "Please Erysah, look at me." Dayton pleaded, he had to try and diffuse the situation before they went anywhere. He did not like the waves of anger that were coming off her.

"Why should I! I'm so mad at you right now!" She resisted the urge for as long as she could. But when his hand cupped her far cheek the warmth of his hand seeped into her, she turned her face towards him, there was no resistance. As her eyes made contact with his she could see his sincerity in his face. "I know you love me and you care, but you need to tell me what's going on. We are going to share our lives together for a very long time. You need to be honest with me." Dayton nodded, she was right. Things were set and were virtually irreversible.

"I know and I am sorry Erysah and to be truthful for the first time in my life I am scared." Erysah couldn't believe Dayton's confession. He was the last person who she thought would be scared of anything.

"Why on earth are you scared Dayton. It's not as if anything will change for you. I am the one who will be transformed into something different." Dayton knew she was right, she was giving up everything for him. He had to try and explain himself.

"Erysah I am scared because I do not know what the future will hold for you. Scared about what will happen when you go through the ritual. We need as much information as we can get. That is why we need to see the keeper." She could see that he was really worried and she understood what he was saying. Erysah nodded sighing.

"Can we go now?" The tension had at last seeped out of her.

"On one condition." She said smiling releasing the death grip she had on the steering wheel, so the blood could find its way back to her fingers. He nodded.

"Name your condition Erysah." He could give her that much. Her eyes bore into him as she pounced.

"Kiss me." Those two words shook him, one minute she was furious with him, the next . . . Erysah was impatient to get going so she just grabbed him by his jacket and pulled him towards her. As their lips touched he enveloped her in his arms. The kiss was deep and searing hot putting fire into his veins. When she broke away he let her go. Turning back to the steering wheel Erysah started the car. "Where to?"

"We are going to a place called Stone Edge, you will need to head towards Aberdeen." Erysah nodded and they started towards home.

Home at Last

After everything that had happened so far that night Dayton was so relieve when they pulled up outside the house. What was left of the moon was high in the sky and cast its feint light over his home, giving it an unearthly glow. It was well past midnight and he was eager to get Erysah inside and show her his home properly, not via a dream. She had been unable to have a good look at the building, because she was driving and had to concentrate on the unfamiliar dark road leading up to the property.

"Welcome to my humble home," he said as he opened the door, stepping aside to let her in. Humble Erysah thought, chuckling, there was nothing humble about it. The place was vaguely familiar, although it was more impressive in the flesh, so to speak. Dayton took the luggage straight into the library, leaving Erysah to take in her surroundings. She stood in the entrance way her trainers making no sound on the cream marble floor, turning slowly she took in the view before her. The entrance hall was spacious; dark oak panelling hugged the lower part of the walls in the corridors, which went in at least three directions. They were topped off with cream plaster walls and ceilings. A deep red plush carpet ran down the centre of the floor, continuing up the staircase, rods spanning the steps to keep it in place. The main stairs were off to the left, sweeping up and around to the right. The wooden balustrade was supported by a rustic metal framework filled with leaves and flowers, which continued along the landing. She could see several doors, all closed. The landing disappeared in two directions and she remembered there were more rooms further down. Erysah eyes were brought back down to ground level because she could feel Dayton watching her. He smiled "You know my room is not up there." amused that her eyes had wandered up towards the bedrooms. Erysah smiled and immediately changed the subject.

"Dayton I know this might seem a silly question, but do you have any food? I'm starving." Right on cue her stomach protested its empty state. Nodding to her he took her hand and guided Erysah towards the kitchen.

"I took the liberty of getting some provisions the day before I left to come and meet you. It will be the first time the kitchen will have been used. I will enjoy watching you prepare and eat something." Erysah shook her head and laughed, she still couldn't get over the fact that this was actually real and not a dream, she would have pinched herself but it would be more fun to pinch him, she thought.

"Well, make the most of it; I have a sneaking suspicion that after the ritual I won't need to eat. Am I right?" Dayton nodded and kissed her hand, pulling her into the kitchen. Erysah was surprised to find it very well stocked. The cupboards and fridge had enough food in them to last a few weeks. There were also plenty of mod cons like, microwave, toaster, kettle, hob and oven. "I'm impressed," she said as she put some bread in the toaster. After deciding to make something that was quick and simple. Spaghetti on toast with grated cheese and a coffee, it was instant but she didn't mind. Dayton sat at the table and watched her every move, every nuance. As she reached into the cupboards for crockery to plate up her food her t-shirt rose to reveal a thin line of flesh, which made him groan silently. He watched the movement of her hands, the sway of her hips and the curve of her bottom. Her breasts undulated gently as she glided effortlessly from one activity to another. When she sat down to eat she looked at him. "Are you enjoying yourself?" Dayton nodded as a huge grin spread across his face. Erysah shook her head in amusement. "I feel like I'm on one of those reality shows with you watching me like that." Dayton just shrugged shoulders and steepled his fingers, he then continued his observations. Not one word came out of his gorgeous mouth as he devoured his Solelil with his eyes. He was still in disbelief that this was happening and not a facsimile, as Erysah had called it. His throat was tight as his heart galloped in his chest. There were no words of conversation in his mind, so he just sat and watched, enjoying the vision before him. He watched as she put a mouthful of food in her mouth and chewed slowly, occasionally licking her lips. The whole thing was mesmerising and when she swallowed well . . . He found it totally sexy.

Dayton's continuous silent observations were starting to annoy her, so she decided it was payback time. But her kind of payback was going to make him squirm until he couldn't think straight. When it came to teasing, he thought he'd won, he may have won the last round but not this one. She was about to prove him otherwise and she was aiming for a completely different type of teasing. Erysah began to eat a little more slowly and seductively. Occasionally she'd let the sauce from the spaghetti run over her lips a little, so she would have to swipe her tongue over them to lick it up. Sometimes she would let it dribble down towards her chin and she would have to use her finger to catch it. Pushing it into her mouth slowly and sucking on it before slowly pulling it out again. By the time she had finished he was looking at her through deep blue lustful eyes. Dayton could not believe that watching Erysah do something as simple as eating could be such a turn on. As he watched her put the food in her mouth and closed her lips around the fork, pulling it out slowly, suddenly Dayton found it hard to breathe. The anticipation of what was going to happen next making his gut clench and his groin ache. The way she licked her lips when the juice spilled onto them, made his groin burn. And when she sucked her finger, well . . . he was lost. He had an ache so bad; he thought it would never go away. He had a sneaking suspicion that she was toying with him. Suddenly Erysah got up and took her plate and cup to the sink, gave them a quick wash and left them to dry. Before she realised it Dayton was behind her closing her in with his body, his hands resting on her hips.

"Now what are we going to do?" grateful he couldn't see her face. Dayton pressed his hard body into hers. 'Yes', she thought. 'That'll teach him to mess with her like that'. By the time she had finished eating he looked as though he wanted to devour her. With him being a vampire there was a very good chance of it. However she knew that he would never hurt her.

"Bed," he croaked hoarsely. Erysah pouted.

"But I'm not tired." She whined unconvincingly.

"Neither am I," he said, with a sly smile and a strained voice. His jeans were so tight that, it was not just his voice that was being strangled. He picked her up and threw her over his shoulder, so she was hanging upside down, his shoulder pressing into her stomach. She thumped his back with fisted hands and kicked her feet, trying to get him to put her down. He did nothing more than smack her rear that was right next to his face. He was extremely tempted to take a bite out of it. It was so soft, plump and tantalising, it made his mouth water.

"Dayton, please put me down, I'm going to be sick in a minute if you keep carrying me like this." Dayton said nothing, but just swung her around in his arms and cradled her in front of him. She put a hand to his face and looked up at him; he was so damn sexy and irresistible. She could feel the heat radiating off of him. As he strode down the corridor to the library Erysah wriggled in his arms, but he held her in a firm tender grip. Sighing she put her arms around his neck and pulled herself up towards his tight-lipped mouth. She could see that he was trying to restrain himself. She couldn't help herself, she was hungry but not for food this time. Her hunger this time ran much deeper and hotter. She hungered for Dayton in every way imaginable. Eventually her lips made contact with his just before they got to the library. He had to stop and kiss her back, how could he not, she had pushed his own need for her into the heavens. He felt the fire within her feeding his own, tugging on her lower lip he sucked it into his mouth. Erysah gasped allowing Dayton entry and he took full advantage, sweeping in with his velvet tongue. She matched him, their tongues tangoing in a sensual battle, revelling in the taste of each other. Dropping her down on her feet he enfolded her in his arms and let her take him away on a wave of pleasure. When they managed to prise themselves away from each other, he picked her up round the waist and she wrapped her legs around his middle, cupping her bottom he continued their journey to his private chambers. The heat of her pressed against his arousal was almost more than he could endure. He placed Erysah on the large bed that sat in the middle of the room, he walked back into the corridor.

"Hey!" Erysah shouted. "Where are you going?"

"To get the luggage, it is still in the library." His voice straining in his throat just as his erection was in his trousers, Erysah nodded. She knew it would only take him a few minutes to get it. She wondered if she would have enough time to get to the roman style bath and get in before he came back. 'To hell with it,' she thought and ran through the door she had seen when she was here in one of the dreams. Yes, it was there. She hurriedly stripped everything off throwing her clothes in a corner and dove in head first into the clear blue water, her skin tingle as the heat of it caressed her naked body. When she came up for air on the far side, Dayton was standing at the edge of the bath with his arms folded across his chest. "What do you think you are doing?" he asked, knowing full well what the answer was going to be, she had not finished her teasing of him. Dayton thought it was about time that he reciprocated.

"I wanted to get clean after our long journey," she swam towards him so she could put her feet on the bottom. She began to walk forwards rising out of the water like some siren of the sea, her wet hair clinging to her body like a second skin. It clung to the curves of her breasts, her nipples peeking through the curtain of hair. Dayton suppressed a groan. "Come join me, Dayton," her eyes enticing him as she leaned back and pushed herself back into the middle of the pool. Her naked body shimmering under the water and her hair pooling around her like fire. That did it for him, he could resist no longer, she was a little minx and she wanted to play. How could he say no to her, especially when erotic images were flashing through his head. And he was not sure if they were his or hers. Before she had even reached the other side Dayton was in the water. He hadn't even bothered to take his clothes off but dived in head first. Erysah tried to set herself upright before he reached her. Dayton surfaced and grabbed an ankle before she could get away and pulled her towards him. She almost sank back under as she travelled towards Dayton as he trod water. Her hair flowed behind her like breath from a dragon. He pulled her back to wear he could stand comfortably in the water. His clothes billowed as the water moved them around, hugging and releasing his body.

"Well . . . here I am, now what?" Dayton asked as he brought her to a vertical position in front of him, his hands on her waist. Erysah laughed so hard she tried not to swallow any water.

"I thought that you might have taken off your clothes first." Her eyes sparkled as the water reflected off them.

"You never mentioned removing my clothes. Your request was for me to join you and that is what I have done." He was trying to keep a straight face but the corners of his eyes were starting to rise. Erysah burst into fits of laughter, her heart soaring with happiness.

"Dayton, I swear you surprise me at every turn." He let her go and she had to kick her legs to keep afloat. She then swam around him towards the shallower end until she could stand without drowning. Her hair pooled out around her shoulders. Dayton began walking slowly through the water, as if stalking his prey. Each step inched his body out of the pool making his clothes cling to him in a crazy pattern. By the time he was within a few feet away nearly all his chest was exposed through the semi opaque material. Erysah reached out and began to undo the buttons on his shirt and dragged it off his wet skin, letting it float in the water. She noticed his skin covered in goose bumps as he shuddered. "Are you cold?" Dayton shook his head, his eyes darkening to an even darker blue. Erysah began tugging at the waist band of his trousers to encourage him to move closer to her.

"Erysah," he made a half hearted grab for her. But as he moved forward she retreated until her shoulders and breasts were out of the water. Her hair clinging to her like wet satin. Unclasping his trousers and lowering the zip he gradually released himself from his wet clothes. The relief was short lived as the warm water caressed his now engorged manhood. It wasn't until Erysah looked down through the water that she realised that he still had his shoes on. She put her hand to her mouth trying to hide the smirk. "What?" Dayton could not understand what she found so amusing.

"Your shoes," she said, choking back a laugh. "In your haste to join me you left them on too." Dayton looked down and groaned. He lifted one foot to try and remove a shoe but lost his balance and toppled over in the water. Erysah burst into fits of laughter. When Dayton managed to right himself, he looked at her scornfully.

"A little help would be nice." Erysah tilted her head to one side, as if thinking about it. She would have to dive down to get them off. Disappearing under the water she yanked at both his feet, bringing him under with her. Pulling off both shoes she resurfaced and threw them onto the side of the pool. When she turned round Dayton was nowhere to be seen. She had expected him to surface just after her but he wasn't there. Worried she started to dive down and look for him. There was no sign of him. The only things she could see were his clothes floating in the water. Erysah began to panic and started shouting.

"Dayton! Dayton where are you? Come on Dayton, this isn't funny." She was really starting to worry. Erysah was just about to get out of the pool when something pressed against her back.

"And where do you think you are going?" Dayton's voice whispered in her ear. His hands slid around her sleek body. She turned round to see him smiling at her.

"What happened? Where did you go?"

"A little trick I am able to do," he chuckled, she pushed at him trying to get away from him because he'd scared her half to death.

"Well it wasn't very funny." Erysah scowled. "It was like you were invisible."

"I was," Dayton said with a smug look on his face, Erysah's eyes widened in disbelief.

"What do you mean you were invisible?" Erysah thought that he was winding her up.

"Watch." He said as she looked at him she could still feel his hands on her body, she noticed he started to fade out, disappearing. She could still feel him but she couldn't she him. Dayton thought that her face was a picture as she was stunned by his party piece. But before he could make himself visible again she managed to grab his erection, which startled him. Dayton gasped as he lost all focus and couldn't reappear. Whilst he was in this state he was unable to communicate with her. Fortunately he could still use the mesh to talk to her. *'Erysah what have you done?' I am stuck like this now and I do not know how long it will last. I have no voice when I am like this.'* Erysah laughed, as she stroke him. She heard his groan in her mind.

"I think this might have interesting possibilities." She couldn't resist saying it out loud, knowing Dayton could only communicate mentally.

"What do you mean interesting possibilities?"

"You'll see, but I won't, if you feel me." She burst out laughing again at her own joke.

'Oh, very funny Erysah.' Dayton's mind was doing overtime, but he had to admit it did have a certain appeal to it. Walking her backwards so that she was against the side of the pool he decided to take the lead and he pressed his invisible lips to hers. The sensation was rather strange. Although he could feel her there was a slight reduction in sensation, as though there was a thin barrier of some sort between them. He turned Erysah so that she was leaning forward on the side of the pool. And began exploring her from behind, her response on the other hand had intensified. Erysah felt as though she had a low level electrical current pass over her skin. Everywhere he touched he caused her to moan, gasp or suck in a breath through clenched teeth. He continued to explore her body with his invisible one. The whole experience felt surreal, he asked her, *'are you alright?'*

"Oh, yesss! Don't stop Dayton, please." She begged, her words came out as gasps. As he entered her there was a shift in his body's response. Once he had joined their bodies together everything increased. Dayton got the full force of the sensation that Erysah had been experiencing. And OMG now he knew why she was reacting the way she was. It was like having a taser hit on your most private parts. Every thrust caused an electrical pulse shoot through them both, almost welding them together. It didn't matter that Dayton was invisible because she had her eyes closed. Erysah was engulfed in the most powerful physical feelings she had ever experienced. Even Dayton whose voice had been silenced had pictures flashing through his mind which carried over to Erysah. They climbed higher and higher like two soaring rockets the current passing between them in a never ending cycle. The sensations increased until pleasure became pain and vice versa, causing them both to shatter. There releases were so powerful, brightly coloured lights to flash in their minds. It was then that Dayton reappeared, his body leaning over Erysah's as they stood locked together.

Neither one of them could speak. The neurons in their minds were still exploding in orgasms of their own. Their bodies shuddered continuously with aftershocks. It took several minutes for them to be able to part. Erysah was the first to speak.

"That was . . . I can't find the words," she was still breathing hard.

"I know," Dayton nodded, his own breath ragged. "What happened?" How did you manage to freeze me invisible?" His mind was numb from the whole experience.

"I honestly don't know, Dayton. All I did was grab you . . . and well . . . well you know the rest." Dayton hugged her to him. "I supposed I was annoyed that you pulled that stunt on me and I wanted to get my own back on you. But I never meant for that to happen. I didn't even know it would happen." Erysah was truly shocked. Thinking about what he had said earlier and all that had happened; she thought it might be a good idea to see the keeper, so she directed the conversation that way. "When were you thinking about going to see the keeper?" Dayton was surprised at her change of heart.

"What changed your mind?"

"What just happened between us and all the other incidents made me rethink things." Dayton understood what she meant. There had been many unusual incidents with regards to Erysah and there was no way they were just coincidental.

"I will contact him tomorrow and make arrangements to visit. All records are kept where he lives." Dayton was relieved that Erysah had come round. Although, tonight was amazing, it was still worrying. Erysah began to shiver in Dayton's arms. "Come on, Erysah let us get out of here and into someplace warmer." Erysah nodded. He lifted her up and jumped out without any effort. She raised an eyebrow at him; he just smiled and shrugged his shoulders. Grabbing a couple of large towels, he wrapped one around Erysah and one around himself. Once in the room he lit the fire while Erysah dried herself off and put on a satin night dress. Dayton was still wrapped in his towel when he came over to sit next to her on the bed. He was unable to resist the softness of her skin; he stroked the back of his index finger down the length of her arm, making her shudder.

"How will you contact the keeper?" Erysah inquired. She knew she still had a lot to learn about the Vardesh. Realising that Dayton didn't tell her everything at once because he wanted her to get used to things slowly, rather than being bombarded with everything and being overwhelmed.

"I will use the channeller. Being the guardian I have been enhanced to enable me to use it. That is why I was surprised when you managed to contact me with it." Erysah understood, why he had panicked.

"Who enhanced you?" Erysah had a feeling she knew what he was going to say but she wanted to hear it from him.

"Sollest, she is the High Priestess of the Vardesh. When she chooses her new guardian they have to go through an enhancement ritual. That way the guardian is able not only to communicate with her, they will also be able to use the channeller to contact the others of our race." Dayton did not see any reason why he should not tell her, especially as she was his Solelil and she would have to understand these things. She would have to get used to the idea that he had certain responsibilities to the Vardesh and Sollest.

"When will I get to meet this Sollest?" Erysah was curious to know. "Will it be at the ritual?" Dayton nodded.

"Yes, although I will have to go and see her shortly and tell her when we need to have the ritual. But first, we need to go and see the priest at the church to arrange our wedding. I would like them on the same night, if you do not mind?" Erysah then remembered that Dayton had asked her to marry him and she looked down at the left hand and began twiddling with the amazing ring he had given her. She had gotten so used to it; she had forgotten she was wearing it. Erysah desperately tried to focus on something else because the thought of marriage was scary, almost as scary as the thought of the ritual and what she would become after it. Even though through her father, she was already half way there.

"You seem to have a lot of rituals; do you have rituals for everything?" Dayton laughed and shook his head.

"No, not for everything, but we do have a few." He leaned over and kissed the top of her head. "Then again humans have a number of rituals themselves, if you think about it". Erysah considered this for a moment. She supposed Dayton was right. She listed them in her head. Birthdays, Marriages, Baptisms, Funerals, Anniversaries, Christmas, Easter and these were just the main ones. Then there were the other ones like, Valentine's Day, Mother's Day, Father's Day, Saints Days and various Bank Holidays. Most of them celebrated ritually every year.

"Wow! Thinking about it we have lots of different rituals and celebrations. On about celebrations do the Vardesh have any?" Erysah wondered if they celebrated things like birthdays, especially as they lived for so long. Dayton picked up on her thoughts and beamed at her, his grin was almost as wide as his face. "What are you grinning at?" Erysah was bemused by his reaction.

"Nothing really, but I do believe that we may just set a precedence."

"What are you going on about?" Erysah was exasperated by Dayton at times. He seemed to find many things amusing.

"Well, because of our longevity we do not tend to remind ourselves of certain things. But I may start celebrating something next year. I may take a leaf out of the human world." Erysah pushed at him, trying to knock him off the bed. It was like trying to push a wall over.

"Dayton you can be so incorrigible at times." But she was grinning when she said it. She had an inkling of what he was on about. Although she tried not to think about it, the question had to be asked. "When . . . ?" Dayton looked slightly confused by the one word question. Erysah continued. "When are we to perform the rituals?" She had used the plural because she hadn't wanted to use the 'M' word. Dayton knew she was avoiding saying the word 'married'. He wondered why she seemed more afraid of getting married than she seemed to be with her transcendence ritual.

"I would like to perform the rituals, as you put it in five days time. But that depends if I can persuade the priest to perform the marriage ceremony that soon." Erysah resisted the urge to visibly wince at his use of the word. She did love him and did want to be with him. She knew she was being silly. Perhaps it was the fact that she had always been taught by her grandparents that marriage was sacrosanct and not to be taken lightly. Her grandparents had been married for over forty-five years before . . . she stopped herself. It made her too sad and angry to think about what had happened. Erysah wanted to look forward to the future, especially now she had one. It would do no good to try and hang on to the past. What was gone was gone and no amount of wishing would change it. Suddenly she thought of Violet, it was almost as if she now went hand in hand with her grandparents. Not surprising really, she was her great aunt, after all. She needed to let Violet know that she was okay, that she had found a new life and was getting married. How would she react to that? It had only been a few days since she had met Dayton. Everything seemed to be moving at the speed of light. She had managed to use the word, even if it was in her head. But she did need to contact them; it was a conversation she wasn't looking forward to. Erysah could just imagine Greg's reaction; he would probably blow a gasket.

He had always been very protective of her. She remembered once when she had filled in for Charlie one Saturday night. He was off sick and she had offered to help Greg and Kenny at the bar. As usual Saturday nights was very busy. Towards the end of the night a couple of young guys who were a little drunk. They started to try and chat her up. Things got a bit out of hand when she had gone to collect some glasses. As she walked past their table, one of them grabbed her, pulling her onto his lap. She tried to get up but his friend blocked her path. The guy who had grabbed her started grinding his already swollen groin into her bottom. Erysah felt sick. When Greg spotted what was happening, he went ballistic. He grabbed the guy who was hovering over her and tossed him towards the door. The other guy let go of Erysah and when Greg had pulled her out of the way he grabbed the guy out of the chair, dragging him to the door where he had left his friend guarded by Kenny. Whilst Greg had hold of the two miscreants, he whispered a few choice words in their ears. Whatever he said to them, was enough to make their faces pale. She knew she would not see them in the bar again; they would be barred for life. That was the only time she had truly seen him angry, normally he was so placid.

"Dayton? Can I ask you something?" Erysah was being cagey. She knew that the existence of the Vardesh were to be kept secret, but surely she could still tell the two closest people to her that she was getting married.

"Of course Erysah, what is it?" Dayton was not surprised by her hesitance. He had been getting the odd thought through the mesh but had not said anything.

"I would like to call my great aunt and my cousin whose bar I work at. Erysah found it strange still to think of them as family. But that is who they were, her family and she needed to get used to it. I just want to let them know that I'm okay and tell them that I'm getting married." There now she had spoken it out loud and it didn't sound that bad, when she said it. Dayton hugged her and gave her a very slow and salacious kiss, which left her breathless. "What was that for?" she gasped, as she held onto him, her arms round his waist.

"For saying the words that have been terrifying you ever since you said yes." His smile was so intoxicating she couldn't help but smile shyly back at him. "Please do not be embarrassed Erysah, if that is what you wish, you can invite them to the wedding." That statement took Erysah completely by surprise.

"It would be fantastic if they could come, but what about knowing about the Vardesh? I thought that you have to keep yourselves a secret." She was now concerned that they might be revealed. Dayton smiled and hugged her tighter.

"Erysah, please do not worry. We still have to interact with the human race to survive. Just because they are invited to the wedding, does not mean that they will find out about who we are. We can make arrangements for them to stay in the town." Erysah nodded, she was relieved by this. "You can ring them tomorrow after we have got a date from the priest, alright?"

"Thank you, Dayton." She was truly grateful that she didn't have to cut herself off completely from people she cared about. Now she was starting to look forward to getting married even more so. She leaned into him and stroked his back; he found it comforting to have her do that. It was a rather strange sensation but he liked it. Time had slipped away from them again, but this time there would be no more disappearing. No more waiting for tomorrow. No rushing, no desperation. He could now sleep holding Erysah in his arms, knowing she would be there when he woke. In just a few short days Erysah would be his wife and she would transcend into being one of the Vardesh. They would then be able to spend the next five hundred years together.

"Sorry beloved, time to sleep. The day is almost upon us." Erysah nodded as she let Dayton bring her onto the bed properly. Lying together in a lovers embrace, they both drifted into sleep.

Preparations

When Dayton and Erysah woke the next evening they were still wrapped around each other. At some point during their rest Dayton's towel had slipped away from his body and in typical male fashion he had reacted with the heat of her body. His erection nudging at her stomach. She squirmed as the heat from the large bulbous head pressed at her belly button, through the silken material. This made Dayton suck in a breath. '*What a way to wake up*', he thought to himself. '*Mmm*', Erysah thought back. She pressed herself even closer and nuzzled his neck. Dayton crushed her to him.

"Regrettably, this will have to wait until later." Dayton said with a sigh.

"Why?" Erysah spoke into his neck her voice vibrating through his body. She kissed her way up his throat to his ear and nibbled, Dayton groaned.

"You are not helping me Erysah." his body began to burn with a slow insidious fire.

"Funny," she said raising her head slightly trying to look at him. "I thought I was helping." A wry smile crept across her face. Dayton could not resist the look on her face, so tempting and with those luscious lips of hers. So he did the only thing he could, he kissed her deeply and passionately. As their tongues tangoed with each other, Erysah raised her leg across his waist trying to get closer to her goal. Before he had even realised it the head of his erection was knocking at her forbidden entrance. His body reacted of its own accord and he thrust deeply into her. He took Erysah's gasp into his mouth, as he did he rolled both of them over so she was under him. Their lovemaking was fast and furious. Erysah seemed to find a kind of desperation in herself. A fire that needed dousing and despite Dayton's protests he was more than willing to oblige. When they were both sated, they washed and dressed ready to head into the town.

"Are you going to be like that every time we wake?" Dayton was curious, because he had to admit it was the best wakeup call he had ever had. Erysah looked thoughtful for a moment. She quite liked the idea herself.

"I don't know, Dayton." She said with a smile. "We will have to see what comes up." Then she burst out laughing and dived out of bed. Dayton lunged forward and slapped her on the bottom, making her squeal.

"You Erysah, are incorrigible," he said, as he slapped her rump again, joining in with her laughter. "Come on, we have to go and see Father Johnston before I show you the town and feed you." He took her hand and led her back up to the library. The thought of going to see the priest sobered her up very quickly.

"What about you Dayton, you need to feed to." Erysah wondered if he had ever considered taking her blood. The thought transmitted a little too loudly. Dayton caught hold of it.

"No, I have not considered using you to feed me. It is against everything I believe in. After . . ." He hesitated.

"After what? Dayton" Erysah pressed him to finish.

"After the ritual I will no longer have to feed on humans."

"Dayton you are really starting to be annoying. Stop beating around the bush and just tell me!" Her frustration was starting to show because she started pacing the room. He sighed, why was he so afraid. She was here with him, she had agreed to marry him and he knew she loved him. Dayton was bemused at her phraseology but understood what she was saying.

"After the ritual we will only need to feed from each other. You will never need to take human blood, unless . . ." He hesitated and changed the directions of his words slightly. "Our bodies will become self sufficient, only needing an exchange from male to female and vice versa." Erysah stopped in her tracks and looked at him. She knew from the conversation she had had with Jarro what the 'unless' was. Perhaps one day. He looked like a naughty boy who had just confessed breaking a priceless vase by playing football, inside the house. She charged at him, jumping up putting her arms around his neck and her legs around his waist. Dayton's breath left his chest with the unexpected force. She had moved much faster than he had anticipated. Hanging off him she held her head back and looked at him.

"Really?" he nodded, feeling quite overwhelmed by her reaction, he was unable to look away from her gaze which held him with such intensity.

"Yes." His voice was a mere whisper.

"Then it will be just you and me, forever." She seemed to glow with the information.

"Well not quite forever, but for the next five hundred years." A look of sheer relief started in his eyes and then spread to the rest of his face, continuing to spread through his whole body all the way to his toes. Erysah wasn't quite sure but she thought she saw tears well up in his eyes. She leaned in and kissed him with everything that she was, everything she felt for him. She poured every ounce of love she had for him into it. Dayton eyes then did well up and as he closed his eyes pale pink tears ran down his cheeks. He felt so blessed; he had not known what he was missing until he had found her. Now he knew how the others who had found their Solelil or Solelae felt. After the kiss ended Erysah let herself down. She had noticed his tears but did not mention them, but took them into her heart. She looked at him adoringly after he had discreetly wiped them away.

"Dayton?"

"Yes," he managed to choke out.

"I just wanted to say something to you." Erysah hoped that she wouldn't embarrass herself when she told him.

"What?" He managed to make his voice a little clearer.

"Oh, nothing much, it's just that . . ."

"Just, what?"

"Oh, just that, I love you, Solelae." Dayton looked at her stunned. He did not even know how she would know the word, let alone what it meant.

"Hhhow . . . How do . . . How do you know that word?" His words stuttering out of his mouth like a man with an affliction.

"Sorry, I picked it up out your head, you were thinking about Solelil and Solelae. And as you call me Solelil most of the time, so I thought that Solelae might have been the masculine version. Did I do wrong?" Dayton did nothing more than grab her in a passionate embrace, returning every essence of what she had given him tenfold. When he released her she asked him breathlessly.

"What do those words mean anyway? You kept calling me Solelil, but you never explained them what it exactly meant." He smiled, his eyes still sparkling with the remnants of tears.

"You never asked me."

"Well, duh!" Erysah smacked the front of her head with the heel of her hand. Dayton looked at her confused and shook his head and smiled.

"The literal translation is 'sunlight of my soul'. I suppose because they bring light, happiness and love to the other person."

"Oh!" Was all that Erysah could say, she was stunned at how poetical it sounded.

"How do you want to travel to town?" He said changing the subject.

"What do you mean how?" Erysah was confused; she naturally thought that they would go in her car.

"Well . . ." he said grinning and wiggled his eyebrows. Erysah shook her head trying to hide her laughter, he looked ridiculous. "I have got some transport of my own, would you like to see it?" Erysah's curiosity was spiked and she nodded eagerly. Grabbing her hand he led her through the house until they reached another door at the rear of the property. Erysah realised that they were at the other end of the building. As she had not really seen the outside of the house properly she didn't know that Dayton had a garage attached to it. As they walked through the door Dayton flicked on the light. There sitting by the side of her car was a low slung black and chrome beast. Erysah's jaw dropped her eyes popping wide.

"Wow! Dayton!" she exclaimed. "What. Is. That!" It was more of a statement than a question, "and please don't say it's a bike, because I can see that." Dayton beamed as he walked over to the machine and stroked it with a fond caress that almost made Erysah jealous.

"This, my beloved is not just a bike, this is a Harley-Davidson Fat Bob FXDF in Vivid black. It has a black engine with polished covers. A teardrop style air box and low slung two into two chromed exhausts. Fat handlebars, chunky 16inch wheels, on a wide slab front end and Bobtail rear fender." He could have gone into more detail but he did not want to bore her with information she obviously would not understand.

"Sorry, my mistake." Erysah chuckled. "Now I know why you like to wear black a lot. But I have no gear to wear."

"Oh, contraire, Solelil," Dayton said as he went to a grey metal cupboard that sat in one corner of the garage. When he opened it Erysah was amazed to see, it was a closet filled with all the different leather jackets, trousers, gloves and helmets. "Come take a look," he gestured, waving his open hand towards her. As Erysah walked over she forgot all about the fact that her car was in the garage. The last time she had seen it was parked in front of the house. But for some unknown reason she had no idea how it got there and she really didn't care. She could feel the adrenaline pumping through her body, causing it to heat up with excitement. Dayton began pulling out a set of leathers, in black of course, that he thought would be the correct size for her. While she put them on, Dayton put on his. The smell and creak of leather was intoxicating and felt sexy as hell. The leather hugged every soft curve of her body. As Dayton turned and saw her in his already tight leathers, he felt a crushing sensation as his body began to swell. Dayton swallowed hard as he stifled a groan and mounted the bike.

Erysah got on the bike behind Dayton and clung to him, arms around his waist holding on like a back pack as the garage doors opened. Dayton twisted the throttle and brought the bike to life. The deep roar of the engine throbbed between her legs as they rode into the night towards the old church. The vibration of the bike did not help Dayton's predicament, if he did not get control of himself, he was going to be in a mess, literally. St. Winifred's was on the far side of Stone Edge, set at the foot of a hill, just off the main street. It took them about twenty minutes to get there. The thrill of the wind travelling past them as Dayton drove them through the streets was invigorating. Erysah was surprised that nobody paid any attention to them as they flew past, especially as the bike seemed louder in the darkness. Then she remembered that Dayton could muffle the sound around him.

He did not drive up to the doors, but pulled up outside a set of very old iron gates that were set into the stone wall which surrounded the churchyard. The gates were still open and Dayton knew the priest was still receiving visitors. With helmets in hand they walked up the gravel path, the stones crunched and shifted beneath their feet as they headed towards the church doors. As soon as they reached the heavy old oak door Dayton pushed it open. Erysah had expected it to groan and grind as it opened, but the large iron hinges moved silently. Entering the church Erysah stared in fascination around her. The inside was both simple and elegant. A centre aisle with pews on either side led down to the chancel, beyond that was the altar covered in a simple white cloth with gold crosses embroidered on it. Stained glass windows lined the walls, each one depicting the image of a man, whom she presumed were the apostles. Behind the altar was another window, this one showing a picture of the Virgin Mary with Baby Jesus in her arms. Stone arches and pillars supported a vaulted ceiling. Erysah found it magnificently beautiful in its simplicity. Down the aisle in the front left pew near the altar sat a grey haired man. When he heard them enter he turned around. Smiling he stood and approached, holding out his hands palms out towards them. He was tall and wily his arms ready to embrace one or both of them.

"Dayton, welcome," said clapping his hands on either side of his shoulders. "You have not been to mass for a while."

"Yes, I know Father. May I introduce the reason why?" Dayton said grinning.

"My apologies young lady but Dayton is one of my favourite parishioners." The priest was thin with a long angular face framed with a small pair of round glasses. The glasses seemed at odds with his face as they sat on the end of his roman nose. He still had a full head of hair, although it was almost white. Dayton placed his free hand at the small of Erysah's back.

"Father Johnston, this is my beloved, Erysah." Father Johnston held out a hand to her which Erysah took. He placed his other hand over the top encompassing it in his almost skeletal hands.

"I am very pleased to meet you Erysah. So it was you that has kept him from my services." Erysah blushed.

"Sorry." Erysah squeaked out, unsure why she felt she had to apologise to him. She didn't even know that Dayton went to church.

"I presume that you have come to see me for a reason, other than a social call." Father Johnston stated, many years of knowledge seemed to reside in his old and wise eyes. Dayton acknowledged him with a small nod.

"I have a great favour to ask of you, Father." Father Johnston nodded and signalled to follow him to the front of the aisle. "We would like you to marry us as soon as is possible." Dayton looked slightly anxious as he made his request. He knew that Father Johnston would think the worst, but he had no other recourse. Father Johnston signalled for them to sit. As soon as their rears hit the wood of the pews, he spoke.

"Is there something you are not telling me?" He asked Dayton with an accusing look.

"No Father. It is nothing like that. Erysah is not pregnant. It is just that we do not wish to wait any longer."

"Is this true Erysah?" The priest asked her. Erysah only nodded, she was afraid her voice would give her uneasiness away. Father Johnston looked at Dayton for a moment, and then nodded in affirmation. "How many will be attending?" he asked satisfied that neither of them were lying to him. Relief coursed through Dayton's veins, grateful he never pressed any further. Dayton had not realised there was tension wrapped around his body until it was released. Over the years the two of them had come to an understanding and even though the priest had no knowledge of the Vardesh's existence, Dayton suspected that the priest knew he was different. Erysah was slightly bemused by the priest's lack of inquiry. She thought he would ask a myriad of questions, especially as he was a Catholic priest.

"Excluding us, three possibly five." Dayton knew that Erysah had not contacted her Great Aunt and cousin yet.

"Okay, but it will take a couple of days to organise. Let me go and check my diary." As Father Johnston went into the vestry, Erysah looked at Dayton with a worried expression.

"Do not worry beloved, everything will be fine." She slipped an arm around his waist, resting her head on his shoulder and clung to him. Dayton's arm enclosed her shoulders. Within a few minutes Father Johnston came back with his diary. Erysah stiffened abruptly, as if she had been caught doing something she shouldn't have been. She felt warmth and a sensation of laughter in her mind. Erysah blushed and wanted to kick him for it.

"How does this Friday sound, most of the afternoon is free." The priest still had his nose in the book while he was speaking, so he didn't notice Erysah's reaction to his return.

"What is the latest time you can do father?" Dayton asked, knowing full well that Father Johnston would know he would ask for a time after dark.

"Well . . . I could possibly perform the ceremony after evening mass, but there are a couple of conditions." He looked up over his glasses as he spoke.

"Name them father, I am sure we can accommodate you, as you are willing to accommodate us." Erysah now realised that was more than asking favours, this was all about bartering. 'You scratch my back and I'll scratch yours' sort of thing.

"The Bell Tower needs re-roofing and re-pointing; we already have half of the funds but could do with a donation towards it." Dayton nodded and knew exactly what the priest was after. Erysah had a good idea too. Father Johnston was happy with the negotiations and closed his diary. "Shall we say eight o'clock?"

"Yes, that will be perfect. Thank you, Father." They shook hands and with that the deal was done. "And we will also attend mass every evening until Friday." Father Johnston knew that Dayton would know that condition without being told, otherwise the bands would not be read. Father Johnston nodded in agreement.

"See you tomorrow evening father." And with that they left the church. As they approached the bike Erysah grabbed his arm to stop him.

"Did you just agree to give him the rest of the money for the repairs to the bell tower?" Dayton shrugged. "Why?"

"Money has never been an issue. I have been around for a long time and have accrued a substantial amount. Also it is just the way we have always done things here. There are a number of clichés that could be used in this scenario but I will not go down that route. Now let us go and get some food. How does pizza sound?" Suddenly Erysah's stomach rumbled in answer to the change of topic and she nodded. They travelled through some back streets until Dayton pulled up outside a little Italian Pizzeria. The building was much like the buildings in the rest of the village, grey stone symmetrical cottages that lined the narrow streets. The only exception was that there was a large multi-paned bay window next to the entrance. The sign over the window said Angelino's. Inside it was quaint and cosy, small intimate tables skirted the walls, covered in blue and yellow checkered table cloths. The central area held four larger tables set for four to six people, one of which was occupied by a family. Dayton led Erysah to a table right at the back near a couple of doors, one led to the toilets and the other she presumed led to the kitchen. As she looked around the place she noticed a few more tables had people sat at them. One table had a couple in the far corner, another had a couple of girls talking animatedly and giggling at each other's words. When the waitress came up to them to take their order she seemed slightly taken aback when she saw Erysah sitting with Dayton. She knew it was his favourite table, he had told her that he liked to observe people and their interactions with each other. He had said that he was a bit of an amateur sociologist, even in church she had seen him sitting at the back watching people. On a couple of occasions she had been late for mass she had seen him watching people with his fathomless eyes. Jez wondered if he ever knew that from time to time she watched him to.

"Hi Dayton, haven't seen you in a while."

"Hello Jez, may I introduce my fiancée Erysah." She glanced at Erysah's left hand and saw the ring there; her whole body seemed to sink at the announcement.

"Hi," was all she managed to croak out. For as long as she could remember she had had the hots for Dayton. She had tried on many occasions to speak to him after evening mass, but he always seemed to be rushing off somewhere.

"Hi," Erysah replied, smiling shyly.

"What are you having?" Jez asked looking at Dayton.

"Just a Marguerita, thin crust," Dayton replied not really looking at her. Jez felt crushed. She had begun to think that he was gay and she had been okay with that. But now . . . now he had turned up with a woman he was engaged to be married to. It was almost too much to bear.

"And for you?" she said turning slightly towards Erysah, trying to hold onto some sort of professionalism, when all she wanted to do was run away and cry. She couldn't bring herself to look at the woman who had, in her mind stolen Jez's dreams away.

"The same please." Jez nodded and walked into the kitchen. Erysah looked at Dayton and raised her eyebrows questioningly. Dayton sighed.

"It is not what you think. I cannot tell you here but I will when we get home."

"What about your pizza? How?" Dayton shook his head. Erysah nodded and knew it was difficult to talk openly here. After about ten minutes the man from the table who was sitting with the woman got up and went into the toilet. Dayton excused himself and followed. Minutes later the pizzas arrived. Jez looked at Erysah, her expression asking where Dayton was.

"Call of nature." She said. It wasn't a lie, as such. It was a call of nature, just not a human one. Jez just nodded and returned to the kitchen. Dayton was back a couple of minutes later. "Is everything okay?" she asked him. Dayton just nodded. For some reason he did not feel comfortable about Erysah knowing what he had been doing. The rest room door open and the man, who had gone in before him came out looking slightly unsteady on his feet. Erysah stared down at her pizza rather than at the man. Her appetite waning. "Suddenly I don't feel hungry, can we go Dayton?" He simply nodded and went to pay the bill.

On the ride home Erysah didn't feel the same exhilaration she had felt before. Her mind kept going back to the man at the restaurant; she wondered how much blood Dayton had taken. When they got back to the manor house Erysah was still feeling queasy. Although, she didn't know if it was from hunger or the realisation of what she knew Dayton had done. Suddenly her legs gave out, before she was halfway to the floor Dayton swept her up and took her into the lounge where he laid her on a chaise. Quickly he went into the kitchen and retrieved a can of orange juice. Erysah was still feeling light-headed as he came back in. Sitting on the edge of the chaise, he faced her handing her the juice.

"Thanks," she said and took a couple of sips. After a few minutes she felt a little better.

"I am so sorry Erysah; I should not have exposed you to my needs like that." Dayton looked mortified that his need to feed had caused her to faint.

"No Dayton don't apologise, I think it was because I was hungrier than I thought. My blood sugar level must have dropped. Perhaps I should have eaten before we went out, instead of seducing you." Dayton laughed, feeling a little easier.

"Is that what you did?" He said raising an eyebrow, she nodded knowing that was exactly what she had done and she wasn't going to deny it. For some inexplicable reason she was drawn to him like a moth to a flame. Every time he was near her she burned for him.

"I'm still hungry, any chance of some food before I waste away to nothing." Erysah teased him. Dayton felt the knots in his stomach relax. He still felt selfish. He felt as though he had put himself before his Solelil. Although she was a constant part of him, he sometimes found himself acting on instinct. He knew he could not do that; Erysah's needs should come before his own. He did not like himself very much at that moment.

"Of course, stay there and I will make you something."

"Okay, while you're doing that, I will ring Violet and Greg." Dayton bent down and kissed her gently, leaving her lips tingling and wanting more. Dayton pressed a phone into her hand.

"I will not be long." He said as he brushed his lips over her temple.

Erysah hoped that someone would be at home this time, remembering that the last time she rang no one was there. The phone was answered on the third ring, almost, as if someone was right next to it.

"Hello," said a male voice on the other end, it sounded gravelly. If it wasn't for the fact that she knew it was Greg's number she wouldn't have recognised his voice.

"Greg?" Erysah still wasn't sure it was him, her voice trembled slightly.

"Yes, who is this?" Erysah was confused; surely he would recognise her voice.

"Greg, its Erysah."

"Erysah, Erysah. Oh, my god! Erysah! Where are you? Are you okay? Mum said that you had gone away. What happened? I have been beside myself with worry." Her heart clenched with guilt but she had been to emotional to speak to him, especially after what she had found out. Now at least she could focus a little better and keep her promise to Violet.

"Whoa, slow down. Calm down, Greg, please. I told Violet that I was going away. She suggested I have a holiday". There was silence as Greg digested what Erysah had just said. It seemed to go on forever. She continued listening for a minute longer then broke the silence. "How is Violet anyway? The last time I rang, no one was in." Erysah had been worried, especially after the last conversation she had had with Violet. All of a sudden Greg yelped.

"Mum, did you have to do that?" Erysah almost laughed with relief. She could hear Violet's voice in the background chastising him for hogging the phone. "Sorry, Erysah mom wants to talk to you. I'll pass you over and speak to you later. I am glad you're okay."

"Okay Greg, thanks." Erysah chuckled to herself, typical Violet. Then she heard a fumbling noise and knew Violet had the phone. "Hi, Violet how are you?"

"Much better now, I was worried when I hadn't heard from you. Did you go to Scotland?"

"Yes. Is Greg still in the room with you?"

"No, I shooed him away, so we can talk freely." Erysah was relieved. "Are you okay?"

"Yes, I'm fine." More than fine she thought to herself.

"I must admit I am curious as to what your mother left you, but I won't pry."

"Thank you for that, it was very personal and it answered a lot of questions, but I won't go into details."

"I understand Erysah. There are some things that you just have to keep to yourself." Violet more than anyone knew that, she still had her own secrets to keep. Perhaps one day . . .

Actually, I have a surprise and a favour to ask both you and Greg." Violet was suddenly extremely curious. Erysah seemed nervous and excited at the same time. How would they react to finding out she was getting married?

"Now you have me intrigued Erysah, what have you been up to?"

"Well . . ." Erysah hesitated for a moment.

"Spit it out girl, it can't be as bad as our last conversation." Violet chided. Erysah thought back to that day, which was almost a week ago. 'Was that all', she thought it had been much longer than that. Taking a deep breath, she let it all out.

"I'm getting married and I would like you and Greg to come to the wedding." Her words rushed out at lightening speed. There was no sound coming out of the phone and for one minute she thought that Violet might have had another heart attack, either that or she hadn't understood a word she had said. "Violet . . . ? Violet? Are you there? Did you hear what I said?" Still nothing, Erysah was starting to get really worried. "Violet!" she almost screamed down the phone.

"There's no need to shout I'm not deaf!" Violet scolded as relief washed over her.

"Sorry Violet, but when you didn't say anything . . ." Violet interrupted her.

"It was just unexpected. I didn't even know you were seeing anyone?" Erysah thought back to when she had first saw him. It had been about seven months ago.

"We have been together for about seven months." She wasn't lying exactly but she was wondering how she was going to get round the question of where they met, because sure as eggs were eggs, that question would come. Then she had a brainwave on how to deflect that question. Erysah had a feeling that Dayton had put that thought into her head. "Do you think Greg would mind giving me away?"

"Umm . . . I don't know Erysah you would have to ask him." 'Yes,' Erysah thought. '*Thank you Solelae*,' she sent to Dayton. A warm rush of love hit her like a tidal wave. Erysah could hear Violet shouting Greg back into the room. Once again there was the fumbling of the phone.

"Hi Erysah, mum says you have something to ask me." Greg sounded wary.

"Err . . . yeah. I'm getting married, will you give me away?" Erysah blurted the words out as fast as she could, so that Greg couldn't interrupt her and then waited for the explosion.

"You're what!" he bellowed, Greg couldn't believe what he was hearing.

"Getting married, will you please give me away?"

"How can you be getting married? You haven't been seeing anyone, not to my knowledge." Greg thought he knew everything about Erysah, how could she have kept this from him. He felt hurt and betrayed because she had not been able to confide in him. He was getting more irate as he spoke; his voice getting louder and angrier. Erysah held the phone away from her ear, Greg's ranting was deafening. She couldn't understand why he was so angry. He was like a brother to her; he had always protected and cared for her. Now he sounded like a wounded beast.

"Greg! Please stop!" Erysah pleaded. "I have known him for about seven months."

"Seven months, how can that be? You have worked at the bar every day for the last three years. You haven't had time to meet anyone!" Erysah thought, '*thanks Dayton, now, what?*' Laughter filled her mind along with the smell of food as he came into the room holding a plate for her. Erysah's stomach growled.

"Here," he said passing her a plate full of scrambled eggs and smoked haddock. "Please, let me have the phone, Erysah." She never said anything; she just passed him the phone. *'On your own head be it.'* She thought to him. Dayton just smiled and winked at her. "Eat!" he demanded whilst his hand covered the mouth piece of the phone. "Am I speaking to Greg?" Dayton's voice was silky smooth and unruffled. Erysah couldn't hear Greg's reply but Dayton's voice had a calming effect on her, so she surmised that it was doing the same to Greg. Dayton looked down at her, again, "eat", he mouthed the word. Erysah sighed and started eating. The food was delicious, *'how could he cook so well?'* The reply came into her mind, *'I loved to cook when I was younger.'* Erysah smiled and nodded with understanding. After all she had met Jarro who had not ascended yet and he ate normally. Erysah found that thought extremely funny, considering she was in the same room as a vampire.

By the end of his conversation with Greg everything had been organised and Erysah had finally finished her food. Greg and Violet would arrive on Thursday evening; Dayton would book rooms for them at the Boars Head (a local pub that had rooms for rent). Violet had insisted that Erysah wore her wedding dress. Violet said it should fit but she would be able to alter it if necessary. Dayton would send a car for them when they reached Aberdeen Train Station, bringing them to Stone Edge. Greg would walk her down the aisle and give her away to Dayton. Erysah felt much better now on all fronts. Her two closest friends, who were also her family, were now coming to her wedding. What Dayton had to do now was contact Garroch and his family to let them know the date and time. After that he had to go and see Sollest, to arrange the 'ritual of transcendence'. Unfortunately, Erysah could not know where the temple was until Friday, when it was her time. Dayton hesitated for a moment, he wondered if it were possible. Would it be too much to ask, he certainly thought she would be willing. And for some inexplicable reason she had made a connection with Melindra. Should he risk it? Would Erysah be in any danger? Suddenly she was in his mind. *'You think too loudly at times Dayton.'* She laughed. He looked down at her. Her large eyes shining a deep emerald as she stared up at him.

"Do you think you could do it?" He asked almost knowing what her answer would be.

"I've done it before, with you." Her reply was simple, factual and to the point. He walked over to a bureau that sat in between the two windows that were at the far end of the room. Retrieving the velvet pouch that was in a small draw in the writing desk, he gave it to Erysah.

"Would you like me to instruct you on what you need to do?" His heart was in his mouth at even thinking about asking her to do this.

"No, Dayton. Thank you, I think I'll be able to manage." She said showing her most reassuring smile.

"I will be back shortly, will you be okay?" Dayton could not help but feel apprehensive.

"Of course, Dayton, don't you trust me?" Erysah looked at him, he had been so over protective since they'd met in Barnard Castle. "Is the temple far?" Dayton shook his head, he was not going to tell her that she was practically sitting on top of it.

"It is not that Erysah, I worry for you, you are still not fully Vardesh and only I am supposed to be able to use the Channeller." Erysah laughed.

"Oh, Dayton," she sighed with exasperation. "We both know from experience that I seem to be the exception to that rule." She couldn't help smiling at the worry on his face. Reaching up she caressed the worry lines from his face. Dayton clasped her in a tight embrace burying his face in her hair, the smell of strawberries and cream filling his nostrils.

"I love you Erysah, I would die if anything to happen to you." His heart was in his eyes.

"And I love you to, but you heard what Kaspir said." He could not deny that episode. It had plagued him then and still did. He kissed her deeply before releasing her.

"I love you; if it does not seem to work, please do not exert yourself. Stop if there seems to be a problem." Erysah nodded and pushed him out the door, laughing at his silliness. She had to wonder though why she didn't find all these strange and unusual experiences terrifying. Even in her mind she seemed to be accepting them, she could understand her heart accepting. But her mind hardly questioned any of it and that was more scary than anything else.

"Go Dayton I don't want to be waiting all night until we are together again." Dayton could not argue with that, because he felt exactly the same. With that he went to see Sollest. As he entered the temple Sollest was already visible through the veil. Obviously she had been expecting him, but there again nothing would escape her.

"So the time is nigh?" she stated. Dayton bowed low in greeting.

"Yes Sollest. We wish for the ritual to be performed at midnight this Friday. If that would not offend you?"

"I think that it would be the optimum time, as it is the beginning of a new moon. You will need to contact the other clans. There will have to be representatives from them all, the wolves, the eagles, the cats and the dragons. Whom would you suggest? Remember there are no ruling pairs. It is only I and my sisters that have that power, at present." Dayton thought it strange that she had used the phrase 'at present'. Was she trying to tell him something in her own cryptic way. With so much on his mind he decided not to query it now, there were more important things to do.

"From the Wolf clan I thought we could request Xron and Benne, from the Eagle clan it could be Sawh and Lavender. Then from the Cat clan I could ask Zeke and Yanska and I have already asked Garroch and Melindra they are coming from the Dragon clan." Sollest nodded.

"You need to contact them tonight if they are to get here on time. Where is the channeller?" Dayton cringed briefly at her demand.

"Erysah is using it to contact Melindra. When we were there she somehow made a connection with her. Somehow she managed to use it to contact me outside of the dream state."

"How is it she has the Channeller?" Sollest question was not one of curiosity but more of confirmation of what she already suspected.

"Apparently Kaspir, her father left it for her". Dayton sighed. Kaspir had been his friend and he had gone against doctrine.

"I did not know it was missing". Sollest briefly remembered allowing him to use its energy to prolong his life by one day so he could get his affairs in order, but no more than that. Obviously he had taken advantage of her generosity, no matter what was done could not be undone.

"Neither did I. Things have been so quiet of late; we have had no need of it". At that moment Sollest stepped through the veil. Dayton jumped back in surprise. "Sollest what are you doing? You only come through the veil for the rituals. And your sisters are not here." Dayton was on the verge of panic, it had not been the first time he had seen her but this was not a ritual.

"Relax guardian, I will be able to contact the others for you, but I need to be on this side of the veil." Dayton understood but he did have one question for her.

"Forgive me Sollest, may I ask a question." Sollest nodded. "Will Erysah be alright using the channeller?"

"I have no doubt she will be fine. Remember she is already part Vardesh thanks to Kaspir." Sollest walked over to the pedestal. On it were four symbols, one on each side, each one representing a clan. There was also a fifth symbol on the top. This was the symbol of renewal. As she walked around the pedestal anti-clockwise she touched each of the symbols with her left hand and then she went back the other way reversing her movements. "It is done." She said as she walked back through the veil. "I will see you Friday guardian. Come to the temple one hour before the ritual to collect what will be needed for the ceremony." With that the veil and Sollest disappeared. Dayton returned to Erysah, who he had left in the living room. He was relieved to find her well and smiling as he entered the room.

"Did you manage to contact Melindra?" Erysah squirmed uncomfortably at his question. "Well . . . what happened, Erysah? Did something go wrong?" He rushed over and sat beside her, clasping her hands in his.

"No nothing went wrong exactly." Erysah felt embarrassed and could feel the heat creep up into her cheeks.

"What happened? Erysah, please tell me." He took hold of her face with his hands and caressed her cheeks with his thumbs. She could see the worry in his eyes along with the love he felt for her.

"Well . . . I . . ." She didn't know how to tell him. How could she tell him that she had been in communication with all three of them somehow she had managed to touch the babies minds too. Although, she suddenly realised she didn't have to. By the way Dayton's face changed, he had got the message through the mesh. His eyes went wide; she thought that they might fall out of their sockets. She raised a hand to his face in a gentle caress grabbing his chin she guided her stunned vampire towards her mouth. Whispering a kiss gently over his lips, she spoke into them. "I'm sorry Dayton I didn't do it deliberately, it just happened." She rested her head on his. "I never meant for it to happened, it seems the more I use it, the stronger the connection. What does it mean Dayton?" He looked at her, confusion in his eyes. He was unable to speak at that precise moment. Erysah brushed her lips over his again, nipping at his lower lip until he responded and came out of his stupor.

"I do not know Erysah, but it is not supposed to be possible. When I spoke to Sollest she did not even seemed surprised that you had used it before and she was certainly not worried about the fact that you were using it again". His thoughts went back to his conversation with Garroch and Melindra; he had to agree with them. "We need more information, we need to go and see the 'Keeper'." Erysah understood that for Dayton nothing was making any sense. After almost five hundred years of continuity, Dayton's life had just been turned upside down. What the next five hundred years would bring, he had no idea anymore. All he knew was he had found his Solelil and had got another chance at life. However, she was nothing like he had expected and he had a sneaky suspicion that there was something more going on. But for the life of him, he had no idea and that made him nervous. He had even admitted to Erysah that the things that had happened with her had scared him. What he could not fathom is why Erysah accepted almost everything without question. Or if she did question it, she never voiced it to him, verbally or otherwise.

Prophecy and Legend

"Erysah, I need to contact the keeper, can I have the channeller please." He seemed extremely agitated after his visit with Sollest. Erysah moved her head to indicate that it was back in its pouch and was sitting on the table. As Dayton got up to go over to the table Erysah grabbed his hand.

"Are you okay Dayton, I never meant to cause problems. I do love you, you know that, don't you?" Her voice was soft, full of emotion, her eyes reflecting her words. God help him but he loved her too, desperately. He tugged at her hand, not to get her to release his. But to make her stand up and come to him, as she did he encircled her within a gentle embrace. He rested his chin on the top of her head and sighed. He felt complete, his life would never be the same again, not that he wanted to go back to the emptiness. He just had a feeling life would get a lot more interesting. Since her arrival things had taken many unusual turns, even more so since she was close to the temple. Was it a coincidence? He did not know, it was almost as if her being here magnified her already extraordinary gifts.

"Let me contact the Keeper and then we will go to our chambers." He picked up the pouch off the table. "Come let us sit on the chaise. You do not need to be away from me for me to do this. In fact you could probably help." He heard the word '*how?*' in his mind. "Just keep hold of my hand." Erysah nodded as they went and sat down. Dayton took the channeller out of the pouch and placed it in his hand. He lifted it to his forehead and held onto Erysah with his other hand, he then closed his eyes. Reaching out his mind he searched for the Keeper. Through the mesh and the physical contact Erysah travelled with him, neither of them realised it was happening. Dayton thought that she might just amplify the channeller, so he would not have to go into the temple which acted as an amplifier.

Reaching his destination he spoke into the mind of the Keeper. It was the Keeper that realised that there were actually two minds contacting him.

'Who is with you guardian? And how can it be possible that both of you are here?' Dayton composed himself, he was starting to expect the unexpected when it came to his Solelil.

'It is my Solelil, Keeper. Her name is Erysah. She is why I . . . we are contacting you'. He corrected. *'May we visit you on the morrow?'* Even though Erysah could hear everything she kept silent. Then the Keeper spoke to her directly.

'Good evening, Erysah.' Shocked Erysah didn't respond at first. After a few moments she replied with one word.

'Hello.'

'I presume . . .' the Keeper continued. *'that Erysah has not transcended yet.'*

'No, keeper but . . . .'

'But what?'

'She is not fully human, she is half Vardesh'.

'What!' The Keeper exclaimed.

'She is the daughter of the former guardian and his Solelil. His Solelil did not transcend but she was with child after their encounter. No one knew.' Well that was not strictly true, he was beginning to think that Sollest knew more than she was telling.

'I will consult the scrolls, come see me tomorrow, you will need to stay for a day. Now go and leave me.'

'One more thing Keeper, Sollest mentioned something about a legend and a prophecy. Maybe that will help.'

'Ah, yes it will. Thank you. Go.' With that the connection was broken. Dayton put back the channeller from where he had originally got it from. Erysah thought the Keeper was extremely terse.

"Everything is now set. Tomorrow we will go and see the Keeper." Dayton would be glad when it was all over. If he was feeling this worried, how was Erysah feeling. Outwardly she seemed so calm, maybe there was a tempest roaring inside.

"So what do we do now?" She asked as she rubbed her finger over his chest in a circular motion. Erysah was hoping for some chill time. Things were going to get very busy, very quickly. Reading her mind he grabbed her wrists and raised her arms and put them around his neck locking them there. He then grabbed the backs of her thighs he lifted her legs and locked them around his waist. As he did Erysah leaned in and locked her lips on his, her kiss was deep and passionate as the fire raged inside her. It took them along time to get to the chamber as Dayton had to stop periodically, so they could catch their breaths. Erysah's long drugging kisses caused him to lose strength in his legs, the blood rushing to his groin like a firestorm. When they got into the chamber, Dayton fell onto the bed twisting sideways so he wouldn't hurt Erysah. He released himself from her grasp and stood at the end of the bed, then began to undress in front of her. She watched him from the bed, rolling over onto her side to get a better view. Her lips parted as her breathing increased, drying them so she had to moisten them with her tongue. Erysah's eyes followed every movement and became heavy with lust. Propping her head up with her hand she him watched intently. Licking her lips in eagerness, occasionally moaning quietly as pieces of flesh revealed themselves. A heat of molten lava began to creep through her veins, gathering at her inner sanctum. She felt the heat and could feel that her sheath had swollen with pleasure, her pants were getting wetter by the second. Eventually Erysah was able to feast on all of him. He stood proud, magnificent and unashamed. Just as she thought he was going to come over to the bed he turned round and showed her his back, which was just as impressive as his front. Dayton then walked calmly into the bathing room. Erysah sat up stunned by what had just happened. She knew he was aroused, it was obvious. Then she heard a splash. That was it, she was pissed off now. She started to take off her shoes, but she was unable to undress fast enough, 'to hell with this,' she thought. Marching into the room bare foot she was ready to give Dayton a piece of her mind. When she looked around she couldn't see him, but she knew he was there. He had pulled his party trick again.

"Dayton I know you are in here. It's not funny. How can you tempt me like that and then just walk away?" Suddenly she felt a push from behind and she ended up in the water, clothes and all. When she rose to the surface Dayton was standing smiling at her in all his glory from the side of the pool. Before she could say anything to him, Dayton had dived back into the pool and was upon her, kissing her complaint right out of her mouth.

"Whatever is the matter, Erysah? You look a bit wet." Dayton couldn't help laughing. She wanted to be angry at him but she couldn't keep it up. As soon as he pressed his naked body against hers, she dissolved. Her hands began to trace the muscles of his back, journeying lower with every rotation until she reached the mounds of his bottom. Dayton moaned as she squeezed one of his buttocks making him buck forward. "I need to get you out of these clothes, now!" And he wasn't joking. He ripped at them like a man possessed. Within seconds her clothes were in tatters, floating in bits on the surface of the water. Once she was naked he took every advantage he could. His hunger was so great that he could not wait to be inside her. She could see it in his eyes and she felt the same way. Grabbing a thigh he lifted it up to his hip and positioned himself at her entrance, Erysah leaned back and held onto his wrists as she brought up her other leg. Moving slowly he entered her, millimetre by millimetre, driving her ever closer to the edge. Dayton needed to gain some control, if he had thrust up to the hilt he would of exploded as soon as he hit home. Her velvet sheath engulfed him sending hot licks over his already very sensitive shaft. It was sweet torture. Erysah squirmed.

"Please, Erysah stop!" he almost begged. Once he was fully inside of her, he was able to breathe through the sensations coursing through him. He pulled her up, bent his legs and jumped out of the pool. Erysah held onto him for fear of slipping on his wet skin, a look of surprise on her face as she gasped. Still impaled by his shaft she bounced on him as he walked them into the bedroom. Both of them were gasping from the sensation that small journey had caused. Dayton leaned her against the far wall for support. "Lift your arms and hold onto the sconce." His voice was husky and demanding. Erysah looked up and saw that she was under one of the wall candles. She moved her hands from around his neck and reached up and grabbed it. Dayton placed a hand under her bottom and with the other he clasped a breast. Whilst he teased the nipple between his fingers, his mouth found her neglected breast. Then he began to move, slowly at first while he lavished attention on her breasts. Once the fire took over he could not focus on anything but the fire. The fire within him stoked the fire within her and she followed him into the inferno. As Dayton thrusts got harder and deeper, Erysah moans got louder and louder. Their lovemaking was pure and unadulterated passion. Her body undulated with the rhythm of his thrusts, rising and falling against the wall. Her arms bent and extended as she hung onto the sconce. Her breasts bounced against his chest, causing her nipples to ache even more from the contact. She could feel her orgasm rising to meet his, as he came he let out an almighty roar, this was followed by her own. Dayton froze in mid thrust, his stomach flipped in reaction to what he had heard. This caused Erysah to come down from her own orgasm like a stone. Still pinned against the wall by Dayton, she stared back at him baffled by his reaction. She could see confusion in his eyes.

"What's wrong Dayton? What's the matter?" her voice trembled.

"Did you hear what just came out of your mouth?" His astonishment was written all over his face.

"Sorry I couldn't help screaming so loud, you are so passionate and create such intense feelings within me. It's hard not to react to the sensations." Erysah was totally befuddled by his questions.

"Erysah you did not scream . . ." She looked at him perplexed by his response. "Erysah you . . . roared."

"I . . . thought that you roared?"

"I did but only once, the second one was you. It was a higher pitch than mine." Erysah began to weep slightly, tears started to stream down her cheeks. '*What did this mean? What was happening to her?*' her mind was in turmoil.

"Dayton, please tell me you have some idea what it means?" Dayton walked the two of them over to the bed and sat with her on his lap as her body still had a grip on his manhood. It was strange that her body was reluctant to let his go. For a period of time they were physically tied together. The first time it had happened was when they completed the body thread and he had thought it was connected to that. But it happened every time they made love, both of their bodies swelling and locking them to each other. He wondered if that would change after the ritual.

"I have a theory," he said. "I am beginning to wonder if it is because you are close to the temple. Perhaps it is amplifying your Vardesh side. Triggering your inner dragon." Erysah thought about his words, they sort of made sense. The way she was able to use the channeller. The fact that if she tried hard enough she could just talk to Dayton through the mesh.

"Well, I haven't got any better idea, but it does kind of make sense." Erysah could not deny any of the facts.

"With everything that has happened I just wonder what will happened after the ritual." It still plagued Dayton, the not knowing. From what he knew from past rituals, even though he was not allowed to attend. The Solelil or Solelae went down human and came up Vardesh. The how's of what happened he had no idea. The phoenix represented death and rebirth. He would only have to wait a few more days before all the mysteries of that particular ritual would be revealed. He had already attended a couple of the other clans ascension rituals. When youngsters ascended from their human trappings into their Vardesh form. Erysah didn't want him to worry, what would be would be. God, she sounded like a fatalist. How was it that she was so accepting of what was happening and he was not. Did it have something to do with her Vardesh heritage? They would know soon enough.

"Please don't worry Dayton. Let's just take one day or night as the case may be, at a time." Dayton nodded. He rolled them over onto the bed. At some point during the conversation Erysah's body had released its pressure on Dayton and he was able to extract himself. Erysah couldn't resist asking the question because she wasn't sure she had heard right, after all they were in the throes of passion. "Dayton . . . are you sure you heard me roar?" He smiled, his face lighting up with it.

"Ohh, yess! It was like your dragon recognised mine and responded." Erysah burst out laughing.

"Well that's good otherwise we might be in trouble." She managed to choke out. Dayton couldn't help but agree and started laughing to.

"Come, sleep we have a long night tomorrow." Erysah still found it strange that she was working nocturnally now. She nodded and kissed him on the end of his nose and snuggled in for the day. The next time she stirred was when she could smell food wafting in the room. Dayton had got up early and made her something to eat, so they could set off as quickly as possible. Erysah's stomach growled.

"Was that my inner dragon?" she laughed.

"No silly, you are hungry. For a human you do not seem to eat a lot." Dayton chuckled. "Now eat. I want to be in Aberdeen by eight."

"What time is it now?" she asked. She wasn't even sure what day it was, she was so confused by day and night now. "And what day or night is it? I've seemed to have lost sense of all time."

"To answer all your questions, it is five thirty on Wednesday 3rd November 2021. Any more information you would like?" He said sarcastically, grinning at her. Erysah threw a pillow at him, which he caught easily. After finishing the food Dayton had brought, she got up to get dressed. Dayton couldn't resist stroking a finger down the bare skin on her back.

"Don't start something you won't be able to finish," she said, as she threw a seductive look over her shoulder. Her hair cascading around her shoulders like a red cape. Dayton groaned and picked up the plate.

"I will meet you up stairs," he growled. Trying to resist the urge to go back and put her over his lap and spank her. He groaned again as that thought had just made everything even worse, as his shaft sprang to life. Fifteen minutes later Erysah joined him in the library. "How do you want to travel?" he asked her. "By car or by bike?"

"I didn't even know you could drive?" Erysah stated remembering that she had driven up here from Barnard Castle.

Dream Lover

"Yes, I can drive but only an automatic. I could never get the hang of a manual gear shift. It took me a long time to get your car in the garage, without crashing it." Dayton felt a little uneasy with his confession.

"I wondered how it got in there." Erysah just hoped that the gearbox hadn't been ground into dust, but she was too polite to say anything. She didn't want to bruise his ego anymore than his confession already had.

"Do you have a car?" Erysah asked, knowing full well that the answer was probably yes. Dayton nodded. "What sort is it?" Erysah thought that it might be something like a Porsche or Ferrari. With a grin Dayton told her.

"It is a two door Aston Martin DB7 Vantage V12 automatic in cobalt blue." '*Wow!*' thought Erysah,' *he likes his classics*'. Dayton smiled and shrugged, he had heard her thoughts. She was hoping that he hadn't heard her previous one.

"Car, definitely car. Yours, not mine." Erysah walked over to him and held his hand. "Lead on, lead on." She gestured with her other hand. She was eager to ride in such an awesome car, even though she actually preferred the DB9. But she wasn't going to quibble over a number.

When they got to the garage they walked over to another door Erysah hadn't noticed before. But there again she hadn't really taken a good look. As they went through she realised it was an adjoining garage. There the car sat in all its glory, deep metallic blue, with blue and white leather interior and walnut trim. The aroma of the leather was inviting, Dayton opened the door for her and she slid right in. Everything was so smooth and silky, like soft caramel. The door clunked shut and Dayton went around the back and put something in the boot before getting in. The seats fitted snugly around them, Erysah stroked the walnut on the dash before putting on her seat belt. Dayton pressed a switch inside of the car and the garage doors opened to let them out into the night. It was now six thirty, Aberdeen wasn't that far away and in this car it certainly wouldn't take that long. Erysah hardly noticed the world rushing past outside, as she luxuriated in the splendour of the DB7's interior whilst the car purred its way along the streets. From time to time Dayton would look across to Erysah and smile. He didn't know why he did it and he didn't care why, he was happy. Yes, that was the word for how he was feeling. Happiness, strange how he had never experienced it before. An emotion so simple, yet so powerful. All to soon he was taking the turn off for the Keeper's abode. It was out in the middle of nowhere, west of Aberdeen. Surrounded by forests on three sides, it sat at the end of a field. It was nothing to look at, a medium sized farmhouse in a large acreage of land. The stark landscape made it look dark and foreboding in the waning moonlight. There were no lights on that Erysah could see and parts of it looked derelict.

"Are you sure we are at the right place?" she asked nervously.

"Yes," he said, as he began to drive around the building. Erysah could see he was looking for something but she hadn't got a clue as to what.

"What are you looking for Dayton? Perhaps I can help."

"Thank you for the offer but you are not yet fully Vardesh and it would be difficult for you to see in this light." 'Great', Erysah thought. 'Night vision'. Finally Dayton stopped the car at the back of the building and climbed out. Holding his hand up flat palm out towards her he signalled silently for her to stay in the car. She nodded understanding his request. And as she had no idea what he was looking for, it seemed best not to argue. He closed the door as quietly as possible and walked towards a group of trees that sat forward from the rest of the forest. Erysah thought it was eerily silent normally the night time could be quite noisy, but not here. The silence was almost deafening. Suddenly a face appeared at her window. She had not seen or heard anyone approach as she was too busy watching the last place she saw Dayton disappear into the trees. Erysah screamed for Dayton both in her mind and out loud. The impish little man, with large bulbous eyes, sagging jowls and milk white skin stumbled backward and fell to the ground. Within seconds Dayton appeared towering over him. Dayton extended a hand to the man and helped him up. Erysah realised that he was not as small as she thought. He must have been squatting down to look into the car at her. Dayton walked over to the car and retrieved the bag he had put in the boot, then he opened the door and helped Erysah out of the car. Her heart was still doing overtime on the drum beat, but she was no longer scared out of her wits. She was just slightly terrified. Holding tightly onto Dayton's hand she reluctantly approached the stranger, he squeezed her hand for reassurance.

"Keeper, this is my Solelil, Erysah." He said as he introduced her to him. The Keeper bowed humbly before replying.

"I am honoured to meet one such as you and am deeply aggrieved that I caused you such distress." Both his manner and his words were very strange. Erysah didn't have time to reply, when he spoke again. "Come Guardian, come," he signalled for them to follow him. They followed him into the only solid part of the building. Winding around half demolished walls, entering and exiting doorways, without any doors. Through what looked like an old iron gate, down some steps and then they came to a very large heavy wooden door. Erysah felt dizzy from all the twists and turns. It was as though they had been led through some kind of elaborate labyrinth. The door didn't look old, it looked ancient. As if it had stood for hundreds, if not, thousands of years. But when the keeper opened it, it made no sound, it was smooth. As if it took no effort at all to open it. It had been the second old door she had seen that opened like that. Erysah didn't think that Dayton was muffling the sound, perhaps these people just knew how to look after things.

Once inside they were greeted by a vast room with a vaulted ceiling. It hadn't seemed possible from the outside. Erysah had been so busy concentrating on where they were going and not getting lost, that she didn't take in her surroundings. Or 'perhaps that was the point', she thought to herself. In the centre of the room was a large round table, it reminded Erysah of the round table at Camelot, it must have been nearly twelve feet across and at least six inches thick. She couldn't see how it was supported because there was very little light in the room. What there was, was focussed over the table itself. Several items were scattered on it. There were very heavy looking leather bound books, numerous scrolls and tablets. There were no chairs that she could see. As Erysah walked around the room in awe, she could see that the walls were lined floor to ceiling with shelves crammed with all kinds of literature. Some had books on, others had scrolls. Some even had tablets and parchments. In this amazing place was information going back probably thousands of years. A whole library full of the Vardesh's history, amazing. There wasn't much light in the room from what she could see, only the small chandelier that hung over the table, like a spotlight. The room's temperature was interesting, depending on what was stored on the shelves Erysah could swear that there was a slight variation in the air temperature there. As she wandered round the room, she began to wonder what information the keeper had found, if any. Dayton had put down the bag next to the table they were standing at.

"What have you gleaned Keeper?" He asked the strange looking man. The Keeper was almost as tall as Dayton, but from his skeletal physique and his sallow complexion you would not think he was of the same race. His hair was long and white, tied at the nape of his neck by a piece of what looked like string. She couldn't even try to guess how old he was. She remembered that Jarro wanted to be the Keeper and was hoping to train with this man after his ascension. Erysah had some idea it would be the fascination of the myriad of information stored here. The history of the Vardesh had to be closely guarded, although she didn't know how. There had been no guards that she had seen or security system. Perhaps they were invisible, able to disappear like Dayton. Or perhaps there wasn't any, one thing's for sure she would have never have found it. It looked like there was information here from the beginning of time, or perhaps it was just from when they settled in Scotland. She had never seen so many ancient documents in one place.

"Ahh, the information that you gave me was of great help. Not only was I able to find the legend of the 'Queen of the Vardesh' or 'Dragon Queen'. But I also found a prophecy which could have relevance." He indicated for us to go around to the other side of the table. As we did, he pulled out some stools for us to sit on. For a minute or two he rummaged around on the table looking for whatever he was looking for. Then he shouted. "Ah ha! Got them!" He moved things haphazardly out of the way, so he could lay everything out for them to see. The lack of respect he showed for those ancient things surprised Erysah. The only things left in view were a stone tablet, which had some kind of writing Erysah didn't understand carved onto it, a wax tablet with the same sort of writing on it and finally two scrolls, one larger than the other. The keeper was very excited by his finds and was eager to share what they contained. He began with the stone tablet. "This tablet contains a list of names, rulers of the Vardesh that lived over four thousand years ago. It speaks of each clan having a lord and then the queen being overall ruler. There were five on the council. The Dragon Queen, Head of the council. The Dragon Lord, The Wolf Lord, The Cat Lord and The Eagle Lord." As he pushed it to one side he grabbed the waxed tablet. "This is just over two thousand years ago. It tells of a great war between the Vardesh and the Avardi. The Avardi were jealous of the Vardesh's longevity. Some of the Vardesh were even able to morph into their clan creature. It was said that because they shared their bodies with another creature it extended their lives even more, maybe two or three times as long. Which meant some could live to be well over fifteen hundred years. It was said that the Queen and the Lords lived even longer than that. Maybe even twice that age, which could make it more in the region of three thousand years. The Avardi only lived for a hundred and fifty years and nothing could prevent their deaths. No matter what they tried, they eventually died." Then putting that aside, he took the larger of the two scrolls. "This one is from just under two thousand years ago. It tells of a great exodus, all the Vardesh lords are dead and 'Sherya' the Dragon Queen has told her people that she can no longer protect them. They had to scatter and find safe havens, live quietly until her return. It says she died of a broken heart when the Dragon Lord, who was her Solelae was killed in the final battle." That just left the final scroll, this was much smaller, as if it was a hand written note of some kind. Erysah had a feeling of 'déjà vu'. "This is from about eighteen hundred years ago. This is a prophecy. It reads as follows: It is said that 'Sherya the Rhysae' would return to reign her people when the time was right. She would be born of a new millennium and her rise would bring back with her, the transforms. Those who among the Vardesh who were powerful and wise to aid her." Dayton and Erysah had sat through the whole thing in total silence, not even a thought passed between them. Dayton then spoke.

"Keeper what you have told us is extremely interesting but what relevance does it have towards what is happening to Erysah." The Keeper got a piece of paper and a pencil, then looked at Erysah.

"Please write your name on the paper in capital letters." Erysah shrugged her shoulders and did as he asked.

ERYSAH

Underneath that he wrote the Dragon Queen's name.

SHERYA

Then he wrote the word rhysae underneath them.

RHYSAE

"Look at the words and tell me what can you see?" Both Erysah and Dayton looked carefully at the three of them. For a moment they didn't notice anything, then Erysah gasped.

"Oh, my God!" she exclaimed. "Are you trying to tell me that I might be the Dragon Queen!" It was then that Dayton came out of his ponderings, a realisation setting in.

"Surely Keeper this is just a coincidence?" Dayton knew that the Keeper would not jest over something so serious.

"I was uncertain until I asked your Solelil to write her name, but what is on the paper is indisputable." Erysah was stunned. You could have hit her with a wrecking ball and she wouldn't have felt it. Dayton was just as shocked by this, he desperately wanted to talk to Sollest on this matter.

"We need to return home." He said abruptly. "I must speak with Sollest." He grabbed Erysah by the hand and picked up the bag he had left on the floor beside the table.

"Yes, I agree," said Erysah.

"Very well," said the keeper and he walked towards the door, which looked much smaller on this side. As he opened the door Erysah saw that they were in the middle of the forest, or at least part way in. But she couldn't focus on that at the moment, she had other things on her mind. Like going to see Sollest herself and giving her a piece of her mind. "Farewell, friends." The Keeper said as he closed the door.

Dayton and Erysah travelled through the trees at breakneck speed. Eventually they came upon the car, still parked behind the building. Erysah didn't even want to comprehend the how's, why's and wherefore's because if she did, it would give her a headache. She already had one, she certainly didn't want another. They rode in silence on the journey back to Stone Edge. Both lost in their owns thoughts on what the Keeper had discovered. By the time they got back to the house it was about four am. As they walked through the house to the library Erysah could tell he was really angry about something. He was never normally this distant from her. By the time they got into their chamber she couldn't stand the silence any more.

"Stop!" she shouted and ground herself to a halt by digging her heels into the carpet, then she pulled back on his hand. It was almost like he had forgot that she was still attached to him. The action made Dayton snap out of the furore going on in his mind. He blinked and looked at her as if seeing her for the first time. He dropped the bag that was still in his other hand and dropped to his knees grabbing Erysah round her waist and began to sob uncontrollably. All his rage and anger came out in those tears. He wasn't even sure why he was so angry. He wasn't angry at Erysah, he adored her, she was his every breath, his life. Was he angry with Sollest? Had she somehow orchestrated all this? Was Erysah the Dragon Queen? He was now terrified for her to transcend. Would she still be Erysah or would she be a total stranger? He knew in his heart that he would rather die than lose her. Did he have the strength to let her go and take himself into the black? Could he leave her to a half life, just like Kaspir did with her mother. All this was irrelevant really, for he knew what the answer was. He did not have to think about it. In many ways he regarded himself selfish on this matter. In his heart and even deep down in his soul he knew he could never let her go, no matter what the consequences. And that thought terrified him more than any other. Erysah just stood there and stroked his hair while he released all the pent up emotions that had plagued him since talking to the Keeper. They remained that way for a long time. Eventually Erysah managed to sit on the floor and Dayton's head resting in her lap. She caressed his long silken locks and hummed a soothing tune. Before the long night was over and they fell asleep.

Getting Married

Dayton stirred on Erysah's lap raising her from her slumber. She automatically started to stroke his hair again. As he turned his head to look at her, she could see that he didn't know what to say. So she spoke first, saying the only thing that was in her heart.

"I love you." She whispered. To Dayton these words were so soft and sweet, not even honey from the bees could have been sweeter. He still could not find the words to reply, so he sat up and took her face between his hands and kissed her. Not a passionate kiss but a gentle and tender one, saying with his lips what he could not say with his voice, as it had deserted him. He felt ashamed by what had transpired when they got home. So much emotion . . . emotion he was not used to and he did not know how to handle it. When he released her and put his arms around her, he rested his head on hers she repeated her words. "I love you."

"Please do not say that Erysah. I have behaved so foolishly." Erysah sighed.

"In what way have you been foolish Dayton? You have lived for nearly five hundred years with very little emotion. Now you are overwhelmed by it. It is not easy to deal with. I have lived with a myriad of emotions all my life and can for the most part cope with it. But you . . ." Her words were gentle and tender and understanding. Dayton could not believe his good fortune, sometimes he thought that he did not deserve her. Erysah picked up on the last thought. "Never think that. I could say the same about you. But . . ." she hesitated. "But for whatever reason fate has brought us together, we will deal with it. Whether good or bad, we will share it. And I don't expect anything less or anything more than that."

Dayton got up, pulling Erysah with him and led her over to the bed and sat down. "How can you be so calm after what you have found out?"

"Dayton, what will be, will be. Nothing or no one can change that."

"But I . . ."

"Feel betrayed?" Dayton nodded. "Why?" Thinking about it he did not really know why he felt that way. She pulled him towards her and rested his head on her breast, cradling him in her tender arms. They sat there like that for a while until Erysah realised what day it was. "Oh, no, what time is it?" She asked almost in a panic. Dayton sat up perplexed by her change of demeanour.

"Nearly nine, why?"

"Oh, dam, we've overslept. We are supposed to meet Violet and Greg at nine, remember?" Dayton sat up. "How long will it take us to get to the Boars Head?"

"If we go on the bike, we can be there in ten minutes."

"Come on," she said pulling at him. "I hate being late and Violet will not be happy being kept waiting." Dayton laughed, as she continued to drag him upstairs. The weight of the previous night melted away into insignificance with Erysah's sheer panic of being late to meet with her family. Joy careened around his body. He found it hilarious that she could cope with vampires, but her family was a different prospect. Ten minutes later they were whizzing through the streets, heading towards the pub where Violet and Greg were staying. Dayton had arranged to have a meal with them, to make it a little easier to get to know each other. They walked in, hand in hand, their helmets in the other and headed straight for the lounge. In the evening it doubled up as a restaurant, especially during the holiday season. Greg and Violet were already sitting at a table in the far corner. Greg seemed to hesitate when he saw them. It looked as though he wanted to get up and give Erysah a big hug, but he was unsure about the person she was attached to. Violet just smiled. There was an almost knowing look on her face that Erysah was intrigued by. She could tell that Greg was giving Dayton the once over, however Violet was giving Dayton a more appreciative look. In his mind he spoke to her '*I feel like an exhibit, put on show, something to study.*' Erysah wanted burst out laughing but she didn't want them to know that they could communicate mentally. So she just smiled at him and told him to '*stop!*' When they got over to the table Erysah freed herself and handed her helmet to Dayton. Then went over to hug both Violet and Greg. Greg took the opportunity to whisper in her ear.

"Are you okay?"

"Yes." She whispered back. In her mind she was laughing and it made Dayton feel warm inside. Standing up she went back over to Dayton who had found a temporary home for the helmets and stood in front of him grabbing both his hands. She guided them round her waist and they went willingly. Despite the fact that his arms were protecting her, he felt like she was protecting him. "Dayton," she said looking up at him briefly. "This is Greg and his mother Violet. My two favourite people and my best friends."

"I am pleased to meet you both." He said and held out a hand to Greg. Who shook it firmly, but briefly.

"Let's not stand on formality, Erysah. You and your young man sit." Violet said. Once everyone was seated, food and drinks were ordered. "Dayton what sort of work do you do?" Erysah cringed inside at the question. A kiss came into her mind from Dayton to reassure her.

"I am a custodian or caretaker if you prefer." Which was not untrue, but not strictly true either.

"And what is it you look after?" Greg chimed in.

"There are several ancient sites in the region. I make sure that visitors respect the ruins and do not cause any damage other than what mother nature deems to inflict."

"Must be fascinating. Have you lived here long?" Violet queried.

"No, only a few years. Before that I travelled a lot."

"Here or abroad?" Greg asked.

"Both, I have had the good fortune to have visited numerous countries. I have an interest in ancient history and archaeology. So when I got this position my experience stood me in good stead." Even if Greg or Violet weren't impressed with Dayton, Erysah definitely was. She could sense that every single word that came out of his mouth was the truth. Dayton had omitted to put a time frame on things. Erysah was starting to learn that it was not the things that he said that were important, but the things that he didn't. He had not lied but had skirted around giving out any revealing knowledge about himself, virtually lying by omission. After the meal, things got down to business. Violet led the conversation, or was she just laying out how it was going to be.

"You will of course be spending tonight here Erysah. I have spoke to the landlord and have changed my room for one with twin beds. There is no way you will see the bridegroom until the ceremony tomorrow." She turned to Dayton. "You understand, don't you, young man." Dayton nodded. *'She is a formidable woman Erysah, wherever did you find her?'* he laughed into her mind. She replied, *'she was left to me by my mother.'* They both looked at each other sheepishly.

"Violet is that really necessary and can you call him Dayton, that is his name." Erysah was slightly frustrated.

"Yes, I do think it's necessary for the bride and groom not to see each other the night before they marry. It's tradition and I hold strongly with tradition. Don't you agree Dayton." She seemed to give him a knowing look.

"I cannot deny that tradition is very important and concede to your values. If we lose our traditions, we lose ourselves." *'And no I will not come to you tonight. You have to be human for them for one more day until after the ceremony. As much as I will hate not being with you in whatever way we are able, I respect Violet and her values.'* He sent a warm hug with his words. Greg was almost beside himself with glee. Although he did try to hide it, but not very well. Because Violet caught it and clipped him round the head for it.

"Ouch!" he complained, although slightly delayed. Erysah couldn't help herself and burst out laughing, followed by Dayton, Violet and finally Greg himself.

"Serves you right, gloating is unbecoming." His mother chastised. "Dayton you should say goodbye to Erysah." Dayton acknowledge the instruction and leaned over and kissed her chastely in front of her guests.

"I will see you tomorrow beloved." He stood up to go and Erysah got out of her chair putting a hand on his arm as he started to walk away. *'Is that it?'* A knowing smile lifted his face leaning down he kissed her again this time a little more thoroughly. Which made Greg gag and he coughed. Both Dayton and Erysah smiled into their kiss.

"Bye, I love you Dayton. See you tomorrow," she added in her mind, *'please don't worry, everything will be fine. I honestly believe that and if I feel that you are worrying too much I will come and seek you out.'* Dayton had no doubt that she would do exactly what she said. *'Do not worry,'* he replied. *'I have to get things ready for Garroch, Melindra and Jarro. They will be arriving soon and I am sure they will find a way to keep me occupied. We all have to get our strength up.'* She knew exactly what he meant by that. She also knew that tonight would be the very last time he would feed from another human. That thought itself was a kind of aphrodisiac, now she really couldn't wait until tomorrow night. Well the end of it anyway, when they would finally be alone. Dayton had not missed that thought and he gave her a knowing smile as he let her go and went to greet his guests.

After Dayton left she followed Greg and Violet upstairs to their rooms. Greg's was opposite Erysah and Violet's, however they all went into Violet's. Greg was itching to bombard her with questions. The major one being what the hell had happened. One minute she was there in Bittern the next she was off to Scotland and to top it all she was now getting married. He had no idea she was seeing someone, she had said nothing. He thought that they were friends and that she could talk about anything to him. But no she hid this from him and he felt hurt. When he had asked his mother, all she had said was that it was not there concern. As long as Erysah was happy that was all that mattered and she had instructed him not to say anything at all. Aggrieved as he was, he respected his mother immensely and loved Erysah like a sister. He would never do anything to ruin her special day and he was secretly very honoured that she had asked him to give her away. Weighing the two things up, giving her away was way better than being pissed off at her. So he would leave it. Violet disturbed his thoughts.

"Can you get the dress for us please, Greg?" Greg nodded and headed off to his room. He came back with a large silver box, on top of that was a smaller gold box and that was topped off with a even smaller black box. Erysah looked at Violet questioningly. Violet got a coat hanger out of the wardrobe while Greg opened the silver box. Inside was the most beautiful dress Erysah had ever seen. The bodice began with a heart shape line for the bust, nipping in at the waist and fitting over the hips. The top layer of lace was embroidered with bows and butterflies. The skirts flowed down to the ankles and out at the back forming a train attached at the back. There was a matching lace bolero jacket which covered the shoulders. As Violet hung it up Erysah wondered if it would fit her, she also thought that it was too good for her.

"Are you sure Violet? It is so beautiful." Erysah was overwhelmed by the sight of the dress. Everything was beginning to become so real.

"Yes, what is the point of keeping it in a box. I will never wear it again and it should be worn. And I have had it already lengthen to your height." Erysah couldn't believe how much trouble Violet had already gone to. She had to admit she was curious to see what was in the other two boxes. Next Greg opened the slightly smaller gold box. Violet pulled out another silver box before taking out a long veil and hanging it on another hanger. Inside the second silver box was a beautiful but simple tiara. It was silver in colour and had three rows of arches, starting with five on the bottom reducing to three and then one. Each arch was encrusted with small white stones and from each arch hung a small teardrop shaped pearl. It was breath-takingly beautiful, Erysah was lost for words. Violet left the tiara in the box. Finally it was the turn of the black box which was the size of a shoe box. Erysah assumed that it held some sort of footwear. She was right but wow what a pair of shoes. They were white satin with jewels sewn onto them in the shape of bows to match the dress.

"Now I know that we don't have the same size feet Violet, where on earth did you get these from and at such short notice?" What had Violet been up to. It was almost as if she had planned this from the very start.

"The shoes are a wedding present from Greg and I. You couldn't wear just any shoes with this dress, now could you?" Erysah had to agree, Violet was awfully good at circumnavigating questions she didn't want to answer and she had accomplished this one rather well. She didn't want to push it any further so Erysah turned to Greg and hugged him, tears welling up in her eyes.

"Thank you," she managed to choke out. "Both of you thank you," she said as she went over and hugged Violet the tears were now flowing freely. Greg handed her a handkerchief. Erysah wiped her eyes and blew her nose. She was overwhelmed by emotion. The joy, the warmth and the love that was in the room. She had never felt so happy. Violet looked over to Greg and nodded over to the door, he knew it was his cue to vamoose.

"See you tomorrow Erysah, have fun playing dress up with mother," he said grinning as he closed the door behind him. Erysah looked at Violet.

"Yes, young lady we are going to make sure that you are the most perfect bride for your groom tomorrow, so get everything off except your pants. You may have to go commando tomorrow, I know I did when I wore it." There was a glint in her eyes when she said that, as if remembering her time as a bride. Or was it how her husband had reacted when he found out that she wore nothing under the dress. She could just imagine what a passionate wedding night they must have had. Erysah stripped completely what was the point of doing things in half measures. She wasn't ashamed of her body and Violet was a woman after all. And she was family, she was her Great Aunt. Violet nodded with approval with Erysah's decision. The dress had a satin lining and was so smooth against her skin. After Violet finished fastening the button up back she came around the front to have a look. Erysah's red hair flowed around her shoulders like a cape. Violet decided that the bolero wasn't necessary. If she did Erysah's hair so most of it was down it would be perfect. She made Erysah perch on the edge of the bed so she could try on the tiara. Violet picked up Erysah's hair here and there and played with the arrangement until she was happy with it. Then she got the shoes out, thankfully they fitted perfectly. As Erysah displayed herself to Violet she could see the tears forming in the old woman's eyes. She looked like a proud mother.

"Wait here," she said to Erysah, her voice tight with emotion. She went out into the corridor and shouted for Greg to come back into the room. "I want to see Greg's reaction when he sees you. It won't do any harm to have a man's point of view." Violet had a mischievous look on her face. Violet positioned Erysah right in the line of the doorway, so that she would be the first thing Greg would see. There was a knock on the door. "Come in Greg," Violet shouted. When the door opened and he saw Erysah, he froze. His eyes widen and his mouth gaped. He stopped in mid word.

"Wha . . ." Violet went over to him and took the door out of his hand so she could close it.

"I think we got the reaction we wanted, don't you Erysah?" She said smiling. Erysah nodded and started to chuckle.

"Wow, Erysah is that really you.?"

"Of course, it's her silly boy. She looks wonderful don't you think?" Greg focussed on his mother.

"Wonderful is an understatement mother, she looks amazing. Your guy is going to flip when he sees you." Greg would have been jealous of Dayton but he didn't think of Erysah in that way, she was more like a sister to him. He just couldn't help the protective streak he had for her and if that guy of hers ever hurt her, then he had better beware.

"Good, that's the whole idea, Greg. Now go, I'm tired and we have had a long journey and it's very late. We need to look fresh for tomorrow and I don't want to rush." Greg nodded and waved goodnight to them both and left the room for the second time.

Dayton arrived at the manor house just in time to see a big black Jaguar pull up outside the front door. He stopped the bike next to the driver side window. The person inside rolled it down and Jarro looked at Dayton. Dayton flipped his visor up so he could talk to him.

"Do you want to follow me, then you can put the car in the garage out of the way." Jarro nodded. He followed Dayton around the back and into one of the garages. He pulled up next to the Aston Martin. Once Jarro cut the engine Garroch got out and helped Melindra out, followed by Jarro.

"Good evening Guardian. Where is Erysah?" Melindra asked.

"She is staying with her friends." He did not want to go into the complications of the fact that her friends were also her family. "And please all of you call me Dayton while you are here. Because we do not want Erysah's human friends to get suspicious."

"Very well, but I do not feel comfortable doing this, especially when we are so close to the temple." Garroch said.

"I shall enjoy that," said Jarro. "I hate all this formality." Melindra gave her son a disapproving look, he just gave his mother his best smile.

"Do you have luggage?" Dayton asked. Garroch nodded and went to the boot of the Jaguar and pulled out two suitcases, one bigger than the other. He gave the smaller one to Jarro and he kept the big one for himself. "Follow me and I will show you to your rooms. They are above ground but they are all secure. This house has been used for centuries to hold various clan members."

"Dayton," Melindra said. "You forget Garroch and I have been here before. We stayed here when it was . . ." Garroch glared at his Solelil.

"Yes, of course you have. When it was Kaspir and Anya's ritual. Both Garroch and Melindra nodded solemnly. They followed him into the main house. "Would you like the same rooms or do you just want any?"

"It does not matter, any will do." Dayton nodded and gave them the first room on the left from the stairs, while he gave Jarro the one next to theirs.

"Tomorrow the others will come for the ritual and stay over until it is safe for them to travel again."

"Who is attending?" Garroch asked. Melindra wondered if she had met any of them before. She knew that there would be representatives from each clan, as there had been last time.

"Xron and Benne from the wolf clan, Sawh and Lavender from the eagle clan and Zeke and Yanska from the cat clan." Dayton stated as if it was a shopping list.

"Good choices, will Xron and Benne bring Jasmine with them? It would be good company for Jarro while the ritual is happening." Jarro cringed. "Do not worry Jarro she is too old for you. She will be due to find her Solelae next year. I feel sorry for our female children, it is much harder for them to find their mates." Dayton had to agree, it was usually the male that searched for their Solelil. They lost many females that way, when they ended their 'year of yearning'.

"When you are ready come to the library and we will go and feed. Jarro you are welcome to explore the house but do not leave, because you will not be able to get back in unless I am with you." Jarro nodded his understanding. All the properties owned by the Vardesh had a unique security system, it was tied into the biology of the current occupant, almost like a DNA scan. But because the Dragon Temple was also there, there had to be extra measures in place. Dayton headed back down the stairs and was reading one of his many books when Garroch and Melindra came into the library. Melindra had taken to wearing more flowing dresses as she increased in size and with the news of twins she seemed to have swelled even more since her had last seen her. It would not be long before she would spend most of her time resting. Only getting up to go out and feed and then eventually Garroch would have to bring her what she needed. Putting down the book he stood. "We will have to go in the Jag because I do not want to feed to close to home tonight. I hope you do not mind."

"No, that makes perfect sense." Garroch said. "Where do you think we should go?"

"We could go to Aberdeen, it will only take an hour or so to get there, we could be back in plenty of time to prepare for tomorrow."

"Agreed. Do you wish to drive?" Dayton held his hands up in confession.

"I can only drive automatics. I could never get on with the gears." Garroch found it slightly amusing but raised only a faint smile.

"I will drive then, will you sit in the back with Melindra?"

"Yes, of course, if that is what you wish."

Down in the garage the three of them got into the Jag and headed north on the main road out of Stone Edge. While in the car Dayton received bits of feelings from Erysah. It was obvious she was feeling strong emotions. There was awe and wonder, love and joy. It made him smile, it also made him wonder what they were up to. And what Violet had planned for tomorrow. He had the distinct impression she was not a person to be unprepared. He was curious, but he had made a promise to keep to the tradition and he intended to honour it. He wanted the time to pass quickly so he could be with his beloved Erysah again. Dayton hardly noticed the journey, his thoughts on his bride. That felt very strange, thinking in human terms. It made him smile. Melindra brought him out of his reflection.

"Why are you smiling?" Melindra asked

"I was thinking about Erysah and tomorrow."

"Were you thinking about the wedding or the ritual?"

"I was thinking about what her and her friends might be up to. Violet gave the impression she had been prepared long ago for the day that Erysah got married."

"Oh, why?" Melindra was wondering about these people.

"She has only a son and thinks of Erysah as a daughter."

"I see, they must be very close then." Melindra tried not to pry but she could not help herself, she was a female after all.

"Yes." He debated whether to tell Melindra or not. Would it make any difference? Probably not. "Violet is actually Erysah's Great Aunt and her son is Erysah's cousin. It is her cousin Greg who is giving her away tomorrow. I would ask that you not mention your knowledge of this as Greg is unaware of his true relationship with Erysah." Melindra nodded.

"This Violet must be a formidable female."

"Yes, I definitely get that impression. She also seems to have a hidden knowledge which is disconcerting." Dayton confessed.

"A hidden knowledge of what?" Melindra was intrigued.

"That is it, I am not sure. And it worries me."

"Surely you do not think she knows about the Vardesh?" Melindra was certain that it was something else. Garroch looked briefly at the two of them in the back of the car, taking in all that was said. From what Dayton had said he too was beginning to have a few concerns.

"I do not know Melindra. I cannot seem to get a lead on anything."

"I would not worry about it, Dayton. You need to concentrate on tomorrow." Changing the subject she asked about Sollest. "Has Sollest given you and Erysah's your robes yet?" Dayton shook his head.

"I have to see her one hour before the ritual. I presume we will get our robes then." Melindra nodded.

"Yes, that sounds about right. Sollest never changes anything unless she wants to." Dayton wondered about that statement. He wondered how much change was going to happen if the keeper was right and Erysah was the dragon queen.

Garroch pulled into a supermarket car park, he went to the farthest corner. Away from prying eyes they could start their search for nourishment. Normally Garroch and Melindra would feed each other but because she was pregnant, Melindra needed extra blood to supplement her young, that was the only reason that Garroch and Melindra were out. Thankfully they only had to venture out about once a week, but that would get more frequent the further on Melindra got. Dayton would be glad that tonight was going to be his last time for a long time. Only if he and Erysah had offspring would they both have to feed off humans. About two streets away there was a night club, people were cueing up to gain entrance. The three of them attached themselves to the end and began talking to some of the girls standing just in front of them. By the time they were half way to the door they had had their fill and left. The journey back was very quiet, everyone seemed lost in their own thoughts. Melindra was thinking about the conversation she had had with Dayton on the way to Aberdeen. Garroch was thinking how long it would be before Melindra would not be able to go out, especially as she was carrying twins. And Dayton was thinking about Erysah and the events that would be happening in less than fifteen hours time.

Violet woke Erysah up at two in the afternoon, she had only been up herself since twelve. She had had a very late breakfast with Greg. Finalising a few things with him, giving Greg one or two extra jobs to do before the wedding. Violet had a bowl of porridge and some cheesy scrambled eggs with toast. A glass of orange juice and a pot of tea on a tray. As soon as Erysah smelt the food she was wide awake.

"Is there anything you can't do? You must have the landlord wrapped around your little finger, to have gotten all this." Erysah laughed.

"Come on eat Erysah, you have a lot to do this afternoon. There are only six hours left and I want you looking your most stunning." Violet was in a serious mood, so Erysah just nodded. She couldn't managed to eat all the food as her stomach was all knotted up, but she did her best and ate a little bit of everything. Half an hour later she was in the bathroom showering, when she went back into Violet's room there was a strange woman with her. She had a big bag and a folding chair. Still wrapped in a towel Erysah was made to sit in the chair. Violet must have had this planned for a very long time because despite the short notice and the fact that they were in Scotland didn't make any difference. She seemed to have everything organised with military efficiency. Erysah realised that one of the many jobs Greg had to do was to find a hairdresser. She didn't know who was more resourceful, the thought of Greg going into different hair salons asking for a hairdresser made her smile. She would have loved to have been a fly on the wall for that. Violet got out the tiara and gave it to the woman, whose name she didn't know. By the time the hairdresser had finished about two hours later, her long red tresses were arranged in large ringlets and the tiara was incorporated into the hairstyle. Some of her hair was up to hold in the tiara in place, whilst the rest hung down either over her shoulders or down her back. Her hair shone like fiery lava flowing out of a volcano. The hairdresser also did her makeup. She actually put very little on. Just enough to accentuate her features, making Erysah look like the natural beauty that she was. By the time she was finished it was well past half past six, only a little over an hour left before she was due at the church. After the hairdresser left Violet helped apply a layer of body butter on making her skin feel extra soft and smell like coconut. Suddenly there was a knock at the door and Violet and Erysah looked at each other questioningly. Both shook their heads, as if to say they were not expecting anyone. Violet went to the door and opened it slightly so she could peer through it. On the other side was a young man she didn't recognise.

"Yes, can I help you?" puzzled by his appearance.

"Are you Violet?" the man asked. Erysah recognised the voice.

"Jarro," she shouted. "Is that you?" Violet looked at Erysah.

"Yes, Erysah." He said through the gap in the door, desperately trying not to peek. "I am here to take you and your friends to the church."

"You are a bit early young man." Violet chastised.

"Yes I know, but I did not want you to worry about the transport. I will wait downstairs in the lounge until you are ready to go." Jarro announced.

"Very well young man, thank you for being so considerate, Greg will be back soon and he will wait with you." Violet admired the young man's diligence.

"See you soon, Erysah." Jarro shouted as the door closed.

"Right, young lady we have about forty five minutes to get you into that dress and finish everything off." Violet stated with determination. Twenty minutes later Erysah was in the dress. "Now let's see," Violet said to no one in particular. "Something borrowed, hmm . . . Something blue," she went to her suitcase and pulled out a little blue garter. "Right leg up, please," she said as she slid the garter just past Erysah's knee. "Something old," she went to her handbag and pulled out a velvet box about six inches square. Inside was a teardrop necklace on a plain gold chain. "This was my mother's necklace it's well over a hundred years old. You can borrow this, as well as it being old. I am leaving this to Greg, It was given to Greg's Grandmother by his Grandfather. And finally something new, well that's the shoes. Well, that's everything I think. You're as ready as you will ever be." Erysah wasn't so sure, now that she was all dressed up, her nerves were starting. Violet had changed into a lemon skirt which was accompanied by a fitted lilac jacket, topped off with a lilac hat with pale yellow flowers on it. To complete the ensemble were lilac shoes. There was another knock at the door and Greg's voice came through from the other side.

"It's time to go, may I come in. I have the other thing that you wanted me to get, mother."

"Yes, yes Greg. Please come in and bring it with you." A moment later the door opened and although Greg had seen her briefly last night in the dress, he was not prepared for the beauty that was standing in the room.

"Erysah . . . you're . . .

"Greg!" his mother snapped.

"Sorry mother." He said sheepishly and produced a beautiful teardrop shaped bouquet comprising of white lilies and yellow roses. Erysah was astounded and took the flowers. Violet went to the door and looked at

Greg. He was dressed in a grey marl morning suit but without the top hat.

"Bring Erysah down now, just follow me, okay. Do you think you could manage not to drool on her. It would be better if you looked where you were going." His mother chided. Greg nodded and held out his arm for Erysah, she rested her hand in the crook of his elbow. As they walked through the corridor, doors began to open of their own voliation as people looked out at the vision passing by. Erysah just concentrated on not tripping on the dress which flowed along the floor. Going down the stairs she could see the landlord, his wife and the hairdresser waiting to see her. She could see the awe on their faces and then Jarro appeared and his chin almost hit the floor. Erysah was the typical blushing bride by the time she got into the lounge. Jarro was suddenly snapped out of his trance when Violet tapped his arm. He was wearing a black suit and tie, with a crisp white shirt, he very much looked the part of a chauffeur.

"The car young man, if you please?" Jarro nodded and went out to the Jag and opened the door for Erysah to climb in. Violet got in the back with Erysah and Greg got in the front with Jarro. The trip to the church took less than ten minutes.

Dayton had been at the church for twenty minutes, he was wearing a suit similar to Greg's. Both Garroch and Melindra had come with him. Garroch had agreed to be his best man, he was wearing a black suit like his son and was standing next to him on the pew at the front. Melindra sat just behind them in a jade green gown which tucked in just under her breasts and flowed generously over her bump. Jarro had been gone for a while because he was being the bride's chauffeur. He had wanted Violet to know that he had made sure their transport was there for them in plenty of time. For some reason Dayton was starting to get anxious and he did not know why. He did not understand why this was so important to him? He had no idea, it was nothing to do with his culture or heritage, it just was. Father Johnston had come out about ten minutes ago preparing for the ceremony. He had on his wedding robes and when he had finished he stood talking to the three occupants of his church. Eventually the church door opened and in walked Violet and Jarro. Violet's arm was nestled in the crook of his elbow. Jarro felt rather strange about it, but Violet had insisted. Funny Jarro felt a sense of pride as he walked the Great Aunt of the bride down the aisle. They walked up to the front of the church, but where was Erysah? Dayton began to panic. Violet saw the look on his face and smiled.

"Don't worry, she's here. I just told them to wait a few minutes before coming in. I wanted to be in place so I could watch her walk down the aisle." Dayton nodded and visibly relaxed. Before another word could be spoken Greg and Erysah came through the doors. When he caught sight of her, his legs gave way and Garroch had to hold him up. As Erysah walked up the aisle she looked like an ethereal beauty, beyond anything he could imagine. Her skin glowed as her dress hugged her body, showing every curve. As she came down the aisle towards him she seemed to glide along, as if on a cushion of air. Dayton was having problems trying to get enough air in his lungs and felt as though he would pass out any second. As she got closer his vision began to blur. He had to blink several times, so he could keep her in focus. Eventually she was standing beside him and Greg put her hand into his. '*Yes*,' he thought. '*She is real.*' Father Johnston smiled at them and Greg went to stand next to his mother. Father Johnston then began the wedding service.

"We are gathered here to witness the marriage between Dayton and Erysah," he began. Most of the ceremony went by in a blur, Dayton was on automatic pilot. Just following the cues that the priest gave him. Before he knew it they were at the most important part. "Will you Dayton, take Erysah to be your lawful wedded wife?" Dayton looked at the vision in front of him.

"I will," he choked out and nodded.

"Will you Erysah, take Dayton as your lawful wedded husband?" She looked at Dayton, who seemed so awestruck by her and said.

"I will." Her voice a soft whisper.

"The rings please?" he said to Garroch. Garroch produced two amazing wedding rings, both had a dragon encircling it. One had a emerald for the eye, the other had a blue diamond. After giving and receiving rings the priest then said. "I now pronounce you, husband and wife. You may kiss the bride."

Dayton lifted the veil with shaky hands, Erysah smiled at him her eyes sparkling with her own tears. He leaned towards her, when their lips met it was the most sweetest kiss he had ever had. Everything that had happened before seemed to pale into insignificance. She was his and he was hers. Whatever happened now there was no going back. Dayton decided Erysah had been right, what will be . . . will be. As long as they had each other, nothing else mattered.

THE RITUAL

Everyone including Father Johnston went back to the manor house for a buffet supper which Jarro had prepared before leaving to pick up Erysah. Everything was set up in the dining room. The long mahogany table was covered in a white cloth which was laid out with salvers full of pastries and sandwiches. There were pitchers of juice and the was a coffee machine on a sideboard. Small talk battered around the room, both Dayton and Erysah tried to be good hosts and circled the small group of people. Eventually around ten o'clock Father Johnston announced that he was returning back to Stone Edge and he asked if Violet and Greg wanted a lift, which they graciously accepted. Dayton thanked the priest for everything and vowed to go and see him shortly.

"I expect you to bring Erysah with you." That was not a request, that was exactly what he did expect. Dayton nodded and bid him farewell. Meanwhile Erysah was saying her goodbyes to Greg and Violet.

"When are you going back to Southampton?" Erysah inquired.

"Not for a few days, we thought that we would have a bit of a holiday while we were here, using Stone Edge as a base. Are you going away on a honey moon?" Violet asked.

"I must confess we have not even thought about one. Maybe later." Violet nodded and hugged Erysah and headed for the priest's car. Greg held her hands and looked at her.

"I shall miss you, the bar will not be the same without you. Oh, and by the way you look absolutely stunning, Dayton is a very lucky man." Erysah blushed at his words, she let go of his hands and hugged him.

"We will see each other before you go home." She said emphatically, Greg gave her a little salute and followed his mother to the car. Dayton came up behind her and slid his arm around her waist and waved with Erysah to the departing occupants in the priest's battered blue Astra. Guiding her inside he closed the door.

"Well Mrs G'nard we have some other preparations to finalise because we will be having some more guests within the hour."

"What preparations and what guests?" She hadn't forgotten about the ritual but it had slipped her mind briefly with the wedding and everything. And she hadn't realised that there would be other people at the ritual. She started to feel nervous all over again. Dayton picked up on this through the mesh.

"We have a little time for ourselves, how about I help you out of that wonderful dress." A mischievous grin crossed his face briefly.

"What about Garroch, Melindra and Jarro?" Erysah knew it was a pointless question but she had to ask it anyway.

"They have their own ways to occupy themselves." He laughed and lifted her off her feet. As Dayton walked through the house, she didn't see anyone else. So she assumed they had gone to their rooms. Once they were in their private chambers Dayton put Erysah back on her feet. He stood there and looked at his wife, it was a strange sensation, but it made him feel warm inside. Erysah saw the love shining in his eyes and all she could do was stare at him, her husband. Her heart was full and her soul appeased. She could tell Dayton wanted to tell her something but all she wanted to do was kiss him. She took a step towards him to do just that but he stopped her. "When you came through the church doors, you took my breath away. I have never seen anything so beautiful. Garroch had to hold me up." He confessed. Erysah's eyes went wide.

"Really?" Dayton nodded.

"Really. You looked like an angel. An ethereal beauty gliding towards me. To use a human turn of phrase 'I thought I had died and gone to heaven.'"

Erysah laughed at his silly confessions but they touched her heart. "I want to explore every inch of you in that amazing dress. I have to say I am very impressed with Violet. She is an amazing woman."

"Yes, she is isn't she." Erysah had to agree with him. Her heart was so full of happiness, she now had Dayton to herself. Nobody could take him away from her.

"Will you stand for me and let me explore you, as if you have never been explored before?" Dayton stared straight into her emerald eyes. Erysah suddenly felt very shy and gave a small nod. Dayton circled her, gently touching her hair. Standing behind her he carefully undid it and released the tiara, putting it to one side. He swept aside some of the flame red ringlets that bathed her shoulder. His touch was gentle and set her skin tingling. He brushed his lips into the crook of her neck and along her shoulder. His hand stroked down her arm and circled her wrist. Raising her hand he kissed the rings that he had put on her finger and stroked the tattoo, then he let her hand go. His hands caressed each side of the bodice, from the waist down going over the curve of her hips. Then he travelled back up again and moved his hands forward over her stomach. Erysah leaned into him, his hands then started to travel north to her other curves. He slowly caressed her breasts through the fine lace and satin. Her low moans seem to echo in the room as she pressed herself even further into him. Releasing her breasts his hands slid to her arms, brushing gently upwards he rubbed her shoulders. Separating her hair at the back he positioned it over the front of her shoulders. He stroked her neck with his fingers making Erysah shudder. Her breathing increased slightly in anticipation. His fingers gently traced along the bare skin on her back. She was sure he was writing something but couldn't make it out. He then traced the edge of her dress. Then pop, a button was undone, it was followed by a whisper of a kiss on a shoulder. Pop, another button came undone followed by another kiss on the other shoulder. Erysah's heart began to beat faster, matched by her breathing. Pop, kiss, pop, kiss. He continued in this manner until he was at her waist.

"Hold your dress beloved, I do not want it revealing you just yet." Erysah crossed her arms around her waist to keep the dress in place. Dayton continued his previous activity. Eventually all the buttons were undone, it was then he saw that she was completely naked beneath the dress. Dayton groaned as he stroked a finger down her naked spine, all the way to the cleavage of her buttocks. Erysah shuddered and moaned with pleasure. Suddenly the clock struck eleven. '*Damn,*' Dayton thought. He had to go and get the robes from Sollest. Dayton placed his hands on Erysah's shoulders and turned her round.

"Erysah," he said sheepishly.

"What's the matter?" Erysah was slightly confused.

"We have to stop for now."

"What! Why?" He had got her blood raging and she was wet with anticipation. Now he was saying that they had to stop, she couldn't believe it.

"I have to go to the temple and fetch the ceremonial robes from Sollest. Our guests will have started to arrive for the ritual." Dayton had not purposely kept her busy to take her mind off it. It was also a distraction for him, he was still really worried about what might happen. Erysah picked up on his thoughts and a kind of serenity past through her from some unknown source.

"I wish you'd stop worrying, everything will be fine. Have you got to go far to the temple?" Why was she so calm, she should have been terrified, but she wasn't.

"No, but promise me you will not follow me." Dayton knew it was a lot to ask. Erysah started laughing. "What is so funny?"

"Well, I am not exactly in a position to go anywhere, am I?" She was still hanging onto her dress, which was quite heavy. She didn't just want to drop it, she needed help in and out of it. "I'll just sit on the bed and wait for you, is that okay?" Dayton nodded and smiled. Helping her onto the bed he made sure that she was completely in the middle before touching the secret button. Dayton kissed her as he pressed it and the bed began to move back. Erysah squealed in surprise and Dayton laughed.

"Do not worry, I will not be long."

"Do you mean to say we have been above the temple all this time." Dayton nodded.

"I am her guardian after all." He kissed her again and went down the stairs. Erysah leaned forward and watched him disappear. When he got to the temple Sollest and her sisters were waiting for him. Each one held something in their hands.

"The gold ones are for Erysah and the silver ones are for you." Sollest said. "Melindra will have to prepare Erysah, while Garroch will have to prepare you, as is proper." Dayton just nodded and took the packages. "Return to the temple with everyone on the stroke of midnight." Dayton nodded again and left. Ten minutes later he was back upstairs and closing the entrance. It was not until he reached his chamber that he realised the Sollest had called Erysah by her given name and not by what she was, his Solelil. He would have contemplated her words longer but Erysah spoke.

"What have you got there?" Erysah asked as he came back up.

"We will find out very shortly. Now I need to fasten your dress back up because we have to go upstairs and speak to Garroch and Melindra." Dayton closed the temple entrance, the bed sliding back into its original place. Erysah sighed and nodded. It didn't take him long to button up her dress, compared to how much time he took to undo it. Fifteen minutes later they were knocking on Garroch and Melindra's door. Garroch open it.

"What is the matter?" he asked.

"May we come in?" Garroch opened the door fully to let them enter. "Has anyone else arrived yet?" Dayton asked.

"Yes, Jarro is greeting everyone for us. I had a feeling we would be needed for something else. Xron and Benne have arrived with Jasmine, which will be great because she can stay with Jarro during the ritual." Dayton nodded in agreement.

"Good. Melindra you need to help Erysah. Garroch we need to go into Jarro's room and you have to prepare me."

"We thought as much," Melindra said. "We had to do it for . . ."

"You can say their names you know, it won't offend." Erysah piped up. "Dayton which ones are mine?" He handed Melindra the gold packages and Garroch the silver ones.

"I have just got to go and see Jarro and let him know where the others have to meet us and what time. Then I will meet you in Jarro's room." He said to Garroch, he gave Erysah a quick kiss. "See you soon, Solelil." Erysah smiled and nodded. Melindra shooed Garroch out the door after Dayton. Melindra put the packages on the bed and carefully unwrapped them.

"What are they?" Erysah asked.

"Your ceremonial robes and jewels." Melindra continued. "Each individual has their own unique set that is made by the 'Sisters of the Phoenix'."

"Sisters of the Phoenix?" Erysah enquired.

"They are the oldest of our race, they live beyond the veil and only come into this realm on rare occasions. They only age in this realm, no one actually knows how long they have existed. They have been our guidance for a very long time."

"Oh!," Erysah was surprised. "Melindra, if you don't mind, can I ask you what my mother wore?" Her curiosity had gotten the better of her and she couldn't resist asking the question.

"I am sorry but I am not permitted to give you that information. It is an honour to be asked to help in a transcendence ritual, each one is sacred." Melindra was saddened at the memory of the last one she attended. Erysah nodded feeling a little disappointed.

"I am sorry I didn't mean to put you in an awkward position." She now felt guilty for asking.

"Do not worry Erysah, it was only natural that you ask that question, I just wish I was able to answer it." Melindra hugged Erysah. Once again they had that communication between each other and the babies. They both smiled. "Come on, we have only twenty minutes to be down in the library." Melindra finished unwrapping the packages and froze when she saw what was in them. The memory of Erysah's mother came into her mind, the robes were identical to Anya's and she had a feeling Dayton's would be the same as Kaspir's. Sollest must have known they wouldn'[t complete the ritual and that these robes were not meant for them but for Dayton and Erysah. Never in their history had a transcendent pair have the same robes as someone else. The sisters endeavored to make them as unique as the individual. What this meant she had no idea, but it made her even more nervous about attending.

"Are you alright, Melindra?" Erysah asked when she saw her reaction. Melindra blinked and focussed on the contents. As she held up the golden material it shimmered in the light. Erysah was stunned, she also wondered how she was supposed to wear it. Melindra lay it on the bed. Next she unwrapped the other package, inside it were two small gold clasps. A woven belt of gold, two armlets with coiling dragons on them and a golden torque with a dragon on one side and a phoenix on the other. They had been concealed in a green hooded cloak.

"Erysah you will have to be naked under you robe." Melindra said solemnly.

"No problem," Erysah laughed. "I am already naked under here." Melindra smiled at her and signalled her to turn around so she could undo her dress. Five minutes later Erysah was standing naked, her back to Melindra. She felt the gossamer material flow over her skin. It was then she realised there was a slit in the material for her head. Melindra started to gather the material at the shoulders and place one of the dragon clasps on it to hold the material together. She did the same with the other side, two straps were formed. There was now a V at the front and the back. Melindra picked up the golden belt and started to arrange the material to cover her breasts, taking it to the sides to cover her hips but right to the back. The belt was fastened at the back under the rest of the material that hung free at the back. Erysah felt a little exposed. Melindra then placed the armlets on her upper arms and the torque around her neck. Finally she went back to the bed a put a hooded cape around her. Erysah sighed in relief, the cape was emerald green with a gold lining. On her feet Melindra put on a pair of golden sandals that laced up her calves. Melindra pulled Erysah's hair forward and raised the hood. Her red hair flowed out the sides like the breath of a dragon against the green.

"You are ready and it is time to go to the temple." Melindra smiled reassuringly at Erysah. "This is your time, Erysah. Come to us and be who you are to be." Erysah was slightly confused by Melindra's words but she nodded and walked with her to the library. She had heard those words before but at that moment she couldn't remember who had said them or when she had heard them.

When they got there, the room was full of people she didn't know and she felt very nervous. There were three other couples and another person in a light blue cloak with the hood up. She could only assume that it was Dayton. On the desk were a number of black cloaks, the other occupants put them on raising the hoods. Everyone else seemed to be dressed in their normal clothes and she couldn't understand why. Garroch went over to the fire place and slid his fingers behind the right side, near the top. The fire place began to move out and slide to the left revealing a torch lit corridor. The four men gathered around Dayton and the four women around Erysah, like an honour guard. The procession began to make its way down into the sacred temple. The journey didn't last very long, only a matter of minutes. Erysah was too nervous to look around, she followed the other figures. All too soon they were in the temple. As they approached the pedestal the robed figures separated and left Dayton and Erysah standing next to each other. A veil of mist descended and through it stepped four beautiful women with white gold hair twisted into chignons, dressed as Erysah was but in white. Each one wore armlets, on their left arm were depicted phoenixes and on the right there was a different depiction altogether. One had a dragon, another a wolf, the third a cat and the last one an eagle. Their hair seemed to be held by a golden comb which also held the image of a phoenix. The woman with the dragon on her right arm stepped forward and spoke to everyone.

"Who brings these two for the transcendent ritual?" Garroch lowered his hood.

"I Garroch of the Dragon Clan bring 'The Guardian'." Then Melindra lowered her hood.

"I Melindra, Solelil to Garroch of the Dragon Clan bring Erysah, Solelil to 'The Guardian'."

"Sisters prepare them." Erysah could only assume that it was Sollest who was speaking. Two of the women in white lowered their hoods and removed their capes. A slight shiver passed over Erysah as the coolness of the air hit her skin. The third woman bound Erysah's left hand to Dayton's right. Erysah wanted to look at him but she was afraid that it would be against the ritual. Once bound Sollest put a chalice on top of the pedestal. It too had images on it of a dragon, a wolf, a cat, an eagle and also a phoenix. Sollest then spoke again.

"Turn and face one another." Erysah was grateful to see his face at last. To her relief he was smiling, she returned the smile. Sollest touched Dayton's head briefly, just enough time for him to receive the ritual words. For the first time since him being made guardian Sollest spoke his name. "Dayton of the Dragon Clan, you will recite the ritual words which your Solelil will repeat." Dayton understood and nodded. Then Dayton began the ritual.

My mind is your mind.

My heart is your heart.

My body is your body.

My soul is your soul.

My breath is your breath.

After he and Erysah had spoken these words he leaned in and kissed her. Erysah thought it was over.

Then Sollest raised their free hands over the chalice and made Dayton hold the back of Erysah's hand, so their wrists were exposed. She took the comb out from her hair and sliced into both their wrists, Erysah flinched. Bleeding them into the chalice. Seconds later these wrists were bound together, cut to cut, mixing their blood. Sollest then sliced her own wrist adding her blood to the chalice. Using the comb she stirred the mixture of bloods. Then Dayton said.

My blood is your blood.

Sollest picked up the chalice and handed it to Dayton. With their bounds hands he took the chalice from her and drank deeply, he then offered it to Erysah. Erysah repeated his words, took a deep breath and then drank the liquid in the chalice. Erysah was surprised, it was not what she had expected it to taste like. It was warm and spicy with a hint of sweetness. Sollest and her sisters then stepped back towards the edge of the veil. The others in the room stepped back against the walls. Suddenly there was a blinding flash of light which made everyone shield their eyes. A second later instead of Dayton and Erysah there were two magnificent dragons filling the entire space, so much so there was little room to manoeuvre. One of pure gold with black claws and emerald green eyes and the other red with blue fronds, claws and ice blue eyes. They both gave an almighty roar that echoed around the temple. The onlookers froze and Sollest smiled knowingly. All her efforts had come to fruition. It had taken her nearly a thousand years of planning and preparation to get here. Now the prophecy was realised and the Vardesh could again grow strong.

The dragons looked at each other when they had heard the roars. They too froze. Thought's flooded their minds, *'Erysah?'*, *'Dayton?'*. Neither of them were terrified by the sight of each other, just curious. Each of them bowed their heads once as if to answer their inquiries. Then another flash of light and the two of them reappeared unbound, still staring at each other. Sollest and the sisters bowed low towards them.

"Majesty," she said to Erysah. "It is good to have you back. Much has happened since you were last with us. Lord G'nard," she said to Dayton. "You are now head of the Dragon Clan, as is your birthright. For you are descended from the Dragon Lords of old." Sollest then turned to those who were standing at the back of the temple. "Behold the queen and her lord have returned to us. Soon all our lords will return and once again the Vardesh will have coherence. For too long we have been without leadership, now we can be a true people again." Although Erysah didn't feel any different, she knew she was. She also knew that she had knowledge of the Vardesh that had been locked away inside until it was released during her transcendence. Erysah held onto Dayton's hand and turned to look at the witnesses. She looked at Dayton and smiled, he nodded back.

"I may be your queen but until my council return we must be cautious. As I have awakened, I am sure the Avardi will soon be aware of my return. Also I am not the same queen of old. I still hold all the characteristics of my pre-transcendent persona and will conduct myself as is prudent for this day and age. With the guidance of my Solelae, Lord G'nard and others I will see us through this difficult transition. It will be up to you to inform your clans of our return and remind them to be more vigilant from now on." Erysah was highly surprised at herself, she was battling with being the ancient queen and herself. "I would ask one final thing before you return to your rooms." This time she spoke to Dayton. "Please present to me those who have come to witness our transcendence." Her tone was soft, just like his Erysah and he knew she was not totally lost, just trying to find a balance. He had been terrified that he would lose her completely. But he had also transcended into the Dragon Lord, just as Erysah had become queen. Even though he himself was having a similar struggle, it was not as bad because he was already Vardesh. He had just been promoted in a way and gained extra knowledge that was his forefathers. He nodded and then looked towards the others and beckoned them forward. The black cloaked figures moved cautiously towards Dayton and Erysah, standing in a semi circle so the pair of them could see them all. Dayton hesitated and asked Erysah through the mesh, '*how shall I introduce them to you?*' Erysah smiled at him and replied, '*how about Erysah may I present to you . . .*' she was laughing in his mind. '*I may be queen but I am still Erysah and always will be. I do not want my reign to be stuffy and staid.*' She could see the relief on his face, he was grateful that his Erysah still remained. Although both of them would have major issues to deal with, but at least they could do that together. Dayton beckoned the first couple towards them.

"Erysah, may I introduce Zeke and Yanska from the Cat Clan." Both of them bowed and said.

"Majesty, it is an honour to have been privileged to witness your return."

"Thank you for attending, I wish for you to be my liaisons with your clan until your lord returns. And even when he does I will instruct him to use you as his advisors." They bowed once more.

"Thank you majesty, we are honoured." Erysah sighed inwardly. The bowing was already doing her head in, but she continued.

"Zeke and Yanska of the Cat Clan whilst we are in private and not amongst the rest of our people, I am granting you a special privilege. You are not to bow to me and please do not call me majesty, I find it annoying." She laughed and looked at Dayton who couldn't help but have a big grin on his face.

"Thank you, err . . ." They were stunned, it was hard to resist tradition. And they were unsure as to what to call her. Erysah started laughing.

"When we are in private you may call me Erysah or if you feel better Queen Erysah, will that suffice?" Both of them seem to relax.

"Yes Queen Erysah." She had a feeling that they would choose that, that was the reason she had added it. They now retreated and joined the others. Dayton then beckoned the next couple.

"Erysah, may I present to you Sawh and Lavender of the Eagle Clan." They bowed automatically. Erysah sighed and tried not to roll her eyes at them. She supposed she would have to get used to it eventually.

"Please, no more bowing. Sawh and Lavender I would bestow the same privileges on you as I have Zeke and Yanska."

"We would be honoured Queen Erysah, it would an honour to serve you." Instead of bowing they nodded their heads once and rejoined the others.

The final couple came forward. Erysah caught the last two words and was about to say something when Dayton spoke again.

"Erysah, may I present Xron and Benne of the Wolf Clan." This time they both just bowed their heads briefly in a nod. Erysah could handle that.

"Ah, yes. You have a daughter, do you not?" They looked at each other in surprise. Erysah laughed and asked Dayton to explain via their mesh. He was happy to oblige.

"Do not be surprised Erysah has the gift of foresight and she knew that you brought her with you." Dayton explained.

"I wish to bestow the same privileges on you, as I have the others. Oh, yes and as for your daughter she has got a bigger part to play in the near future. As yet, I am unable to ascertain what. But rest assured we will not lose her." Benne looked at her Solelae, tears sparkled in her eyes.

"Thank you Queen Erysah, you have given us hope beyond hope." Xron replied. "We would be honoured to serve you." Again with the 'serve you'.

"Not serve, Xron. Assist. I will have no one serving anyone. We will be working as a team, a council. Making suggestions and advising each other as to what we think the best course of action will be for our people, whatever the given situation."

"Understood, Queen Erysah." They both bowed their heads briefly and returned to the others.

"Garroch and Melindra step forwards, please." Erysah said. "You have no need to be introduced to me, my friends. You to shall be advisors, even though Lord G'nard has returned, we shall have need of you and your son Jarro. I see difficult times ahead and Jarro will be key in all our futures. Oh, and if you call me Queen Erysah I shall not be best pleased. You have done much for me before my transcendence and friends do not use titles. Both Dayton and I will be known to you and only you and your son Jarro, as Dayton and Erysah. You may find my ways difficult but I assure you I will do the very best for our people. Now I suggest you all retire. I have need to speak to the sisters in private." With that they all nodded and left. A few minutes later they were alone. Erysah turned round to face Sollest and her sisters. Dayton looked slightly concerned. '*What are you up to?*' he asked.

'*Do not worry, just do not be shocked by what happens next.*' Sollest could tell that they were conversing via the mesh.

"Sollest, where are the scrolls?" Erysah was direct and to the point. Sollest was suddenly anxious she had a feeling that something was amiss. She had not anticipated that the queen would know about the scrolls.

"Scrolls, majesty?" she hesitated. What did Erysah know of the ancient scrolls?

"Sollest, by now you will have realised that not only do I have foresight but I have back sight too. And if you do not give the scrolls to me I will come and get them." Dayton gasped and Sollest looked confused. Dayton looked at Erysah in shock.

"You cannot go beyond the veil Erysah!" Dayton exclaimed. Erysah smiled at him.

"Oh, but I can." She smiled mischievously.

"How? Only those selected females of the Phoenix Clan can travel beyond the veil." Sollest was really confused now and wondered what she was going to do. She desperately tried to think back to the first scroll and what it contained, but her mind was a blank.

"True, but with all your meddling and calculating you misjudged a few things. Just over five hundred years ago when you decided to try and speed things up, pretending to be a human and seduced Kaspir's father. Then giving birth to Kaspir abandoning him to another family, ensuring his survival. You increased the phoenix blood line, so when I was born I had enough phoenix blood in me already to do extraordinary things. The fact that the closer I came to the temple and you the stronger my powers got, was a little disconcerting to say the least. Then of course you had to give me your blood again to aid the transcendence and so I have as much phoenix blood in me as I have dragon blood, maybe even more. I am the only other person apart from you and your sisters that will be able to travel beyond the veil and return." Suddenly the realisation of what she had done hit her. Not only had she brought the queen back but she had created the first new phoenix clan member in millennia. "We are leaving now, but I shall return tomorrow evening. If you are here with the scrolls then I will have no need to prove to you what I say is true. It is your choice. Sisters." Erysah nodded to them in acknowledgement and then turned and walked away with Dayton in hand. Leaving Sollest and the sisters to deliberate on what had just happened.

The New Queen

A few thousand miles away in the mountains of western Italy, Jebediah stood in front of the whole village. They were preparing from the coming Winter Solstice. Jebediah and his followers were an unusual group of people, living very basic lives, using the land and nature as people had done eons ago. The Avardi as they called themselves concentrated on beliefs that would be frowned upon in the modern age. Believing in Alchemy, Witchcraft and Pagan rituals. For over sixteen hundred years they had been endeavouring to extend their lives through any means at their disposal. Eventually they even included the science of biology into their midst. In the beginning their beliefs were centred around the legends of mythological creatures called vampires who were said to live for hundreds, if not thousands of years. But then a man discovered the Vardesh, that they were in fact the stuff of legends. They were the elusive vampires of old. Once discovered the Avardi made a much more concerted effort to find and capture these creatures in the hope they would aid their cause. Over time the memory of them had faded in obscurity as they went into hiding after the great war. They now had become things of imagination, along with werewolves and alike.

As Jebediah raised his hands towards the crowd, suddenly white hot pain seared through his body causing him to collapse on the floor. The people congregated there gasped in horror as they watched their Shamans body twitch and convulse. Joshua one of the Assists spoke.

"Please be calm everyone. I am sure the Shaman will be fine. Please make your way to your homes, so we can take him to his rooms." As Joshua spoke Aaron, Isaac and Nathanial, along with the Lower Assists ushered people back to their homes.

"What happened?" a voice shouted from the crowd. Joshua tried to see who it was.

"We don't know. As soon as we know anything we will let you know." Joshua didn't know what else to say. No one knew why the Shaman had collapsed and why his body continued to be rocked by spasms. Despite the grumblings of the crowd they returned to their homes, but in no great hurry. Before the crowd had dispersed Aaron and Isaac had managed to get Jebediah back to his bed chamber. Moments later Nathanial returned with a Maiden Healer. She knelt by the cot and rested her palm on his head. Despite him sweating profusely he was cold to the touch, shivering periodically.

"Fetch me some blankets and hot water. He is feverish and I need to brew a tonic to break it." Esther said to no one in particular. Seconds later Jebediah screamed. Three words coming out of his mouth.

"SHE IS BACK!" Then he fell into a troubled slumber, mumbling the same three words as he thrashed about on his cot.

"Does anyone know who he is talking about?" Isaac asked as he stared at his Shaman. Raising his head he looked at the rest of the in the room. They all had the same look on their faces, total confusion. Esther leant down with the brew and Joshua raised the Shaman's head slightly to make it easier for Esther to administer.

"This will help him sleep. Rest and warmth is what he needs now." She said as she walked to the door. I will send someone with a thin broth to help him keep his strength up and I will be back later to check on him."

"Is there anything else we can do?" Nathanial asked his brow creased with worry. Esther shook her head.

"Time will tell, but we need to find out who 'she' is." On that point they all agreed. How they were going to achieve that was another matter. They followed the Shaman without question and were lost without his guidance. No one had been prepared to take his place. Normally the Shaman would choose his own successor and would train him accordingly. But none of the Assists were advanced enough for the position, even on a temporary basis. If the Shaman didn't recover it would be the first time since they were founded that they wouldn't have a leader. Their whole society could disintegrate, the Shaman was the glue that kept them together. It would now be up to Aaron, Isaac, Joshua and Nathanial to try and keep the Avardi from falling apart.

When Erysah and Dayton got back to the library, Dayton closed the entrance to the temple. Turning around to face both his new wife and his queen.

"What is happening, Erysah? What was all that about?" During the ritual she hadn't noticed what he had been wearing now she did and found his attire very appealing. She couldn't help but give him a salacious look as she saw his muscular body draped in a simple silver toga, that hung from one shoulder with a silver clasp at the top. Around his waist was a silver plaited thong belt. "Erysah do not look at me like that." He wanted to be serious for a moment, what he had heard in the temple was a major revelation. He had already had his suspicions about Sollest's involvement with Erysah's life, but not to the extent Erysah had revealed. Her knowledge and powers were scary and he wanted to talk about them. Unfortunately for him she had no intention of going down that road at the moment. She was having a difficult time trying to put the two people together as one. Trying to find some middle ground, so both would accept each other. But for now she just wanted to be with her Solelae. As a woman with a man. Erysah found the other button and opened the passageway to their chambers and disappeared. Dayton was exasperated with her, he had his own fight on his hands trying to reorganise himself and become the man he was now destined to be. Dayton G'nard was now Lord of the Dragon Clan. But he was also a man who loved his Solelil. A voice whispered into his mind, *'come Solelae, be with me. As we should be, it is our wedding night after all.'* He felt the sensation of a kiss brush against his lips. That was all it took for his shaft to react, it started to twitch into life. With a relenting sigh he followed Erysah. As he entered their chamber he found her leaning against the far wall, looking every bit the woman she was. Fiery, feisty, beautiful, ethereal and regal. She smiled as he entered the room and opened her arms to him. He went willingly like a lamb to the slaughter.

"My love we are both struggling with what has occurred. I wish to forget for a short while and just be two people who love each other. Can we wait until tomorrow to solve our dilemmas, I beg of you." Erysah spoke so softly and Dayton noticed that she did not contract any of her words. She spoke as a Vardesh. She had changed, yet she was the same. The same could be said for him, only his change had not been so drastic. He kissed her neck and felt an ache in his teeth. Yes, of course they would feed off each other from now on and she had yet to do so.

"Erysah, it is time for our first exchange." She looked up at him and nodded.

"Dayton there is something you should know before we do." He looked at her wondering what she was going to reveal now. "When you feed from me you will also take in my phoenix blood, there is no way to separate it. The phoenix blood from Sollest is more potent in me because she is my grandmother. To be honest my blood is more phoenix than dragon, be prepared for another change in you. This is something that I did not reveal to Sollest. However, she may eventually work it out. The more we feed off each other, the stronger our blood becomes. During the ritual she gave us both her blood and with you taking mine, you will eventually also be able to go beyond the veil too. Unfortunately, I do not know when that will be, but it will happen, that I am sure of."

"You have always been full of surprises Erysah. Ever since I found you, you have not been what I expected. You have always been more and it terrified me, because I thought that I would lose you. I see now that you were right, we have to be who we need to be. And you are my Solelil, Queen of the Vardesh and I am your Solelae, Lord of the Dragon Clan. Whatever I gain from our sharing will only benefit our people and I will follow you without reservation. We are and will be as one."

"Yes, Dayton. We are one. One mind, one heart, one soul, one body with one breath and one blood. As it should be, for you are my king." Dayton shook his head.

"No, it cannot be Erysah. We have never had a king. We have always had one queen and four lords."

"We will talk about this tomorrow. For tonight, can it be just us?" There was a weariness in her voice and a sadness in her eyes. Dayton picked her up and carried her over to the bed. He lay her gently down and lay on his side next to her.

"By the way did I tell you how beautiful and sexy you look in that robe." Dayton smiled his voice tender.

"No, but you look damn hot in yours. Are you as naked as I am under there?" A sparkle lit up her emerald eyes.

"Not telling you," he said mischievously. "You will have to find out for yourself." He teased. She laughed, *'thank you'*. "You are welcome." Erysah rolled onto her side to face him. "Do you want to feed first or . . ." Dayton never had chance to finish his sentence, because Erysah's hand had worked its way under his robe. Her fist had closed around his hard length and had begun moving along the length of it. Dayton moaned as the fire started in his groin, spreading slowly through his body. He placed his hand on her thigh just above the knee and brushed away the gossamer material to reveal her skin. He slid his hand over her smooth flesh and hooked her leg behind the knee, bringing it up onto his hip. His hand then travelled the length of her thigh until it reached the mound of her firm buttock. He massaged it and slid his fingers round into her secret crevice, it was Erysah's turn to moan, as an ache only Dayton could ease awoke. Dayton slid across her hot and wet entrance. Erysah gasped, he then rolled both of them over so he was on the bottom. She was sitting across his thighs, still holding onto his erection. Dayton moved the golden fabric out of the way so he could look at her. He began stroking her fiery entrance causing Erysah to writhe and moan with pleasure. Dayton was doing his own moaning as Erysah was administering to his needs. Stroking and teasing his shaft, suddenly she licked the centre of her hand so it was nice and wet and placed it over the head of his erection. Moving it in a slow circular motion, causing electricity to pass through him causing him to buck uncontrollably.

"Erysah!" he screamed. "Stop, please! It is too much." She smiled at him enticingly.

"And what . . . will you . . . do if . . . I do not . . ." she said between gasps. He could not keep himself together and longer, he had to have her or explode. He grabbed her by the waist and lifted her off him and partially sat up. Then impaled her on him Erysah screamed as her orgasm took her over the precipice. But Dayton was not finished yet, he pulled aside the golden cloth that covered her ample breasts. Her nipples were hard and enticing, a rich ruby against her alabaster skin. He took both of them into his hands and brushed the nipples with his thumbs. Then he bent forward and latched onto a nipple with his mouth. The taste was so sweet that he moaned along with Erysah. Slowly she began to rock back and forth, the friction of the movement teasing her sensitive bud. She adjusted herself so that her feet were under her. Squatting over his sword she began to move her sheath along the length of him with long slow movements. Reaching the very tip before coming back down, she only managed it half a dozen times before Dayton could take no more and grabbed her ankles when she was down. This caused him to plunge into her up to the hilt, he sat up completely and put his arms around her back and held him to her. He began kissing her neck, her throat, her chin and then he found her mouth. Long sensual kisses, deep drugging kisses, tongue battling kisses. When they eventually came up for air, Dayton whispered in her ear.

"It is time beloved, you cannot wait any longer." Erysah nodded, she knew exactly what he meant. "Together, we will do it at the same time. Have you the knowledge?" He felt unsure about asking, because she had received a lot of knowledge when she transcended. She nodded and stroked her teeth with her tongue, they were there as she knew they would be. Her arms encircled Dayton's head and he tilted to one side as she tilted hers to the other. She licked his neck sensuously and kissed the spot, Dayton repeated this action on her. Then they both positioned their mouths on each other's neck and bit down. The biting action triggered their feeding incisors to shoot out and pierce into the vein. The sensation was erotic in itself which stimulated them both into a tantric movement. Although their bodies did not move they used their sexual muscles to bring each other to climax whilst they fed. Releasing from each other's neck they roared in an explosion of sensation as they climaxed. They had fed for much longer than they should have, so were exhausted and collapsed into a deep and intoxicating slumber.

Beyond the veil where time had no meaning, Sollest and her sisters were laying on their chaises in their lounge.

"Was it true what the queen said, and if so, how was it possible?" asked Ziolae, the Wolf priestess. Sollest looked at them wondering how to answer them.

"Come on Sollest," said Leonyra, priestess to the cats.

"Yes, Sollest, we would really like to know how you managed to deceive us and manipulate fate!" Kystrel the Eagle priestess said with irritation. Sollest sighed knowing she would have to confess all but she had thought that she was doing the right thing at the time. They had been too long without their queen and clan lords. They needed coherence again.

"When I became the dragon priestess and your high priestess after Pendesa chose to go into the black. I found some sacred scrolls hidden in her quarters. I came across them whilst I was going through the ritual cleansing of her rooms. They were sealed in a bejewelled box, beneath her bed. I assumed they were personal items, but when I opened the box I found the scrolls."

"Are these the scrolls that the queen asked for?" Ziolae inquired.

"I presume so, they were written by Pendesa. I know she had the gift of foresight. She must have written down what she saw."

"Where are the scrolls now?" asked Kystrel.

"They are still in my rooms. Do you wish to see them?"

"More to the point is should we all read them?" They sat quietly contemplating what they should do for the best. "Do you think that the queen could come beyond the veil to us?" Leonyra asked.

"I have no doubt that she believes so, but whether it is possible. I do not know." Sollest replied.

"Is it something worth testing?" asked Ziolae.

"I do not believe so, because if it is so, what will become of us?" Kystrel was worried. "If she spends a significant amount of time here, it will extend her life even more." They all agreed on that account.

"I suggest that you give her Pendesa's scrolls and that way it will at least give us more time to evaluate the situation." Ziolae suggested.

"Just one question," Kystrel asked. "How many scrolls are there and have you read them all?"

"There are five scrolls and no I have not read them all, they were numbered for some reason."

"So how many have you read, Sollest?" Leonyra looked intently at her, as did her other sisters.

"Two, they are quite long and it took me a while to decipher the first one. I have yet to decipher the second one. I will go and get the box and you can see for yourselves." The other women nodded and Sollest went to retrieve the box from her room. Ziolae looked at her sisters, worry reflected back at her.

"Why did she not mention the scrolls to us?"

"I do not know Leonyra. Perhaps she thought it was her responsibility as High Priestess to . . ." Ziolae couldn't finish the sentence because she had no idea what Sollest was thinking.

"To what?" asked Kystrel.

"What I would like to know is how did she manage to give birth to a child without us knowing." Ziolae interjected.

"Yes, I know," agreed Leonyra.

"Does it matter, what is done, is done." Ziolae and Leonyra pondered momentarily over Kystrel statement. "More to the point," Kystrel continued, "is do we want to know what the scrolls contain before we give them to the queen."

Sollest entered her chamber, it was just the same as all the rest. This was despite the fact that she was the High Priestess. The only difference was the position of it. Although you could not see the outside of the building, it gave an impression that it was a conical formation. The lowest level housing the pre-ascension initiates, above that were the chambers of the Lower Priestesses. Rising even higher was the rooms of Kystrel, Leonyra and Ziolae, just above them was the veil room and their meeting room. And at the top was Sollest's chamber, as High Priestess she rose above them all. She had moved the box from its original place under the bed and put it into one of the niches that hid behind golden curtains. The niches were set out at regular intervals around the room, there were no windows. The golden curtains gave an impression of stripes running vertically down the walls. Sollest retrieved the box and sat on the bed with it. Opening it up she checked briefly to make sure that all the scrolls were still there. With a sigh she stood up and made her way back down to the meeting room where her sisters waited for her.

When Sollest entered carrying the black ebony box which was encrusted with jewels, the other priestesses turned to face her. Sollest placed it on a glass table in the middle of the room. On each side of the box there was an image representing a particular clan. On the front was a dragon, the back had an eagle. The left side had a cat and the right had a wolf. Which left the lid which held the image of a phoenix. As the sisters stood round her Sollest lifted the lid to reveal its contents. Inside sat five yellow scrolls, three at the bottom and two on top of them. These two had broken seals. Sollest hesitated as she went to pick one of the scrolls up. Ziolae put her hand on Sollest's.

"We have decided not to read the scrolls. Your meddling has already caused some unexpected results."

"Yes, Sollest. You also forgot to take into consideration what effect it will have on Lord G'nard." Said Kystrel.

"Of course," gasped Leonyra staring at her sister. "He will be sharing her blood. What if it becomes possible for him to come here? What then?" Sollest stared at her sisters in horror. Had she miscalculated that much? Sollest closed the box and stepped away from it a look of horror on her face. No male had ever survived that had been born of the phoenix clan or let alone entered the veil.

"I have let our people down and betrayed them I do not deserve the position of high priestess." She sat on her chaise her head in her hands, stunned unable to comprehend her error. Her sisters gathered around her, Ziolae sat next to her and put her arm around her shoulders. Leonyra sat on the other side of he and placed a hand on Sollest's arm, whilst Kystrel sat at her feet and rested her head in her lap. She looked down at Kystrel and shook her head. Ziolae spoke.

"You have guided the Vardesh for over a millennia and we have survived. No one is perfect, Sollest."

"But what if my meddling has brought our destruction?" Sollest was despondent.

"But . . ." Kystrel started. The others looked at her, questioningly. She continued, "but what if this was what Pendesa saw? Who are we to interfere in fate?" Leonyra shook her head.

"No, Sollest has been following what she has interpreted from the scrolls. So they have guided her actions. If they are scrolls of prophecy, we need to leave them sealed. For our own protection. Give the queen the scrolls, then we will not be responsible for what happens in the future. The queen is back and it is now her responsibility, as is her right, to look after our people." Sollest sighed.

"All of you are right, it is not our responsibility any more. Will you all come with me to give her them?"

"Of course, we will Sollest." They said in unison. They had been so focussed on the distraught Sollest that they did not notice anyone enter the room.

"Come sisters," said a voice from behind them, it was Ayriel. She was one of the initiates that looked after the sisters and saw to their needs. "Your repast awaits." The sisters looked at her and nodded. With that she bowed and left, but not before looking once more at the ebony box, sitting on the table.

"Wait, what of the box?" inquired Kystrel, "we cannot leave it here no matter how much we trust the initiates."

"Yes, Kystrel is correct. We must either take it to the temple now or keep it with us at all time." Leonyra stated.

"I agree, I saw Ayriel looking at it curiously, when she came in. Who knows how long she has been standing there before she spoke." Said Ziolae. "None of the initiates can travel through the veil, it would be safer in the temple." They all stood and Sollest collected the box from the table. Walking through a double set of doors opposite from where Ayriel had come from, they entered the veil chamber. In each corner stood a statue of one of the clan images, then in the centre stood a phoenix. Each sister went to their clan effigy and touched the heart stone with their left hand. Placing their right hands on their own hearts they went to the phoenix and placed their left hands on the statue. A mystic veil descended around them. Within seconds they were standing behind the veil of light in the temple.

At first when they stepped through they thought that they were alone. Then suddenly they saw a phoenix bird sitting in the corner, in between the two entrances to the temple. The sisters looked confused, they had only seen the bird in statue form. As far as they knew there had never been any phoenix transforms. Taking its cue from their thoughts, the phoenix rose and walked towards them. There was a blinding flash of light and Erysah stood before them. Stunned by what they saw, Sollest nearly lost grip on the box she was holding.

"What are you doing here?" asked Sollest, her voice shaky.

"Waiting for you, I see you were not expecting me." Erysah replied. The sisters nodded with a look of awe on their faces.

"How is it possible that you are awake at this time?" Leonyra asked. Erysah looked at her and smiled.

"It is possible because I am the queen and . . ." she stopped before she revealed too much.

"How is it possible that you can take the form of a phoenix?" asked Kystrel.

"Curious, is it not? I have been experimenting, while you have been deliberating."

"What about Lord G'nard?" Ziolae inquired.

"Ah, yes Lord G'nard. There has been a little development on that score." The sisters looked at her warily. But before she was prepared to finish telling them about the changes she needed the box from Sollest. She held out her hands, "the box if you please Sollest." Sollest asked one of the sisters to open it and show Erysah that the scrolls were indeed inside before giving it to her. When the box touched the queens hands all the images started to glow. The sisters gasped in terror. "Someone else has touched this box, an initiate. How has she had access to it?" Queen Erysah did not look best pleased. The sisters looked at each other and wondered how she could possibly know. Even they had not realised Ayriel had laid a hand on it. "I will want to see her, at some point, regarding this matter. Now return, I will contact you when the time comes." They bowed and return through the veil. Erysah went back into the bed chamber where Dayton was still sleeping. She knew there was a secret panel at the foot of the bed. Opening it up she placed the bejewelled box that contained the scrolls inside it, until the time was right. Dayton would be awake soon and she wanted to be ready for what was to come.

Printed in Great Britain
by Amazon